"I've missed you more than any other person or place in this world. I know what will make me happy. You, in Atlanta, with me. What will it take to convince you?"

Mira covered her face with her hands. "We don't work. We want different things, Rob. If you love me, please consider that I have built the life I've dreamed of, here, in Miami." She stood. "It's like I'm alive here. I don't want to give that up."

Alive. She was alive here.

Rob wished he didn't know what she meant.

Mira was smart. She knew what she wanted, and she was asking for it.

Rob wanted to make her happy, but no intelligent man would watch her walk away without a fight.

"I'm not signing those papers tonight, Mira." Rob rose slowly. "I believe in us too much to give up that easily, but I've never been able to tell you no. Let's make a deal."

Dear Reader,

What is your favorite Christmas-morning tradition? I remember waking up (early, of course) and walking out to find my grandparents and aunts waiting for me in front of the tree, an audience for the sweet surprise of Santa's visit. I had no idea how difficult that was to accomplish until I was tiptoeing into my brother's house before the sun was fully up to surprise my nephews the same way. Cool aunts, lucky aunts, get to do things like that!

Mira Peters is lucky, too, and surrounded by family now that she's home in Miami. This year, she's braving the Santa-themed amusement park with her energetic nephew, while her not-yet-ex-husband tries to convince her they deserve another chance. Loving him is easy; living with him will take some holiday magic. Rob Bowman is certain of only two things: he can't lose his wife, and the romance of a Key West Christmas can change everything.

If you'd like to know more about my books and what's coming next, enter fun giveaways, or meet my dog, Jack, please visit me at cherylharperbooks.com. I'm also on Facebook (cherylharperromance) and Twitter @cherylharperbks. I'd love to chat!

Cheryl Harper

HEARTWARMING

Her Holiday Reunion

—

Cheryl Harper

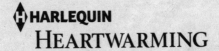

HARLEQUIN
HEARTWARMING

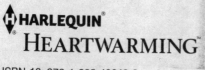

PLEASE RECYCLE • THIS PRODUCT IS RECYCLABLE

Recycling programs for this product may not exist in your area.

ISBN-13: 978-1-335-42648-2

Her Holiday Reunion

Copyright © 2021 by Cheryl Harper

Harlequin Enterprises ULC
22 Adelaide St. West, 40th Floor
Toronto, Ontario M5H 4E3, Canada
www.Harlequin.com

Printed in U.S.A.

Cheryl Harper discovered her love for books and words as a little girl, thanks to a mother who made countless library trips, and an introduction to Laura Ingalls Wilder's Little House books. Whether the stories she reads are set in the prairie, the American West, Regency England or Earth a hundred years in the future, Cheryl enjoys strong characters who make her laugh. Now Cheryl spends her days searching for the right words while she stares out the window and her dog, Jack, snoozes beside her. And she considers herself very lucky to do so.

For more information about Cheryl's books, visit her online at cherylharperbooks.com or follow her on Twitter, @cherylharperbks.

CHAPTER ONE

MIRA PETERS PACED in front of the classroom full of tenth-graders as she waited for the last bell of the afternoon to ring. Most of them were dividing their time between staring at her and watching the clock. One final check of the time convinced her to start the exit procedure immediately. Her class was about two minutes away from freedom and Christmas break. They were like a combustible chemical reaction, bubbling with energy, ready to escape.

"Everyone pass your tests forward to the front of your row." Mira was impressed with how well they followed directions. At the beginning of the semester, that had not been true. What a difference a few months and consistency made. "Push your chairs under your tables before you leave, please."

The bell rang and the thunderous rumble of chairs and feet was punctuated by occasional screeches as twenty-five teens grabbed books and bags and rushed for the door. "Enjoy your break. Grades will be posted next week. In January, we'll study genetics!" She'd raised her voice, but it was a waste of energy. No one was listening, even if it was possible that she could be heard.

Then they were gone. It was quiet and peaceful again.

"A narrow escape. You could have been trampled," drawled Linda Burns, the retiring teacher who'd been partnered with Mira. Teaching her first semester of biology had been bumpy, mainly because of changing state guidelines, too many duties and not enough money for supplies and resources, but it was also exactly everything Mira had dreamed of, thanks to Linda.

Linda was a teaching veteran who'd spent thirty years navigating the pressures of the system. She'd seen it all, done it all, and nothing shocked her anymore. She patted her hand over her salt-and-pepper curls. "Learn to observe from a safe distance, kid. Workers' compensation won't cover stampede injuries."

Mira dipped her chin and ruffled her stack of papers. "I've seen war zones, Linda. Africa. Afghanistan. My family's fight for the last of the kulkuls at Christmas. I can handle two dozen kids."

Linda frowned. "Kulkuls. Those doughnut bites you brought for the potluck, right? I loved those."

Mira tilted her head to the side as she considered the description. She couldn't come up with a better one, even though Linda's didn't encompass the amount of work that had gone into making them, so she nodded as she hustled around Linda.

Faint jingles rang with every step. They were both wearing their best attempt at Christmas finery. Linda's T-shirt said, "Don't make me put you on my naughty list" and showed a disgruntled Santa holding up a long scroll. Mira's sweatshirt had thirty jingling bells attached, each one in the center of a felt snowflake.

"Air force medic. Sure. I get it. You know how to fight." Linda nodded. "But these kids? They do not know or follow the Geneva Convention. Take no prisoners? That's a phrase invented by a high school science teacher after one too many chemistry explosions."

Mira had to laugh. "I guess it's a good thing I haven't faced any chemistry experiments yet. I need to build up my thick skin and buy protective goggles."

"Yes, you do," Linda agreed. "The sooner you learn that lesson, the better. Here, the only weapons you have are your mouth and sharp wit. Sometimes, your opponent is mouthier and sharper." She held up the remote to turn off the projector.

Were her students opponents? Linda framed every day as a battle. Mira was still new enough to hope everyone in her classroom was on the same side of the fight. Linda had never mouthed off to a drill instructor, neither had Mira, but some of her best friends had struggled with authority and come through on the other side. These kids would, too, if Mira was good at her job.

"Big plans for the holiday break?" Linda asked.

Waving the stack of papers before she shoved them into a tote bag, Mira said, "Grading tests. Recording those grades. Working on lesson plans for next semester so you can review them when we get back. Packing up to move." It was a lot to accomplish. This was what she'd been working for, the second career she'd planned while she was deployed and wondering if she'd make it home. A classroom like this had been her daydream when the heat and sand had driven her to the edge.

Then, more than once, she'd imagined how satisfying it would be to grade tests and write bright red scores across the top, visual proof of the success of the important work teaching children.

Some of these kids would learn only what they needed to in order to pass the state-required standardized testing, while others would fall in love with biology and a few would make it all the way through medical school to save lives, discover cures and fulfill Mira's original career plans of becoming a doctor.

The plans she'd made when she'd been the same age as the kids in her current class.

If any of them eventually mentioned meeting with military recruiters or enlisting, Mira would employ every single bit of her wits to make sure they knew what they were getting into. Air force life was good, but it wasn't easy.

If she was learning the same thing about teaching and civilian life, well… She still had hope.

"And?" Linda drawled. "Homework. Housework. There has to be more than that."

"Running?" Mira said, although it was more a question than an answer. She was sure Linda wouldn't accept that as a suitable activity for her holiday break. If she was being honest, it had lost some of its challenge, too.

Linda's gusty sigh was confirmation. "Listen, Peters." She used her last name like every air force squad and veterans group she'd ever come across, not to mention the pack of friends Mira had collected since her air force retirement. Linda did answer to her first name, but only because Mira refused to use her last. "Work and working out? You gotta find something else. If you don't set good boundaries now, this job will eat you alive. Get a hobby. Get a boyfriend. Get a dog. I don't know which you need the most, but hear me now or believe me later."

Linda raised her eyebrows to demonstrate how seriously she wanted her advice taken.

"How are you spending your time off?" Mira asked sweetly. She bent to check her emails on her computer to make sure she hadn't gotten any questions from parents or students regarding the end-of-the-year schedule.

When there was no answer, Mira glanced up. Linda's lips were pursed tightly in displeasure. So, her plans were as simple as Mira's.

"Do as I say, not as I do, young'un." Linda pressed a hand to her hip as she stood slowly. "I put off all those things until I hit retirement. Now that it's here, this part hurts, that part doesn't work so well, and I'm too tired for the rest of it. As the Bard said, 'Seize the day.'" She sauntered toward the door.

"I'm not sure that was Shakespeare. Carpe diem. He didn't write in Latin," Mira murmured as she shut down her computer and pulled the tote straps over her shoulder. The heft of those papers and her files was satisfying, and some of the promise of two weeks away from school was bubbling up.

"Good thing I teach science instead of English or Latin, then." Linda paused at the doorway. "You're doing good, kid. Remember you're in this for the long haul. These kids need good teachers like you and me." Her lips curled slowly before she disappeared down the hall to her office.

Mira shook her head as she followed Linda. She stopped to survey her classroom. She'd cleared the whiteboard at the front of the room while everyone was finishing the test, so it was ready for the next lesson. The students' desks were fairly neat. The plants that lined the high cabinets along the back wall had been watered. Indiana Bones, the human skeleton model that she hadn't used yet, had a hand raised in a jaunty farewell. It was either a greeting or goodbye, depending on which way she was going, and Mira loved it. One of the kids had added a Santa hat to make him more festive. Mira had never discovered which student was responsible, but she hadn't tried too hard.

Everything about her classroom was perfect.

She waved at the other teachers who were getting ready to leave.

Maneuvering Miami's Friday busy afternoon traffic was easier this early in the rush hour, but it was always a pleasure to drive home to Concord Court. That the Court was fairly close to the school had been one of the biggest selling points of this teaching contract over her other two options. Everyone at the Court had become a second family, which was nice.

Her first family? After her parents retired from air force life, they'd returned home to Florida. Most of her sisters were spread out all over South Florida, but they managed to gather at her parents' place sandwiched between Homestead and the Everglades for every official holiday and any celebration her father invented. It was good to be that close to both families but choosing where she wanted to buy her first place had been easy.

All she had to do was get packed up, travel not too far away and unpack. Then everything would be settled. Happily settled.

No one could order her to pack her things and move before she was ready. Painting the walls in every room a different color was her only immediate DIY plan; no more standard greige of base housing or apartments in her life ever again. She was thrilled.

Leaving Concord Court, her latest temporary home, would be hard, but the excitement of the new place was helping her overcome that.

As she slid out of her car and slammed the door, she saw Sean Wakefield driving into the Court's parking lot. She raised her hand in greeting.

"Hey, Mira, assign a lot of homework today?" He rested an elbow out the truck window. Mira could hear his phone dinging. As the person in charge of all the maintenance, construction and grounds at Concord Court, Sean never had a lot of free time. He was also one of her oldest new friends.

"No homework. It's the end of the semester, gave the last test today. I'm still trying to find the perfect mix of tough enough that they'll learn something, but wanting to keep things fun—" she held out her noisy sweatshirt as proof "—partly so that they might still vote me favorite teacher. I want to be voted Best Teacher in my first year. No assignments over Christmas break was a sound decision for them and for me." It might seem a silly goal, but Mira had always pursued goals. This was one she could win. She brushed each shoulder and smiled.

"Good plan, Teach. Everybody deserves a break."

Mira agreed in theory. She'd never been good at stopping or resting. There was usually too much to do. "I guess. Packing and moving into my new house will keep me occupied anyway." The silence stretched between them. Saying goodbye to Concord Court was one of those bittersweet things that life put in a person's path. She'd loved it here. Her best friends were here. But her time was up.

She'd been the first resident of the townhome community the Montero family had built to offer veterans leaving service a free place to live until they could take their next steps, whatever those might be. The only requirement to living in the complex was to go to school or find a job. Mira had finished her degree, earned her teaching certification and had been able to get a place of her own, so she was ready.

That didn't make leaving home any easier.

It was comforting that the band of brothers she'd joined through unofficial group hang-outs at midnight around the swimming pool would miss her being at Concord Court, too. Not that they'd ever come right out and admit it. The serious expression on Sean's face was her best clue to how he felt.

"Run in the morning?" he asked, shaking his head immediately as if he were urging her to say no.

She nodded instead. "Since it's so cool these days, we should begin training for that marathon next year."

"I do not do organized sports," Sean said with a sniff. "I need my freedom to express myself."

Mira rolled her eyes. "Okay, so we'll stick with our usual run. Stretch it to ten miles?"

He frowned. "I'm a busy man. I don't have time to agree to anything other than our easiest run." Instead of waiting for her answer, he grinned and drove away.

"We'll see about that," Mira muttered as she climbed the steps up to her town house and unlocked the door. Learning to stand firm in front of the loud groans of those at the Court who did not want to participate in extra running sessions had been excellent training for teaching high school biology. Sean was the biggest complainer in the group. He was also her best friend.

Inside, Mira dropped her tote on the overstuffed chair that was her favorite spot in the whole place. Filling her one-bedroom townhome had been easy enough, thanks to her father's habit of never getting rid of anything. He'd taken her to his unit in one of her grandfather's storage rental buildings, unlocked the sliding door and threw it open to reveal his collection of odds and ends, rejects, hand-me-downs and too-good-to-pass-up purchases.

Being related to a pack rat when you no longer had to live in their home was nice.

Her father had been in the air force, too, so his collection had true international flair. This overstuffed chair was solid leather, had enough padding to swallow a person whole and was nestled perfectly in the cove of the window, bookshelves on either side.

A reading nook that Mira had often dreamed of and had created for herself.

She'd enjoy using this chair to sit in to grade today's tests, log on to her laptop to enter the grades, and then spend the rest of the weekend sorting and packing up her kitchen. Easy.

But first, the mail.

Mira left and cut across the courtyard on her way to the mailboxes. The days might be shorter in December, but Miami sunshine was still warm. The pool hadn't been covered, so it sparkled in the setting sun. Wreaths made of red cedar and pygmy date palm branches were attached to every other post of the wrought iron fence that surrounded the pool. The ends of the bright red bows on the wreaths stirred in the slight breeze as she passed.

As she reached the flagpoles flying the United States and Florida flags, as well as the flag of each branch of the military, Wade McNally exited the Court's office.

After their one perfectly comfortable blind date, they'd settled into a solid friendship.

"You ready for help yet?" Wade asked.

That was how he'd started every conversation since she'd mentioned finding her new house. He was determined to lend a hand. Wade would also round up a moving team when the time came. What a super friend to have.

"Not yet, but I'm getting there. I've got this school break, and it's time to get serious. I will let you know when." She nodded firmly when he looked skeptical. "I mean it. I'm not going to be one of those silly people who refuses to ask for help." She'd spent the last year walking her friends through easy solutions to problems that boiled down to "Ask for help." Maybe she'd learned the lesson, too.

He glanced back at the office. "Good. We've got plenty of those around."

"Trouble with true love?" Mira asked in a singsong. She was happy for Brisa Montero, who ran the Court and was now in a relationship with Wade. Really, she was. And she was happy for Brisa's older sister, Reyna, who was dating Sean.

Though, being swallowed in a stifling cloud of love whenever they were all together was a lot.

And when they were at odds? Mira enjoyed fireworks but not at such close range.

He shrugged. "Brisa has a plan, but she won't tell me what it is. Her only confidante is Thea, but how much can a ten-year-old contribute?"

Since Wade's daughter, Thea, was wise beyond her years, Mira had a feeling she'd be a good assistant.

"What if it's a Christmas gift for you? Then neither of them can tell you. You can't help with that." Mira watched it sink into Wade's brain that she might have a solid suggestion.

He inhaled slowly, held it and exhaled. "Good point. Trust you to always have a good point."

"And trust Brisa and Thea both to know when they need your assistance." Or her for that matter, but she wasn't going to say that. In her time as the leader of their band at the pool, Mira had learned that letting them come to the realization on their own some-times saved everyone a lot of time and emotion. Plus, they got annoyed at how often she was right.

"Run in the morning?" Wade asked. He didn't complain, she knew, because he wasn't going.

"Yep. Brisa and I want to convince the

rest of the group to train for a marathon." Mira laughed at the loud groan Wade let out.

"A marathon?" He closed his eyes before muttering, "I'll be the guy dating the woman who literally runs circles around him."

She was still giggling when she opened her mailbox. A water bill, a ragged sale paper for the local grocery and a postcard from her dry cleaner. That was it.

It wasn't time to worry yet. Every day she expected to find the large self-addressed envelope with signed copies of her divorce papers, but this wasn't the day, either.

"He still hasn't returned the paperwork?" Wade asked. He'd been the first one to learn about her absent husband. In fact, that weird conversation had been part of her perfectly fine blind date with the former navy trauma surgeon. Consequently, she went on to tell her closest friends gathered at the swimming pool, but she'd required vows that they wouldn't badger her for details. The promise had held strong for months, so she'd told them a week ago that the divorce should be final any day.

Mira assumed it was true. It had been

almost a full year since she'd spoken to Rob Bowman in person. She'd mailed all the paperwork to him a month ago. All it would take is a signature and this marriage could be done.

The self-addressed, stamped envelope should have removed the only barrier her "husband" could make to mailing back the documents.

But he still hadn't returned them.

This year, what she wanted for Christmas was to be divorced. Being set up on a blind date with a handsome, extremely eligible nice guy had shaken something loose in her. More than two years of separation was enough. Mira needed to move forward.

Marriage had never been on Mira's mind at all. Then Rob's path had crossed hers and everything changed. Her life in the air force and his in the army meant they had both been moving fast for a proper romance, so they'd leaped into marriage without a real plan.

The time had come to remedy that.

When Mira realized she hadn't answered Wade's question, she shook her head. "No, I haven't gotten the paperwork back yet. The mail is slow. At the holidays, it can slow down." She pasted on a smile. "Santa could bring it down my nonexistent chimney on Christmas Eve."

Wade crossed his arms over his chest. "You want to go get his signature? Atlanta's a nice drive up the coast. Sean and I can go. We'll put on suits, dark sunglasses, scowl a lot."

Mira grinned as she tried to imagine her husband's reaction to her arrival with a couple of bodyguards. All three of them would end up in trouble, what with Rob being an Atlanta cop. "Let's give Santa a chance first."

Wade sighed. "Can't help Brisa. Can't help you. Guess I better go hang out in the emergency room. They never turn down my help there." He said goodbye and followed the path that led into the courtyard.

It was nice to have friends who had her back. But if it came down to it, she could face her ex without any real concern. They had both walked away from the relationship at the first sign of trouble. He'd stopped in Atlanta. She'd made Miami home. There was nothing left between them except miles.

She'd check the mail again tomorrow.

Her disappointment was easy to forget as she settled into her routine. Hot tea, a stack of tests to grade and her favorite red pen. Hunger was reminding her that dinner was one of the four or five most important meals of the day when she heard a car come to a stop close to her town house. Curiosity got the better of her.

"Two tests left. I was so close," she muttered as she stretched and stood. Whoever it was might have a dinner invitation. The promise of food immediately prompted a happy smile. She'd surprise whoever it was by yanking the door open before they knocked.

CHAPTER TWO

ROB BOWMAN WINCED. He slowly got out of his truck after a long day behind the wheel. He'd been released to travel and return to active duty for only a day, not even a full twenty-four hours, but he'd had no choice. Waiting a month had taken such a toll on his mental outlook that he couldn't wait a second longer. He needed to see his wife.

His boss hadn't been happy to get his leave request so soon after his recovery. Rob owed former Master Sergeant Laurence Booker some loyalty. The guy had been a mentor while they served together and had offered him a job in Atlanta, but he also lived for the job. Book had probably never taken a solid week of vacation in his life. If he wasn't careful, work would replace Rob's life, too. He had already ignored three texts from Book asking him to cut his trip short. Training a new recruit was important, and

Rob was glad to have the opportunity to prove his skill.

He couldn't put off visiting his wife any longer. Getting the divorce papers had changed everything.

She was the only one who could answer the question that had been distracting him ever since he'd opened the package she'd sent.

Had his wife fallen in love with someone else?

Waiting for her to...settle somewhere hadn't been easy. Losing her would be worse.

Facing her front door was a relief. He stretched his right arm carefully, breathing through the pain as the muscles in his still-healing shoulder shifted. One of the prescription painkillers the doctor had insisted he'd need would hit the spot, but that would have to wait.

He still had to figure out what to say to Mira.

"Honey, I'm home," he muttered. He'd imagined saying that to her after a long day with the Atlanta police. Too bad it didn't work here in Miami.

Nothing he'd imagined about making a life in Atlanta seemed to be coming true.

The key to that had to be convincing Mira to give their marriage another shot. If he could come home to her every day, his frustration with the job would fade. Mira made life better; *he* had been better with her. Smarter. Stronger. Happier.

Rob leaned against the truck and tried to unclench the tight muscles in his jaw.

"Come home." That's what he wanted to say. Two words. Simple. Easy.

Getting Mira to compromise had never been simple. Not once since he'd met her in a bar off base in Djibouti had she ever easily gone along with him. That place had been hopping with a collection of military men and women from several different countries, but Mira had drawn him to her, almost like a light glowing only for him and he was the foolish moth who couldn't escape.

Her face, her petite frame, they fooled people into believing she was soft and weak.

Then she hit them with her sharp strength and intellect that could slice like a knife. That night, she'd been tough, careful and so irresistible that sweet-talking her into letting him buy her a drink had become his goal.

The woman who was happy on her own? Mira hadn't made it easy.

Charm. That had been her weakness. Teasing. He used to be pretty good at that. His only hope now was to find that talent again. Rob pulled the red gift bow and elf hat complete with gigantic pointed ears from the front seat. His charm might be rusty. It was a good thing he'd brought props.

Rob carefully put the hat on and waited for any embarrassment to subside before slapping the bow on his good shoulder. Would Mira be amused? A few years ago, he would have bet on it.

Rob climbed the steps and took a deep breath. It was a simple knock on the door, but he might as well have been waiting to jump out of a plane, parachute strapped to his back. This was going to be a big leap.

"Knock on the door, coward," he muttered to himself and then jerked back as the door opened abruptly.

Rob managed to swallow the wince as

sore muscles in his shoulder objected to the sharp movement and forced a slow smile.

Once the pain let up, the smile was easy. He'd missed Mira.

So much.

She was framed in warm light. Her hair was in a weird, sloppy, adorable clump on top of her head. She had zero makeup on, and bells jingled as she froze in place.

"Rob."

That was it. That was all his wife of over three years had to say about this reunion.

He wanted joy and surprise, not shock. That joy? It was spreading in his chest, warming him from the inside. "I'm a Christmas gift, right on your own doorstep."

"What are you doing here? All you had to do was put the signed papers in the mail." Her lips were a tight line.

"We've been through too much to let that be how this ended. Signatures exchanged in the mail? Can I come in to talk?" Rob asked.

She motioned him in.

"Are you jingling?" he asked. "Wait. Why are you jingling?"

"It's called Christmas spirit. My classes

enjoy teachers with Christmas spirit." She crossed her arms over her chest, muffling the bells.

The need to wrap his arms around her was an ache in his chest, but he had to go slowly.

To buy time, he moved slowly through the small space, a combination of living room, dining room and kitchen with a set of stairs to the side. It was nice but it didn't compare to the multistory brick home he'd bought them in Atlanta, the one she'd stayed in for less than two weeks before grabbing her bags and running away.

"Good thing I remembered to dress for the occasion," he said as he pointed at the hat.

When she didn't answer, he added, "Impulse buy from a gas station near Fort Lauderdale." This time he waited for her response until the silence grew awkward. "Good thing the guys on the SWAT team can't see. I'd never live it down."

They weren't exactly welcoming him with open arms after a year of trying to prove himself. Landing his spot on the team had been easier because of his connection to the team leader, a guy he'd served with, but that's where the easy part ended.

Bringing up the job filled the empty silence, but it did nothing to smooth things over with Mira. Rob cleared his throat. He needed better conversation.

Charming conversation.

Everywhere he looked here, there was a piece of Mira. What she lacked in space, she'd made up for with style. The walls of their house in Atlanta were still bare. He'd never mustered the energy to solve the problem himself. Besides that, he preferred... minimalism.

Mira's style? Not minimal at all. Her furniture was mismatched but put together well as if it might have been a careful choice. The odds and ends scattered on tables and the pictures reflected a lifetime of moves. He'd expected Mira's military brat training to make it easy for her to call any place home.

Apparently, that had been true of Miami but not Atlanta.

Boxes lined the floor under the bar. Was she packing?

"I didn't know you liked Christmas this

much," he said. He ruffled the fringe on a blanket thrown over the arm of her cushy couch. It had a scene of Santa's workshop, complete with a line of busy elves assembling toys. Everywhere he turned, there was something else to frown at. "I never realized someone could like the holiday this much." A Christmas village lined the top of the eat-in kitchen bar. He counted three Christmas trees in the room: one traditional live evergreen, one metallic hot pink with white ornaments and a tiny one perched on top of the refrigerator.

When he faced her, she was perfectly framed. A bookshelf on either side of a comfy chair with a stack of papers next to it. Three or four shelves were crammed with paperbacks. The rest displayed snow globes in a variety of sizes.

To buy precious seconds to form clear thoughts, Rob swept off the elf hat and ran his hand through his hair. He was pleased at the way her eyes tracked every movement. Until he tossed the hat down on her stack of papers. Her eyes were still locked to his hands.

Then he saw her notice how long she'd

been staring. Pink lit her cheeks and she straightened.

"The clutter is killing you, isn't it?" Mira asked as she plopped down in her chair. "Don't feel like you have to make polite conversation on my behalf. I read your last email about all the hours you're working in Atlanta on the task force you joined. All I need is the signed paperwork."

This was where they'd always gotten along. Neither one of them danced around the issue.

"I haven't signed them, Mira." Rob moved one of the reindeer throw pillows out of the way and sat down. Soft, warm comfort immediately swamped him, and he had to admit her furniture choices were a lot better than the ones he'd made. Sitting on his couch at home was like being in a doctor's waiting room. No one stayed any longer than they had to.

She closed her eyes to inhale slowly. That made it easier to catalog the changes he'd missed since they'd been apart. They were hard to find. Mira hadn't seemed to age. In fact, some of the restless tension that he'd always observed in her shoulders had eased. Her new life was suiting her well.

"Why not? That makes no sense." She untangled her arms. "We're living separate lives. This should be painless."

"Painless," he repeated. There wasn't much about his return home that he'd call painless. Giving up a job he loved to build something brand-new had been hard. Disagreeing with the one woman who could convince him to make a decision like that had been hard. Remembering how tears sprang up when he told her he'd left the army only because she asked it, giving up the thing he cared about most...

Yeah. That kept him up at night. Mira never cried. She took life's jabs on the chin, got up and fought back.

Watching her walk away to get some time and space and understanding about the adjustment required after leaving military life had been hard.

Opening the envelope with her signed divorce papers had been devastating.

In one minute, she'd knocked down the walls he'd built to adjust to his new life.

Nothing made sense anymore.

Well, nothing except one thought.

He couldn't lose her. That last step was too much.

"*Painless* is not a word I'd use to describe life lately, Mira." Rob felt irritation and anger boiling up, but he had to control that. This mattered too much to let emotion take over. "If it's a one-word description you're after, I'd have to go with…*empty*. Or *waiting*."

She sighed. "I understand. Lately, my life has been waiting, too. I'm moving to my first house after Christmas. I have found a job that I'm good at and I love. You have the same, Rob. There's only one thing holding us both back from ending the waiting." She met his stare without backing down.

"Sure. Living in the same city," he drawled, hoping to defuse some of the tension that was building. She'd always used logic, reason, and he found it hard to keep up.

Then Mira did the thing, the one thing that had always hit him straight in the heart. She snorted.

His beautiful, smart, tough wife snorted

like a teenage girl to show him how little she thought of his answer.

And they both laughed, like they always had.

"Not what I meant," Mira murmured as her lips twitched. "As you very well know."

He nodded and bent forward to brace his elbows on his knees and ignored the pull across his shoulder. "I've missed you more than any other person or place in this world. I know what will make me happy. You, in Atlanta, with me. What will it take to convince you?"

Mira groaned. "We don't work. We want different things, Rob. If you love me, please consider that I have built the life I've dreamed of here, in Miami." She held out both hands as if to show him. "It's like I'm alive here. I don't want to give that up."

Alive. She was alive here.

Rob wished he didn't know what she meant.

Mira was asking for what she wanted. The short time they'd been together in Djibouti, they'd argued more over what they hadn't said than what they had, but she was laying her cards out now.

Rob wanted to make her happy, but no intelligent man would watch her walk away a second time without a fight.

This time he understood what he'd be missing if he couldn't change her mind. He had to buy some time to convince her she belonged back in his arms.

An idea suddenly occurred to him. The perfect solution. He had one thing she wanted: a signature on their divorce papers.

"I'm not signing those papers tonight, Mira." Rob stood slowly, conscious of the fatigued muscles that protested leaving her comfortable couch. "I'd like the chance to prove to you that we deserve another shot. I gave up too easily the last time, so let's make a deal."

CHAPTER THREE

WHEN ROB STOOD, so did Mira. She hadn't expected this answer from him, so she was unprepared. Over a lifetime navigating unfamiliar territory, she'd learned to match her opponent's energy. Rob was calm. She could be, too, but she couldn't let him box her in.

Finding him at her door had stirred up that aching memory of how safe she'd felt next to him. Her first instinct had been to touch him. Even now. Would that ever go away?

To keep her eyes on the plan, to free them both up to create real, full lives, she needed to get him out of her space.

"We don't need to negotiate, Rob. We aren't going to agree on this. I understand," Mira said as she pointed to the door. "You can go ahead and leave. I don't have to have your signature on those papers. This was the easiest way to get the divorce done, but it's not the only way."

Rob bit his lip. How many times had she watched him do that?

When would it lose the power to stop her in her tracks?

This guy, who knew how to charm people into agreeing with his decisions, showing any uncertainty caught her every time.

When he'd offered to buy her a beer to introduce himself in the hot, loud bar off base, his sheepish look had caught her off guard. Her clear "no, thanks" had been unexpected.

Another man might have been taken aback at her polite brush-off, but Rob had never been like any other man she'd ever met. He'd paused before saying, "I should have gone with my first impulse, then."

Mira remembered fighting the urge to ask what that would have been. Most guys wandered away. Seeing a new approach from someone had intrigued Mira.

He'd sighed heavily before muttering, "I'm going to regret this." Mira had watched him slide onto the stool next to her and brace himself. "Where do generals keep their armies?" Then he'd held up his fingers for the bartender to bring two beers. "In their sleevies."

Mira had stared hard at the sweating beer mug the bartender set in front of her before giving in.

She'd laughed way too hard at the tired joke, but it hit at exactly the right time in the right place and that grin had unlocked one of her gates.

Tonight, he shook his head. Whatever the options he was considering, so far, they were disappointing and didn't compare.

"No, I don't want divorce the hard way, either." Rob held out his hand. Mira had to fight the reflex to slip hers into it. "I don't want that, either. I don't want us to be enemies, Mira." She could hear the pain of heartbreak in his voice and it matched her own.

"Don't do that," Mira whispered as she crossed her arms again. "Saying my name like that…" She huffed out a breath. He'd always had the power to stop her in her tracks with one word in his deep, husky voice. It was unfair.

His understanding of that was reflected

in the warm glint in his eyes. Ever since Mira had opened the door, she'd seen the flash of different emotions in that familiar hazel gaze. Worry. Irritation. Confusion. This gleam of warm pleasure was familiar, too, and dangerous.

She'd made up her mind that this was the right thing for both of them, but his eyes, that voice could convince her to reconsider.

He took a step closer. "Don't say your name? Mira." Then he winked as she frowned at him. "Okay. I won't do it again. Promise." Then he held up both hands. "Let's have a temporary truce."

The loud rumble of her stomach caught them both by surprise.

"I'll make my case in a hurry, before my wife starves." Rob offered her his hand again, this time to shake. Mira stared at it suspiciously. "Give me until Christmas to change your mind. If I can't manage it, I'll sign your papers on Christmas Day and go back to Atlanta. I promise."

Mira moved around the coffee table. She could shake his hand if she wanted to from this spot. There was no need to move closer.

She took another step anyway. She had to get closer.

"Why? What will a few more days change?" Mira asked. "We know. We don't work in the real world. That's no one's fault, but why draw this out?"

He didn't argue. He also didn't lower his hand. "We've never had a chance in the real world, Mira. Let's spend some time together to make sure before we throw what we have away."

One of the things she'd always appreciated about Rob was that he didn't lie, not even to smooth things over, not even when a small lie would have made life easier for everyone involved.

And he was right. She'd hated every minute she'd spent in Atlanta on her single visit. The house had been boxy and cold, felt nothing like any home she'd ever had. He'd given her the tour of the busy police headquarters and training facilities, and all she could see was the uniform and weapons that had replaced army issue and fatigues. She'd met coworkers who reminded her of those she'd patched back together in battle.

Every moment had been overshadowed

with the knowledge that the man she'd fallen desperately in love with would never be happy without the adrenaline rush of putting his life on the line.

The nightmares became worse than ever.

But that was who Rob was and she should have been tough enough to shut this down then, before the first drink, the first dance, the first "I love you."

This mismatch was her fault. She should insist on the divorce so he could find someone who accepted him the way he accepted her.

Rob wasn't asking for that, though.

"The last time we talked, you insisted I come home. You meant Atlanta." Mira pointed to the room. "But this is home for me. A job. My family. Good friends. I know that now."

They'd had versions of this conversation over the phone, via email and shouting in person. She knew what the answer would be.

"Give us one last shot," he said as his hand moved to slip around her waist. "Some things are different, that's true. Those we have to work out, but you and me, we're as good together as we have ever been."

Mira knew what was coming next. His eyes were locked to hers. His hand urged her closer, and it was the easiest thing to stretch up to meet his lips.

The world fell away when they kissed. It always had.

Whether it was the dry heat of Africa, the coldly impersonal house he'd bought in Atlanta or her cozy but cluttered townhome, nothing mattered except how his mouth matched hers, how his lips softened against hers, and the incredible mix of comfort and excitement that sparked all the way through Mira.

She reached up to grip his shoulders and blinked her eyes open as he moved back.

It took her too long to realize what had changed. Losing his warmth from the one second to the next was confusing, but it was also a gift. She pressed her hand to her lips as she evaluated her options.

"No more kisses, Rob," she said slowly and ignored the sinking feeling that settled inside her. Shutting down the affection was the adult thing to do. It also hurt. "I can wait until Christmas to get your signature because it will be better for us both to do this quickly, but we aren't a married couple anymore. Just…keep that in mind and let's be…friends." There. That sounded better. Friends didn't kiss. They didn't destroy each other in messy divorces. They could stay in contact via social media and it would all work out.

He held his hand out to shake again and she took it. "I accept your conditions. I'll be glued to your side to prove that, and on Christmas, you won't be able to bear the distance between us anymore."

"Fine. If you come at me, lips all puckered again, I'll have to break your nose." Mira smiled sweetly. He knew she could do it.

He pursed his lips and nodded. Mira decided to lose the battle of wills to stay in the war and stepped away as her stomach growled again.

"Why don't I check for food in your fridge?" he asked, the corner of his mouth curled in a not-quite grin. "Have you gotten any better at taking care of yourself since the first time I stayed over at your place? That apartment barely had room for a hot plate as I recall. You've upgraded." He turned toward her kitchen.

Mira didn't follow. She knew what he would find. She and cooking had an uneasy relationship going on for decades now. As soon as she'd moved out of her mother's house, she'd given it up except for special occasions and bare necessities.

"And as long as I've known you, you've never had a coffee maker," Rob said as he pointed at hers on the counter. "This is a good sign."

Mira shrugged as she hopped onto the stool across the counter from him. "Someone taught me to drink coffee, so I have another bad habit and a machine for my kitchen."

Rob braced his arms on the counter. "That was me. I taught you how to make good coffee."

Mira met his stare until he stepped away this time. "What's in here?" He opened the refrigerator and clapped his hands. "Breakfast for dinner. Our favorite."

It was almost the only thing the two of them could make, so it had to be their favorite. She didn't argue as he pulled out a carton of eggs, cracked every egg and crafted two beautiful, fluffy, large omelets with cheese.

"How do comedians like their eggs?" he asked as he glanced over his shoulder at her.

Which was incredibly attractive. She hadn't forgotten that, either.

When she sighed in response, he shook his head. "Funny side up. You always were a tough audience."

Mira didn't want to. Really. But it was funny!

As she laughed, he held up his spatula like a sword in victory, then dropped bread in the toaster as he dished up the omelets and placed the butter on the counter. When he'd served them both steaming cups of coffee with flair, he claimed the barstool next to hers.

"Yours is bigger than mine," Mira noted as she cut into the omelet.

"I'm a growing boy," he answered as he slid the sugar closer to her. "For your coffee."

They were silent as they ate, and Mira wondered how many times they'd been able to savor a simple meal in comfortable silence with each other. It was hard to recall.

"How did you get so much time off from work?" Mira asked. When they'd spoken last, he'd talked to her about how important his job was as leader for the Atlanta Police Department's SWAT team and tactical response unit. It sounded like he barely slept, much less could take a nice long vacation at the holidays.

"I had some vacation time coming. I couldn't leave the day I got your paperwork. Had to wait on a good window," he said, before sipping his black coffee.

Mira nodded as she worked on demolishing her omelet. She'd been hungry and he was good at eggs.

"How about a trip to Key West? Have you been there? We could explore it together like we toured London." He didn't face her as he waited for her answer. Did that mean he didn't care about the trip? Or that he cared too much?

Mira finished her toast and thought it over. Staying in Miami would show Rob very clearly why she belonged here and he didn't.

That would make getting the signed divorce papers easier on them both in the end.

Refusing a fun, romantic trip with the man who'd been the best adventure partner she'd ever had made perfect sense.

Going away with him would make saying goodbye harder. Rob knew that, too. That's why he was asking. He was planning his victory while he drank his coffee.

Mira knew it was a mistake to agree.

But some mistakes had to be made no matter how enjoyable they'd be and that she knew how it would all end.

"I have family obligations before I can go, and final grades are due." She watched him closely. "But we could go for a couple of days next week." She wanted to see Key West. More than that, she wanted to see it with Rob. Would that ever change?

He shot her a glance, long enough to see his smile. He thought everything was going according to his plan.

Ha.

"I'll do the dishes," Mira offered. That had been the bargain they'd ironed out in their very first argument over who would fix dinner. He cooked; she cleaned.

"I've gotten pretty good at doing both," Rob murmured as if he could read her mind. He opened the dishwasher. Mira waited for his usually disgruntled sigh, but he loaded all the dishes inside. She thought he was going to let one of his old pet peeves go. Maybe he had changed, after all.

Then, before he added the soap, he took all the silverware out and rearranged it in the basket. All forks were together, all spoons and all knives, each in their own compartments. It was his thing. She smiled and shook her head as she sipped her coffee.

"I didn't say a word," he said as he closed the door, stared at the buttons and started the wash cycle. "Look at how I've grown."

He moved to rest against the counter, his hands propped up behind him, and there, in between one second and the next when he'd controlled his features, Mira watched pain shoot across his face.

"What's wrong?" she asked.

His minute shrug reminded her of how quickly he'd ended their kiss. Why? Because she'd gripped his shoulder. His right shoulder, specifically. "What did you do to your shoulder?"

"Some soreness." He waved his left hand as if waving away the question. "It's nothing to worry about."

Before he could come up with a better lie, Mira rounded the counter, grabbed his left hand and led him to a seat at her tiny dining table. He was too tall for her to examine well if he sat on a stool.

"Really, it's fine." The last part of whatever he meant to say was muffled because she'd tugged his long-sleeved T-shirt up over his head. Getting his left arm untangled was fast, easy, and then she slowly worked the shirt down his right arm.

And saw a fresh, bright pink wound that had to be from a bullet.

As an Air Force medic, she'd seen hundreds of these wounds, had cleaned and bandaged them, after stopping the bleeding.

But she'd never seen one on her husband's body. Thinking of Rob in pain jarred her. Mira inspected the healing wound and did her best to breathe normally. She'd always prided herself on never panicking during difficult times, but two years of quiet civilian life had weakened her defenses. Her heart raced, but she could get control of it.

"No infection," Mira said, her voice rougher than before.

"See. It's fine. No blood. It's tender. That's all. Driving all day tightened up the muscles, and I forget sometimes, move the wrong way." At this distance, his mouth so close to her ear, his soft voice caused a shiver that she tried to cover by stepping away. "I'm okay, Mira."

She had to clasp her hands tightly to stop the urge to grab him and yell at him that this was everything that was wrong between them. Right here. This was it.

When she could finally meet his stare, she knew that he understood everything she was holding in.

"It's your shoulder, this time, but it could have been your head. Easily. Or your heart." Mira swallowed hard as the memories of fatal wounds washed over her. Her knees melted so she folded into the chair across from him. How could she face a lifetime of this worry and weakness? Rob could be gone in a single blink.

"But it wasn't. I'm good at my job." Rob wrapped his hand around hers and squeezed tightly.

"Bullets don't care, Rob. You can be the best. All it takes is one in the right spot." Mira closed her eyes. Despite their time apart, nothing had changed. He was going to insist on keeping his job on the task force in Atlanta. She understood ambition. But she wasn't going to live with this for the rest of her life. On Christmas Day, she knew he'd keep his word, sign the papers, and she'd have everything safely back to the way it was.

"I hadn't planned on telling you. I know what this does to my chances," Rob said as he squeezed her hand a second time. "You think you're right, don't you, about my job?"

Mira breathed out slowly. "Yes, but I've always been right, so don't worry. No change to your chances at all." His injury was an excellent reminder of how far apart they were now, regardless of how well Christmas and Key West went. She stood up. "I guess if we're going to waste our time with this last-ditch effort, you can sleep on the couch. Do you have a bag to bring in?" All business, that's what she'd be. She'd be friendly. And he'd keep his lips and his hands to himself. Her only worry was his voice.

"Yeah. A hot shower might help with the muscles. Do you mind?" Rob followed her. He wasn't going to keep arguing his point. That might be a small change from their usual pattern, she noted. "I'll go get my stuff," he said.

She nodded and opened the door for him. For some reason, she stayed and watched him.

"Worried someone would get me on the way to the parking lot and back?" Rob asked as he paused in front of her on the steps, his bag in hand.

Why had she done that? It didn't make any sense. He was a big boy.

"I considered slamming the door and turning the lock." Mira let him in.

"Scared I might change your mind?" Rob asked, his head bent toward hers as they stood in the narrow entryway. This close, he was overwhelming in the way that made it hard to think logically. He'd always done that, entered her space enough that she could feel his heat, smell his scent and touch his skin if she were brave. Rob left the decision up to her, and he'd always been so easy to choose.

Only distance had made it easy to say no.

"The bathroom is upstairs. In my bedroom. There are towels in the closet next to the tub." Mira licked her lips and stared hard at the floor. "I'll make up the couch for you."

She waited for whatever he would say. It would be sexy or sweet or…something, and her walls would fall.

But he stepped away from her. The difference was immediate. The temperature seemed to drop whenever he moved away. Before she could come up with anything else to say, he was climbing the stairs.

Mira flapped both hands in front of her face in an effort to cool her cheeks. Why had she agreed to his staying here? Oh, yeah. Easy divorce.

The water turned on upstairs and she clenched a hand to her jingling sweatshirt.

Make it to Christmas. That's all. Be strong for a few more days and this can be resolved easily.

Mira lost track of how long she stood in her living room repeating those orders to herself. When the water turned off, she realized she better move. She went to the laundry room and found a clean set of spare sheets and a quilt. They would do for the night, so she hurried back to the couch and had them waiting when Rob came down the stairs.

"I've got tests to finish grading and scores to enter. Can you entertain yourself? The remote is on the table." Mira sat, perched in her favorite comfy chair before she glanced up to meet his gaze.

It was an incredibly good thing, too. He was wearing gray sweatpants and no shirt. His hair was still damp. If she'd been standing, her knees would have failed her for sure.

"I've got a book." He pointed to his bag before setting it down next to the couch. "I don't want to bother you."

Bother. He didn't want to bother her.

Mira swallowed whatever words might come out of her mouth because she was capital B Bothered, but he didn't get to know that.

Mira plopped the stack of tests in her lap, slipped Rob's elf hat on her own head and forced herself to settle in to finish grading. The ears muffled little noise, but made it easier to ignore how efficiently Rob made up the couch. Then he dug around in his bag to produce a paperback, the latest of this bestselling thriller series she hadn't had a chance to start yet.

Mira opened her laptop because she was busy and had an important job.

Rob stretched out on the couch, his book in one hand, and slid on glasses. He was wearing glasses and reading a book while dressed like that on her comfy couch.

This was nothing new. Well, the glasses were new. They fit him. It was like watching the superhero turn back into his everyday, cuddly self…if she ignored the bullet wound.

The rest of it? She'd seen it before. Everything was fine. No worries.

Mira wanted to fan herself again, but she refused to let her hands leave the laptop's keyboard.

It was going to be a long night. For some reason, grading the final two tests took twice as long as the rest of the class had.

Some reason. She knew very well the reason.

Rob Bowman had walked through her door and her common sense had shut off.

He'd always been able to do that.

This time, it was going to be different.

CHAPTER FOUR

ROB STARED UP at the faint shadows cast on the ceiling by the pale morning light reflected off one of Mira's snow globes. Last night, after she'd closed her laptop with a snap and tossed his elf hat on top of her stack of papers, Mira had said good-night and marched upstairs.

He'd read or tried to for a while and then prowled around the room hunting up switches to turn off and plugs to unplug for all the lit trees and Christmas decorations. As he'd stretched back out on the couch, Rob realized he'd missed one but decided it was good to have some light in a new place.

He'd gotten up a second time and taken the glowing snow globe off the shelf. Now it sat on the coffee table, tiny Big Ben and a red double-decker bus surrounded by glittery falling snow, within easy reach whenever he wanted to give it a shake.

He'd been with Mira when she'd bought it, but he hadn't realized she had such an extensive collection or the full extent of how much she loved the holiday.

That bothered him.

For most of his adult life, his own holiday decor had been limited to the photos his sister sent of his nephew and niece screaming on Santa's lap or the whole family posed in front of some seasonal backdrop and the old stuffed Santa that had lived under his grandmother's tree when he was a little boy.

Seeing that Santa had always been an important part of the holiday for Rob as a kid. The last time he'd unpacked Santa, worn spots on the suit had worried him. Was that Djibouti? Rob closed his eyes as he tried to picture which apartment that had been. Mira had fallen in love with his ragged Santa and placed it in the only position of honor in his tiny box of an apartment: right on top of the TV.

Almost had to be Djibouti. Had it been that long since he'd unpacked the few mementos he carried with him always? And why hadn't it occurred to him to do more in Atlanta?

If he closed his eyes, he could picture the spindly tree his mother always put up. He hadn't been home to see it in years, not since he'd refused to return to take over the farm after his father died. Farm life didn't fit him. He'd joined the Army to get out of there, and his brother-in-law was the perfect choice to add to the mix.

He still knew where the Christmas tree would be—in the corner of the living room. Nothing there changed much.

Maybe army life had made it easier to live without over-the-top Christmas decor or collections of anything.

Or maybe he was missing something.

He didn't own a single flashing, blinking plug-in decoration.

He had to admit that this light was kind of nice. Darkness had never bothered him, but this soft happy glow reminded him of Mira, her touch on this place, and added some magic.

"Atlanta is missing some magic," he whispered and yanked the quilt closer to his chin. Mira could fix that.

Rob picked up his phone to check the time. Not quite six in the morning. That didn't surprise him. His internal clock was strict and reliable, even if he was on vacation and might like to stretch the limits by sleeping in.

"Now what?" he wondered. He had options. First, he could reverse his steps and light up Mira's living room like the North Pole before she came downstairs. That might be nice. There was also the reminder that he'd used every egg in the house to make dinner and breakfast was looming. He didn't know where the closest grocery store was, but it couldn't be hard to find one.

Rob had almost convinced himself to head for the store and return via a coffee shop with pastries when the stairs squeaked. Anyone who served in tight spots around the globe learned early on to decipher stealthy maneuvers from the normal night sounds.

His wife was sneaking down the stairs.

Why? Rob closed his eyes and shifted slightly so he could watch the stairway without alerting her. Eventually, slowly, Mira made it down the last step and into the living room. In the faint glow, he could tell she was carrying her running shoes in one hand.

Was she going to wake him up to tell him where she was going?

Or invite him to join her?

He watched and hoped for the latter until she opened the front door, stepped through and quietly closed it behind her. The lock turned with a final snick.

"The hospitality of this bed-and-no-breakfast leaves something to be desired," Rob said as he tossed aside the quilt. Mira had her routine. Of course she did. She went running every day before the sun came up. Today she could have company, but she insisted on going her own way. Irritation made it easy enough to decide what to do next.

Rob grabbed his duffel and pulled out a sweatshirt. Yanking it over his head reminded him of the tender spot in his shoulder, but that wouldn't keep him from running. He put on socks and running shoes before grabbing the elf hat. "Some vacation. Awake and running before sunrise."

He managed to get the door locked behind him and stopped to stretch on the sidewalk. The hat settled on his head with barely a twinge of embarrassment this time. Mira might enjoy that embarrassment, too.

As soon as he found her.

This side of the townhome complex was quiet, so he walked back toward the office and the main entrance. Wherever Mira had gone, she hadn't hesitated. Sun was breaking the horizon as he made it to the driveway. From his spot, he could see one runner disappearing around the bend in the road. It was a man, but that could mean it was a common route.

Running had always been a requirement. Military service and working SWAT required physical fitness. He'd never loved it the way Mira did, but Rob realized she had nice scenery. Everything here was lushly green, even in December. No sand. No punishing wind. Catching the guy he'd seen didn't take long, but a curve in the path showed he was the anchor for a line of six runners. Four men jogged steadily behind a slim brunette, and they all fell in line behind a petite woman with a swinging, long dark ponytail.

Mira was setting the pace.

Of course she was.

She had built her own group, taken the lead and had zero to worry about as far as company went.

Mira was smart. She didn't need him watching out for her, even though that wouldn't stop him from trying. Rob didn't pour on the speed, although it was tempting to race to the front of the line and in front of Mira.

Just to show her he could.

And to show the guys behind her that he could.

Unfortunately, it was too easy to imagine Mira's frustration at such a maneuver. So he yanked off the elf hat and draped it across the first available mailbox and kept pace with the group.

When she turned to go back home, Mira's eyes met his as they passed. She didn't stop. She didn't acknowledge him.

But she did snort.

That made it easier to grin at each curious look he got from her followers.

When he made it back to the mailbox, the elf hat was gone. As he turned back into Concord Court's parking lot, Mira and her group were waiting for him, hands on hips.

The elf hat mystery was solved. Mira was wearing it.

"New neighbor or…" the man closest to Mira drawled and slanted a glance at her.

Rob wanted him to fill the rest of that in. Or what?

Mira shook her head as if she couldn't find any way out of answering. "My husband. Rob Bowman." She met his stare, and he could see some of the annoyance he'd expected. "This is Sean Wakefield. He works here at Concord Court." She pointed at the guy who'd asked the question. He frowned at Rob. "Peter. Marcus. Jason. Brisa." She completed roll call. "These are my friends, Rob."

No one offered a hand or a smile.

Either they were a shy group or Mira had told them a divorce was in the works. The frowns they wore helped him answer that question.

"Nice to meet you. I'm glad Mira has good friends here in Miami. I was not surprised to spot her in the lead this morning." Rob crossed his arms over his chest, trying to signal he wanted to eliminate the awkwardness of an unfriendly introduction.

"Must have burned not to race to the front and take over." Mira fluttered her eyelashes at him and it was easy to remember how they'd jockeyed for position on the runs they'd shared.

"It's enough to know I could have," Rob said with a shrug. "I don't have to win all the time."

This time, Mira's snort was a little less cute.

The guy next to her, Sean, whistled loud and long, as he casually draped an arm over Mira's shoulders.

As if he'd done the same thing a thousand times.

Had Mira already fallen in love with someone else? Was that why she'd had the divorce papers drawn up?

Mira's hard shrug answered the question before jealousy or panic could take over. Sean's arm slid away and he held his hands up as if surrendering.

"You don't have to win every time. Right." Mira turned on her heel and walked away, done with the whole conversation.

Leaving him alone with five hard stares.

"Why didn't you mail back the paperwork, man?" Sean asked. "Mira's happy here."

Rob raised his chin. He still had his pride. "I don't blame you, you know. I understand how easy she is to love, Sean. I want a fair shot at keeping my wife."

Sean nodded. "Seems like you've had plenty of time to leave Atlanta behind. Before the papers, that's all it would have taken. Now, my best friend's moving on without you. Accept it. Make us all happy. Well, all but you, I guess, and we can live with that." He followed Mira away down the sidewalk.

Rob wasn't sure what else he would have said anyway.

"Best friend," Rob murmured. That was better than he'd feared.

Then he realized he still had an audience.

"She's the heart of the place," the woman said. She was a beautiful woman, perfect model-like features despite the run. He'd been introduced, but couldn't remember her name. Her slow grin convinced him she knew that, too. "Brisa. Montero. I run Concord Court with Sean's help. If my sister had believed his pretended connection to Mira, her face might have matched yours."

As he absorbed that, the other guys shook their heads. They weren't involved with her, either. The way his shoulders immediately relaxed was irritating. Even eliminating these guys didn't mean she wasn't falling for someone else.

"She's not dating anyone. Trust me, I know. I set her up on her first date in forever," Brisa said. "And if you meet a tall, dark-haired guy with a scowl on his face, that's Wade. He was her blind date. He's with me now. He won't like you, either. Say what you want about Mira's friends, they know loyalty better than anyone. They'll move mountains for her." She put her hands on her hips. "Or help her get your signature on those papers."

Rob was determined to maintain a stiff upper lip.

"As soon as she's divorced, I might try setting her up again. Her heart might be in it this time." She winked.

Confused, Rob exhaled slowly. First, she'd warned him Mira's friends might commit mayhem if she needed them to, but...

Was she throwing him a rope? If Mira's heart hadn't been in the blind date, could she still be unsure about the divorce? "You ever made a mistake, Brisa? One you'd like to rewind and then do over?"

Brisa blinked before laughing loudly. Rob had expected chuckles. This was guffawing.

Was it at him?

Brisa immediately pointed at him with one hand and clutched her stomach with the other.

So that answered his question.

"So many mistakes, Rob. If you need to feel better about yourself, we can go and get a cold drink and compare lists." Brisa straightened. "What was yours?"

"I never should have been okay with her leaving Atlanta. I thought time apart would make it clear we needed to be together." Rob cringed. "I'm here to bring her home."

Brisa nodded and wrapped her arm through his, as though he were escorting her through a fancy ballroom. She waved at the guys, who faded away in the distance behind them. "Now, I don't want to do anything to hurt Mira," she said slowly as she squeezed his arm, "but I have a soft spot in my heart for people who need a comeback. That's you."

The urge to argue was strong, but she was laying everything out in black and white. He might as well see where she was going.

"Can you help me convince her to come home?" he asked. He'd take whatever help he could get. "I'll appreciate any tips."

"If I thought that was the answer…" She wrinkled her nose. "The thing I've learned lately is…sometimes you need to look at the problem from a different perspective. My problems? They came from always taking the easy way out. I would want to help, so I'd jump in…and then I had a mess I had no hope of cleaning up, so I bailed. To make the change I needed, I had to do the hard work. Stick it out. Even when it seemed impossible, too messy, and I was sure I was going to fail." She blinked up at him. "I didn't want to fail. Yet I kept failing over and over."

Rob watched her talk, but her words didn't compute.

He couldn't imagine going through life as the screwup. This decision to split with Mira wasn't the norm for him.

"You're staring at me as if I arrived from another planet." She grinned. "I get that a lot but it's usually more complimentary." They continued along the sidewalk and turned the corner.

"I don't…fail. Not like this." Rob frowned as she pulled her arm away and gave him a knowing look.

"Overachievers. This place is lousy with people like you! The military must attract men and women who are good at everything," Brisa said, the pretend disgust on her face cuter than it should be. "Welcome to the real world."

Rob rubbed his shoulder as he considered that. "More like, the military figures out what we're good at, locks us in there and trains us until we're the best." Ever since his father had made it a habit to show up for his high school football games because Rob Bowman was one of the hottest quarterbacks in the state of Oklahoma, Rob had understood that being the best at something earned respect, attention, rewards, and he'd embraced it.

A blown ACL the summer before his senior year hadn't changed that, either. That accident, courtesy of falling after long, hot hours of putting up hay, had convinced him that his life was going to lead somewhere other than Keen, Oklahoma.

As soon as his leg was rehabilitated, he'd made plan B and set out to be the best enlisted soldier the army had. Later on, life as a part of the military police force had suited him. No one had gotten better marks or reviews for the job.

Brisa sniffed. "Life in the real world has got to be hard." She held out a hand. "I like you and I don't even know you. Messes like me? We can totally get away with that. My advice to you is, keeping Mira is going to require a different outlook."

It made a twisted sense, even if Rob had no idea what she was suggesting exactly. "Like what?"

"You may have to give up what's best for you to get what's right." Brisa frowned. "Don't ask me to explain that yet. I don't know where it came from, but... Say you're dress shopping. Stay with me here." She held up a hand to ask for patience. "You're out shopping for a special night on the town, my favorite. You tell the salesperson you only want to buy couture, one of a kind, the most expensive dress in the shop. No one else will be wearing anything like it, which is totally the goal, in case you were wondering, but it's too tight and it's yellow." Brisa stuck her tongue out. Clearly, she wasn't a fan of yellow.

She continued. "You resolve to not eat ever again or at least until the day after your event and you max out your credit card because this is the best dress you will find. Everyone will agree it's the best the shop has." Brisa paused and waited for him to nod that he was following her. It was a weird analogy but not hard to keep up with. "Now you're paying for the dress and a salesperson shows you her favorite dress. It's less expensive, less exclusive, but it's deep purple, which is the best color for you, fits like a glove and is on sale. It's perfect. You might never have seen that dress on your own because you were so focused on what was best. You were focused on the wrong thing." She glanced up as if to search the sky. "I should have tried *Goldilocks and the Three Bears* instead of creating my own metaphor. Go before I get another message from the mothership."

Rob was still rubbing his forehead when he closed Mira's front door. She was standing in front of the refrigerator. "There's no food in here, but there is water." She glanced over her shoulder at him, so he nodded.

"You okay? Shoulder hurt? I thought you might sleep in this morning."

Rob forced himself to stop turning Brisa's words over in his mind. There was something to what she'd said, but he wasn't any clearer on it than she was. Was she calling his plans for Atlanta "best" in her analogy? Had to be. If he gave those up to find "right," where would he start?

Rob answered, "Nope. Too much to do today." The water hit the spot. When Mira drank and then exhaled with pleasure, the urge to wrap his arm around her was hard to ignore.

"Yeah?" she asked. "Like what?"

Rob held out his hand to count on his fingers. "While you shower, I'm going to the grocery store. I will buy easy-to-cook food there and bring it back here. Then I might take my wife out to breakfast." He sighed happily. "Then, I'm stuck to you like glue."

She frowned. "Was that what I signed up for? It doesn't sound like me."

"You did sign up for it. You should spend more time reading the terms of service before you pick up your pen." Rob stepped closer to her. He'd said he wouldn't kiss her.

If he was clever enough, she might kiss him. He'd make sure she didn't have to go far, just in case.

"My mother sent me her recipe for sticky toffee pudding as a request-slash-order that I bring it for my sister's birthday dinner tomorrow. I do need to go to the grocery store, but there's no reason for us to both go." Mira didn't smile, but her wary assessment had faded. "Stay here. Get some rest. Try a real vacation day or something. I'll shower and change quickly."

"Let's go together, pick up breakfast on the way back. You're as hungry as I am."

Mira wanted to argue. He could see the impulse on her face, but she nodded and headed for her room. The night before, she'd marched up the stairs, each foot hitting each step solidly. Aggressively? Maybe, maybe not.

But today, she moved slowly.

As if she was still thinking about him and his plan. At the top of the stairs, she paused to look down at him. "If we were in Atlanta, would you be doing this? Reorganizing your whole life to spend time with me?"

Rob was still trying to find the correct answer when she closed the bedroom door.

CHAPTER FIVE

MIRA FROWNED AS she read her mother's recipe and wondered if she shouldn't have requested something easier to bake. After tossing and turning most of the night, busy thinking about Rob and afraid sleep would mean returning to the old nightmares, she was tired. Running should have cleared her mind, but there he was. She might have discussed his surprise visit with her friends to regain some clarity, but not while Rob was listening. She'd gotten used to her space. The last thing she wanted to do was go grocery shopping with the man.

Especially since he was so determined to be charming and helpful. It was too much for early Saturday morning.

"So, a neighborhood *mercado* instead of a big-box grocery store," Rob said as he pulled two baskets out of the stack near the door and offered one to her. "I would have gone with the boring chain store near the interstate and picked up drive-through doughnuts somewhere."

Mira slipped the recipe back in her pocket and gathered her patience. She and Rob had a deal. Starting a fight now to get breathing room would make everything harder. "That would have been fine, too, but the bakery here inside the market sells amazing breakfast empanadas. If you are lucky enough to know about them and get here before they sell out, you understand why the parking lot outside is nearly full at this time of day."

She watched his head turn as if he was scanning the tops of the aisles to narrow in on the target: the source of the spicy chorizo inside the *mercado*. The shelves were cramped with the usual items and some specialty ones, too. The three checkouts each had someone ringing up customers and special displays of Mexican snacks and candy, and most of the signs were in Spanish.

When Rob's eyes locked on the exact spot of the tiny bakery, which was impossible to see from the front of the store, Mira laughed.

"Focus," Mira murmured, "you made a list on the way over, remember?"

Rob nodded but Mira wasn't sure he was following the conversation. "Coffee, eggs, milk, other stuff." He glanced at her and smiled. "I was thinking we should divide and conquer, see? If there is a limited source of empanadas and those are the main reason we are here, we should take care of that first."

"Or we could not waste time and do both." She pointed at the back wall. "Go down this aisle and grab some coffee on the way. I'll meet you in produce, where we need to find dates for Gina's birthday dessert."

Rob clicked his heels, turned and marched away, swinging the basket in his hand as he went. She wiped the smile off her face as he glanced over his shoulder to see if she was watching him.

Was it bad that she couldn't look away from him?

Determined to get her head together, Mira went quickly through the dairy section and turned the corner into produce to see Rob talking to a short teenage boy.

Marco was usually stocking produce when she came in. As she wound between tables, she chose two mangos and added them to her basket.

"Dates. Where are your dates?" Rob asked again. Apparently he'd taken her advice to heart and was focused on getting to the empanadas as soon as possible.

The kid juggled the apples in his hands before adding them to the small stack for sale. "I don't know, man. I heard the freezer section's the best place to pick up women." He dipped his chin, a big grin on his face as he waited for Rob's answer.

"For a recipe, kid." Rob did that thing men sometimes did where they tried to get bigger, more intimidating, and narrowed his eyes. "You think I need help getting the other kind of dates?"

Marco wrinkled his nose. "No way, man, but if that's your lady, I'd cool it, quick."

"Hey, Marco, ignore him." Mira bumped Rob out of the way with her shoulder. "Dates. They're sort of like…figs? Or if raisins are like grapes, dates are like figs?" Realizing that both the kid and her husband were staring at her as if they were worried about her, Mira shook her head. "You don't carry them?"

Marco shook his head. "No figs. No dates. Not here." He held his arms out as if Produce was his domain and he knew every one of his subjects.

"Okay, thanks," Mira said as she wrapped her hand around Rob's wrist to lead him to the bakery. They'd have to make a stop at the bigger grocery store, but no one would be complaining about it as long as they got their empanadas.

"Why are you frightening children, Rob?" Mira asked as she watched him put cookies that were definitely not on the list inside his basket. Then she noticed chips and two different types of bread. He'd deviated from the plan, clearly, and they hadn't even made it to the candy yet.

He looked serious, then a genuine smile spread across his face. "We do not accept the poking of our ego lightly."

"Oh, no, not the royal we!" She pressed a hand to her chest. The flutter there reminded her of how much she'd loved this, standing near Rob and bantering. They'd been great at it once upon a time. "I've never bought dates, obviously. Finding them in Produce made sense, but Marco would have known better than to suggest I needed any help finding a real date." She raised her nose in the air.

"Well, no, of course not. You don't have to find dates at the grocery store. You have Brisa." Rob took her basket as they stopped behind the short line at the bakery counter and waited for her to answer.

"Somebody told you about my date with Wade, huh?" Mira didn't mind that it hadn't remained a secret, but everything was so unsettled between them that she didn't want to add more kindling to the fire yet. "Don't worry. She was fooling herself at the time, but they've fallen for each other hard and Wade is totally invested." Not that she'd ever been interested in him anyway. He was a good man, a great friend and the kind of guy a woman could love.

Unless she was already in love with someone else.

"She mentioned she was ready to set you up again," Rob said and nodded at the young mother with a stroller who stepped away from the cash register, a large bag in one hand. "I guess you have to get rid of your husband problem first. Not that having a husband stopped you the last time."

Mira frowned at him. Husband problem? Rob made it sound like she was eliminating a minor inconvenience. Had she experienced mild guilt over that husband problem at the time she'd gone on the cool bike tour of the Wynwood Walls art district with Wade? Yes. Was she going to admit that here? Never.

"I guess you've spent every moment of almost two years by yourself, Wade?" she asked, braced to accept his answer without letting him know it hurt.

"Well, no. I've spent lots of time at work and occasional barbecues and tailgates, trying to become a part of this new team in Atlanta, build camaraderie in the real world. You don't have the military drills, the 24/7 lifestyle, although it's close. To me, that's the hardest part of the job, getting into the team. Turns out, having a connection to the guy who can give you the job helps you get the job, but it might not make you popular with your coworkers." He frowned back at her.

Rob was struggling in Atlanta. Coming

home hadn't been a seamless transition for him, either.

Mira wanted to ask him more about that. For some reason, she'd never imagined Rob would have trouble with any part of his career. He'd always been a top soldier, a top officer, a man to respect. Her new life had meant a new beginning, and that made sense because she was changing jobs. Rob hadn't changed careers. Starting all over again at the bottom, on the outside, might be even harder.

"But I haven't been on dates, Mira. I missed my wife. No one else would do."

Surprised, she met his stare. He meant it. Rob was telling the truth.

"Ah, Mira, *como estas*?"

Shaken, Mira turned back to smile at Julia, the woman who baked all the items the *mercado* sold during the day. "*Muy bien*, Julia, gracias." Before she could ask for her usual order, Julia had bustled away to the case that displayed everything on sale. She was humming to herself as she filled a bag.

Rob bent close to her ear to say, "We aren't finished talking about this date."

Mira couldn't have answered even if she'd known what to say. Her mouth was too dry.

"I tripled your usual," Julia said when she returned with an admiring glance at Rob. "Do you think that's enough food?" Her saucy grin brightened her whole face.

Rob held out some cash. "That should do it, senorita. Thank you."

Julia nodded and made change.

"Ah, one more question," Rob said, "do you know if dates are sold in the store?"

Mira ducked her chin as she watched Julia flutter her eyelashes at Rob. It was adorable, and the slow grin he gave Julia thrilled the older woman. "Baking aisle." She winked. "Where all the good things are kept."

Rob ducked his head as if he were a courtly gentleman. "*Muchas* gracias."

Julia was still giggling when the next customer stepped up to the counter and Rob turned down the aisle with the baking goods. Mira couldn't help but shake her head. That was how Rob Bowman got a woman.

Who knew respect, good manners and a

genuine appreciation for other people was so sexy?

"What are you shaking your head about?" he murmured as he studied the raisins and then did a weird victory shimmy when he found the package. "Dates! We did it."

Mira held her basket out. "Put them in here. Yours seems to be full." She raised her eyebrows.

"Growing boy." Rob tapped his abdomen. "Who needs an empanada soon."

He locked in on the shortest of the lines, tossed four different types of candy in their baskets, took care of the bill and carried the bags to her car. Once they were back in her kitchen, he brewed the coffee and pulled down two plates.

Neither one of them said anything until he'd had his first bite. "Mmm. Chorizo. Flaky pastry. I'll have to get more serious about running if there are more of these in my life."

The sound of his pleasure at the food filled the tiny kitchen and Mira's ears. She dropped the brown sugar she'd pulled from a cabinet.

"Slow down. We'll make your pudding in

a minute." Rob held an empanada up and waited for her to take a bite.

After she'd chewed, swallowed and remembered what she was doing, Mira said, "We? Who is baking this? And it's actually more of a moist-cake thing with a sauce than a pudding."

Rob nodded and put the snacks he'd grabbed in the cupboard over the refrigerator, the one she couldn't reach without climbing on a chair.

When she stared at the cabinet and back at him, he laughed. "You can have whatever you want. I'll move everything to a lower shelf when the pudding is done." He poured them both cups of coffee. "You cook, I'll clean. Then you say, 'We made it' for the party or whatever and I don't feel like a jerk for showing up empty-handed." He waggled his eyebrows.

Mira shook her head as she sipped the coffee. He'd stirred in exactly the right amount of sugar. "You don't have to wash dishes. I accept your terms."

Rob finished putting away the groceries while Mira mixed the cake. It was all so easy.

Maybe easier than they'd ever managed before. That didn't make sense.

Each time he reached around her to put something away, his body brushed hers until she was struggling to concentrate and happy when he ran out of things to do.

This morning when Rob leaned against the counter, the motion seemed easier for him. He didn't wince, and she'd made sure to watch. They were so close together in her compact kitchen that she couldn't miss his expressions. His breaths. The way he studied her.

Too closely.

"I get why Brisa picked you. For the guy she was fixing up. Any man would be happy to find you as his blind date. What I don't get is why you went along with it." He grabbed the spoon she knocked off the counter before it could make a worse mess on the floor, then turned to wash it and tidy the spill.

"We're back to this." Mira sighed. "I was helping Brisa. She'd gotten herself in a mess by sneaking around behind her sister's back and trying to set Reyna up. Wade was her target, the guy she catfished for her older sister's sake, and he demanded her help finding someone new." She put both hands over her heart. "Air force medic turned high school teacher seemed too perfect for a navy surgeon with a precocious daughter."

"That wasn't my question." He didn't back down but waited for her answer.

Nervous with how the world shrank to contain only the two of them, his face and hers, Mira licked her lips. "I love my life here, but something's…missing."

He nodded and tossed the damp towel he'd used to dry dishes across the faucet. "That's why I'm here. Instead of looking for someone new who might come close to making me feel the way you did, I'm here. With you. Asking you not to give up on us."

Mira tried to ignore the ache in her chest at his words. Whatever their problems might be, Rob had loved her. "I only agreed to go on the date after I negotiated ruthlessly to have Brisa join my running group. Me against that many guys? I can totally handle it, but there is so much less complaining now that I have backup. I say 'let's go for ten miles today' and Brisa agrees. Not a single one of them wants to back down after that."

Mira cleared her throat as she stepped back. The urge to take a deep, calming breath was strong. She needed space. "Thank you for the help. If a career in law enforcement doesn't pan out, you have a bright future as a scullery maid."

"Scullery maid, huh? I didn't know we still had those outside of fairy tales and/or European castles," Rob said.

The silence between them became charged, awkward.

As if they were both thinking loudly but didn't want the words to escape.

"Since we made it through baking successfully, let's go out somewhere fancy tonight. We didn't get to do that often enough while we were in the service. What do you say?" Rob asked.

"I can't. I have plans." Mira watched him and waited. When he didn't ask for details, she decided to save them both. It was tempting to leave him thinking the worst as some kind of proof that she'd gone on with her life, but that kind of passive-aggressive power play was wrong. He was being honest with her, and he deserved better.

"Family thing. You can stay here, or I'll

give you the names of some great places to eat," Mira said. There. Easy enough.

"The pudding family thing? I thought that was tomorrow?" He frowned.

"It is. I promised my nephew Jackson that I would take him to Winter Wonderland this evening to see Santa. Tonight and tomorrow's lunch will satisfy my family's requirements until Christmas Eve. As soon as I get back tomorrow, we can go to Key West or… whatever you like, but I can't miss this."

"Dress casual, then? Tonight? No concept of what the dress code is for a wonderland," Rob drawled, "but I wouldn't want to offend Santa. He keeps a list. In fact, I heard he even checks it twice."

Wait. Was he saying he was coming along?

"This is not your thing, Rob. Silly sweaters. Kids screaming. Things blinking and goofy music… Take a rain check and enjoy your evening." She would enjoy hers as well because she wouldn't be dragging him along with her.

"It wasn't my thing before, but I don't want to miss a minute I could be spending with you." Rob picked up his elf hat. "I brought my own hat for the occasion, remember?"

Mira wanted to argue. If he went, things would get so complicated.

The best thing about Miami was how uncomplicated it was for her to live here.

Making friends had been simple.

Finding her purpose had been simple.

Getting through school and landing a teaching contract… Everything had been so uncomplicated, thanks mainly to the support provided by living at Concord Court.

Taking Rob with her was going to create a tangle that would hurt to work through.

His slow smile said he was prepared for any of her arguments.

From their first moment together, Mira had strived to challenge him and keep him on his toes.

The only way to do that in this instance was to give in, at least for now.

"Okay," she said with forced cheer, "but I hope you know what you're getting yourself into."

CHAPTER SIX

ROB GAVE HIMSELF a mental pat on the back for being an excellent passenger. Mira maneuvered the car through Miami's traffic as if she'd seen someone drop a checkered flag. He hadn't expected that, but he should have.

Mira drove like she did everything else: capably and quickly. He knew he'd caught her off guard by skipping the argument over who would be driving. She knew the town. It was uncomfortable to be a ride-along instead of the one hitting the gas, but he could deal with it. Mira didn't need to know that. It would only confirm her suspicion that he couldn't let go of control.

"It's fair to give you one last shot at jumping ship," Mira said as she pulled into a driveway in a nice cookie-cutter subdivision. The orange sun was setting. "Jackson is six. He's very…kid-like."

Rob considered that warning and tried to decipher her meaning. "As opposed to... what?"

"Good question." Mira put the car in Park and faced him. "You and I never spent much time around kids when we were together."

"Zero time. We spent zero time around kids." He'd been happy to keep it that way, too. The world was filled with too many exciting things to try. Kids would slow them down, and as it was every minute he'd spent with her felt exactly right.

"Therefore, I'm guessing this excursion to Winter Wonderland is not going to be your cup of tea." Mira sighed. "I don't want to ruin your night."

"I don't like tea period. Too weak." He raised his eyebrows to see if she'd laugh along with him. When she dropped her chin and gave him her most patient stare, he cleared his throat. "I haven't been around kids much. Even my niece and nephew are quick interruptions when I call my sister, but I am a mostly well-functioning human person. I can handle one kid."

Reading between the lines, Rob was sure she also didn't want him or his presence to possibly take away from her time with her nephew. He got that. He'd be on his best behavior. Wanting to impress Mira was his number one priority. If he failed in convincing her to come home, he wanted to know he'd given it his best shot. Being the world's most pleasant escort would help.

He reached across to squeeze her hand. "I'll be happy to be with you, Mira. That's all I'm looking for. And if Jackson is a kid-like kid, as you say, you could use reinforcements. Kids move erratically. Right?" Rob waited for her to answer. Her rolled eyes were good enough. "I'm surprised his parents trust you to take him to a wild place like Santa's forest by yourself." He heard the sarcasm in his tone and knew she would, too. In his mind, this place had one of those poky little trains kids loved, some lights and a guy in a red suit who posed for pictures. That would be about the right speed for a six-year-old. How wild could it be?

Her slow laugh would have sent chills down his spine if he hadn't been certain any kid attraction would be...well, child's play for two decorated military veterans, one of whom was currently serving on one of the country's largest police forces.

And the other one was a high school teacher.

What did they have to fear from Santa Claus? The two of them together, with their very particular set of skills, made an elite babysitting team.

"What that answer tells me is that you have not spent nearly enough time in Florida." Mira stretched in her seat. "What you're picturing? It's a photo opportunity with a man in a red suit. There's a backdrop, a painted village or something, a few lights and staff dressed in elf suits."

She raised her eyebrow and waited.

The way she'd nailed his expectation on the first try? Hot.

It was also a good reminder that his wife was smarter than he was. Always had been.

Rob wished the lighting was better in the dark interior of the car. He wanted to see the teasing that was coming through the tone of her voice lighting up her eyes, too. He had to imagine it was there. Fortunately, Rob had seen it often enough that he could do that easily.

Before he could answer, a loud yell and thump against the car window shook him. Rob's heart raced as he stared into the dark eyes of a small boy with an impressively crisp haircut, a gaping smile with one front tooth missing and his hands curled into claws like a small, loud, terrifying monster.

"Auntie Mira, who's this?" The boy demanded answers, his voice muffled by the glass.

When his window started to go down, Rob fought the urge to tell Mira not to lower his only protective barrier.

"Yes, Mira, who is this?"

Rob swiveled his head in the other direction to find Mira's sister Gina with her elbows propped on the car door. They'd never met in person, but Rob had endured the third degree via one very long video phone call with all of Mira's sisters. Gina was Jackson's mother. That answered one question. The other sister who lived in Florida was Kris. The youngest, Naomi, lived…

Did all three of them have kids? And their husbands' names were lost, too. If anyone gave him a pop quiz on the Peters family, he'd fail.

Then Gina said, "Oh, it's the long-lost husband. Hello, Rob, long time, no see." Her lips curled but it wasn't a friendly smile. "Did you tell us he was in town?" Gina shook her head to indicate that Mira had not.

"Hi, Gina, I surprised her yesterday," Rob said. He would have opened the car door and moved around to take the car seat she was holding but the small monster had hung both his arms through the window and was staring hard at Rob's face.

Gina raised her eyebrows. "Hmm. Mum is going to be beside herself tomorrow, isn't she?"

"Mom, Mommy, Mama… We lived in England for four years, Gina. You don't have a posh accent and there's no reason to call her Mum." Mira sighed and motioned at her sister to move back so she could open the door. "Don't you tell her Rob is here or I'll dump your sticky toffee pudding in the garbage and then I'll get even."

Her sister feigned an apologetic look as Mira opened the back door.

Rob smiled at the kid who was still

watching him while the women wrestled the car seat into the back.

"Hey, I'm Rob." He held out his hand for a manly handshake. The kid slapped it in a high five and ran around to the open door to clamber into the car seat.

There was some kind of conversation going on in angry whispers. Rob ducked his head to see better, but that was enough of a warning that they had an audience that the sisters broke it off and exchanged mean glares.

Then Mira was sliding behind the wheel. "Gina, we will be back by nine."

Gina stuck her head in the window. "Be good." She swept a glance through the car. Rob thought she was talking to Jackson but it was hard to say. Her gaze lingered on him for longer than he was comfortable with. "Make sure to get me at least one good picture of him with Santa. Everything else is a bonus."

Mira saluted. "I learned my mistake last year, sir. Won't happen again."

"Good. The kid's a mess but he's mine. Can't lose him." Her sister nodded and then stepped back. Jackson was waving wildly as they exited the driveway. Everyone was silent until Mira stopped at the end of the road.

"Auntie Mira, I'm hungry." Jackson kicked one foot. "I want one of those stick dogs we had last year, okay?"

"Sure, Jax, we'll get one first thing," she said as she turned left and merged with traffic. "Which ride should we go on first?"

Rob tipped his head as he considered that. The place had rides? The train. It had to be.

"The Blizzard, the Blizzard, the Blizzard!" Jax shouted emphatically.

Mira's sharp glance at Rob reminded him to hide his wince.

"That's right! Santa's Train! We'll go there first," Mira said sweetly. "The Blizzard is a roller coaster and your mommy will never, ever let me bring you back here if you step foot on a roller coaster. So, where are we going?"

"Santa's Train," Jax said dully. "After the stick dog."

"Correct," Mira said. "Food always comes first for us, doesn't it, Jax?"

Once the volume was turned down, it was

cute to hear Mira talking with her nephew. She was good with him.

The fact that he didn't know how good his wife was with children bothered him.

Before this trip, he would have said he and Mira were perfectly matched in all ways, but they'd never discussed kids. They'd talked careers and travel and places they'd been to or would love to visit. Had she been keeping this part of herself covered up?

Rob tried to name one thing he'd hidden from her, but he couldn't find one.

"Florida doesn't do anything halfway, Rob," Mira said as she stopped at a traffic light. "Here? Santa's village has more than one roller coaster, as well as corn dogs and every flavor of midway food and game you can imagine. You want to win a humongous stuffed snow leopard?"

"I do," Jax shouted from the back seat.

"You can do that tonight," Mira said to him, her low voice seemingly for his ears only, sending a sweet shiver of awareness down his spine. "And on top of all that, you can write a letter to Santa, have your picture taken, enjoy about a million twinkling lights and have holiday music seared into your brain." She sighed as she joined the line of cars waiting to enter a large parking lot. "One visit to Winter Wonderland and you're never the same. I learned that last year."

The quick grin she flashed in his direction was a fine reward for all his good behavior.

"Don't think I'm joking, Rob," she warned.

"I don't but it's adorable how good an aunt you are." Rob watched her head jerk up at his compliment. She shrugged.

"Learning as I go. I was a sucker last year. Jax asked, and I was so excited I said yes right away and told my sister." She raised both eyebrows. "You should have seen how Gina jumped at the chance to avoid…all this." She motioned broadly with her hand before she stopped at the small booth where an elf was taking the parking fees. "This year, as my father was carving the Thanksgiving turkey, the kid told everyone we were coming back. No question mark needed. Knowing that the kid remembered and wanted to do it again with me… No way I could get out of it. Actually,

I didn't want to get out of it." She rolled up the window and handed Rob the map. "Do some reconnaissance. This night might be better with advance planning and tight logistics."

As he accepted the map, Rob tucked away the memory of how her voice softened when she talked about her nephew and his excitement over spending time with her. Mira was strong and independent. Finding the softer, sweeter side had always been special to him. She wouldn't appreciate his calling her on it here or now. Vulnerable Mira had been for his eyes only once upon a time.

"Logistics. My specialty. Initial targets— corn dog vendor and Santa's Train," he said crisply.

"Affirmative," Mira said with a quiet laugh. "Jax, what are you not going to do this year?"

Rob studied the bright map while he waited for the boy's answer. So, Mira had been amused at his assumptions of what constituted winter wonderland in Florida because he'd been *way* off. This one had three different roller coasters, a haunted toy shop and enough food vendors to feed all the elves at the North Pole.

"I am not going to let go of your hand unless I'm sitting down." Jax sounded as if he were repeating a script. "And when I sit down, I am not going to move unless you say I can."

Rob glanced over at Mira as she nodded. "Worst minute of my life since I've been here in Miami happened in the shadow of Santa's Mailbox. Jax darted off to mail his letter to Santa. I looked up and he was gone. They move fast and fade into the crowd. No need for any camouflage when you're the shortest kid in the group."

She was giving him tips, whether she realized it or not. Helping her track Jackson could prove how good they were together.

Mira pulled a small wallet out of the car console and checked her cash.

"What did you do then?" Rob asked. He wouldn't know what to do in that instance. Find an employee? Shut the place down?

"By the time my life had finished flashing before my eyes, I spotted his haircut in the milling scrum of kids shoving letters into the mailbox. Jackson goes every other Saturday with his father to the barbershop and he gets his hair cut the same way his father does. Easy to remember and spot. Then all I had to do was convince my legs to work again." Mira pressed a hand to her chest. "The only other time I remember my heart beating like that, throbbing in my ears, was a night rescue in Islamabad. It's that sick panic that sometimes wakes you up after a nightmare, you know?"

He did know. This was the kind of thing that he'd always been able to share with her. It wasn't romantic. It wasn't sweet, but it was important.

"So, for the rest of the evening, I made him repeat what he just said. Apparently, it stuck, as well as the memory of all the fun we had, too." Mira took a deep breath and put one hand on the door handle. "Are you ready to conquer Winter Wonderland?"

Rob was struck by how beautiful she was in that instant.

It was only another night, one that hundreds of people would enjoy along with them, judging by the size of the parking lot.

But Mira was unforgettable. He'd planned a romantic dinner in his mind: wine, candlelight, dressed for the occasion. Instead, they were both wearing jeans with sweatshirts for the cooler evening air. She'd chosen a neat ponytail and little makeup.

And she was perfect.

His mouth dried up and he had to wait for his brain to kick-start before he could answer.

"I will follow your lead, Commander," Rob said briskly, determined to remind her of the fun *they'd* had together and how strong they were when they were facing the same direction.

For that evening, the plan was simple.

Following Mira was easy. He could entertain her and her nephew at the same time to earn some goodwill.

"Sir, I've already plotted the shortest distance to the food vendors. Does this route meet with your approval?" Rob asked as he bent down on one knee to trace the path leading to the most likely position of the stick dog Jackson had demanded.

If he didn't do something to win over Mira's nephew, the whole night would be weird and awkward.

The boy pinched his lips together and sidled a step closer. Then he traced a finger behind Rob's and nodded firmly. "Good job, soldier."

Rob's lips were twitching as he stood and met Mira's sparkling eyes.

"He's planning to be the first four-star general in the family. How did you know he had such leadership qualities?" Mira held out her hand and waited until her nephew slipped his inside.

"I hope you're planning to go army, Jackson. That's what I did, too." Rob carefully folded the map for easy reference and waited for Mira to pay for their admission. He'd reached for his wallet but her narrowed eyes convinced him to drop his hand. Fine. He'd follow her here, too. "Although I guess air force will work, too. I'll bring up the rear, Master Sergeant Auntie."

Jackson's giggles at how Rob had tacked on Mira's family title to her rank made him feel like he was totally crushing the uncle thing with almost zero training.

"I told Jackson I'll still love him if he goes army, but we'd have to have a serious talk if I hear any mention of the Marine Corps."

This teasing between them felt good. Mira gave him a wry look and slid through the turnstile, but he was certain she was amused, too. In the early days, he'd moved slowly, testing each step he took with Mira.

He'd made a mistake when he'd gotten ahead of himself and accepted a job and bought a house without having her on board, certain he knew what was right for both of them. Serving in different branches of the military meant they'd never had to learn how to live together before they both left the service, but he'd been determined to give Mira everything she deserved: a husband with a good job and a nice home. Mira's unhappiness when she'd joined him four months later should have opened his eyes.

When had he begun to take her agreement for granted? Tonight, it was easy to resolve to never do that again, but it might be too late. Mira led Jackson through the gates with certainty. She made her own decisions easily. How was he going to convince her to wait for him?

The worry over that big question dimmed the happy anticipation that always built when he and Mira were together. Her questioning glance over one shoulder convinced him he'd have to come up with answers later.

As Rob stepped through to the other side of Winter Wonderland, he wished he'd taken a deep, calming breath on the quiet side.

Because on this side...

Children screamed from every single compass point.

Bright lights flashed overhead and left and right. Rides blared competing music along with the clank and whoosh of speed. The sensory overload was familiar, like the first seconds of an operation. He held his breath to steady his nerves.

Then Mira's voice broke through the noise.

"Jax, take Rob's hand. He's going to get lost. Amusement park is not his normal habitat." Mira waited for Rob to open his eyes before giving her nephew a stern "follow orders" stare.

"Auntie Mira gets upset if you wander off. Don't wander off." Jackson grabbed his hand. "I'm starving. Let's go."

Then he stepped up to take point, a strong little boy towing two adults behind him.

Jackson maneuvered through the crowd, his memory of the map and his nose leading him unerringly toward a combination corn dog–funnel cake–lemonade vendor. The kid had gotten some of his aunt's bossiness. It was cute on both of them at the current level.

Mira already had her credit card out and at the ready.

So all Rob had to do was keep an eye out for the way to the train.

While they made sure he didn't get lost.

He'd spent a lot of time leading. On the football field and in the army, he'd been strong and fast and smart. That made it seem natural to step to the front and make decisions.

And now, he'd landed a good spot on a special team in one of the most competitive forces in the country. He'd make more hard decisions. He'd make them quickly and fairly. And most of the time, they'd be the right choice.

Tonight? He could fall in line and be the anchor to their party, the one who only had to ensure they all crossed the line together at the end. It was nice, this following the leader. He hadn't expected that.

Jackson was the expert in getting the full experience of Winter Wonderland.

Mira was the expert in not losing small children in milling crowds. Rob would have never guessed she'd volunteer for such an outing, much less grin with excitement when she was handed her own massive corn dog from the vendor. He thought she would appreciate white linens and wineglasses and had given her those every chance he got, but she was squirming with happiness as she squirted mustard on her corn dog.

Mira and Jackson were giggling and hopping up and down together as they each took a bite of their corn dogs. It was a sweet sight, even to a crusty grump who would have preferred a nice steak instead of a stick dog. Rob swallowed a sigh and slathered his dinner with the tart yellow spread.

A corn dog for dinner. He'd eaten worse.

And every single night he'd spent apart from Mira in Atlanta had been quiet, joyless, empty. Winter Wonderland was none of those things.

When Mira reached over to wipe a spot

of mustard off his lip, their eyes locked and something important clicked for Rob.

It didn't matter where they were—serving in Africa, traveling in Europe, settled into a brick home in the 'burbs or thronged by a crowd in the midway—he wanted to be where Mira was. That was where he belonged. He had to change her mind about a future for them.

He'd enjoy the ride, fight every single urge to run from the chaos and prove to his wife that there were parts of him that might surprise her, too.

CHAPTER SEVEN

MIRA HAD BEEN mentally prepared for her second visit to Winter Wonderland to feature a meltdown by an overtired little boy hopped up on too much fried food. The previous year? She'd been scared out of her mind to see Jax's empty seat, and when she'd found him in the crowd, the adrenaline coursing through her veins had produced a tone the poor kid had never heard before.

She and Jax had worked through it there at Santa's Mailbox. The rules had been easy enough to come up with; her parents had laid them out clearly for their daughters when they were little and had been stationed in Germany. With four of them so close together, they'd made a long train, her father leading and holding one of Mira's hands while she connected Gina to the chain. Gina held Kris's hand, Naomi followed, and their mother kept an eye as the rear guard.

In distress, Mira had fallen back to what she knew, and eventually she and Jackson had finished their outing with giggles and a hot chocolate.

Afterward, Mira had convinced herself that she was not meant for solo outings with her nephew ever again.

That conviction had lasted only until he'd gripped her hand and given her pleading eyes after he'd made his dinner-table announcement that they would be making a return visit to Winter Wonderland. How was she supposed to say no?

Was that why she'd given in so easily to Rob's assumption that he was joining them? Having backup would be nice. Having strong, intuitive backup that understood the stakes was even better. It was almost possible to relax and enjoy how Jax celebrated his corn dog and endured the Santa train with the other "babies."

The fact that Jax had repeated word for word what they'd agreed on as the correct procedure the previous year had reassured her, too, even if it also pinched at her confidence. Mira wanted to be the best at everything, including being the World's Most Awesome Auntie.

Being stern with him about sticking close to her had seriously lessened her chances of winning the title.

So tonight, she'd watched Jax carefully, on the lookout for cranky anything.

It had never appeared.

A lot of the credit for that could be laid at Rob's confident feet.

"Thank you for taking me into the Haunted Toy Shoppe, Rob," Jackson said as they rejoined her outside the building lit only by the glowing eyes of a bad elf. For sound effects, this place had only rhythmic ticking interspersed with a long pause meant to ramp up a person's anxiety, no doubt.

She'd successfully managed to skip it last year, in fact. Jackson was sure it was a new addition, but she'd spied it on the map on their first trip and steered a wide berth around it. Mira wasn't afraid of much. Haunted anything took up the first spot on her "Not Doing That Ever" list.

The list existed in her head, so it was easy to rerank the items as necessary. Tonight, showing Jackson anything scary or haunted took top spot.

Rob had been the guilty party. Mira was off the hook for this one. Did she feel guilty that she'd escaped both Jackson's vocal disappointment if she'd said no and her sister's righteous payback for any nightmares?

Only a little. It wouldn't keep her up at night, unlike the memory of the creepy elf.

"I'm not sure why Master Sergeant Auntie Mira wouldn't take you in," Rob drawled, "but now you can tell her she's got nothing to worry about inside there."

Jax nodded wisely. "I mean, it's an elf, Auntie Mira. What could go wrong? There's not even blood anywhere. It's a house for babies. No monsters, just the elf and some toys that dance and sing and stuff." He shrugged at Rob, very grown-up in his assessment of the fear factor he'd faced. Jax would be desperate for a ride on the Blizzard next year.

"Oh, good, no blood! But will you sleep tonight and if not will Troublemaker Uncle Rob get in trouble?" Mira asked as she tickled Jax's sides. The kid was fascinated with scary stories. She would have held firm in her no for the haunted ride if Rob hadn't pointed out that the attraction was rated safe for kids of all ages.

"No, Auntie Mira," he said as he gasped for breath. "Rob told me what to do if an elf comes after me."

Mira turned toward Rob, curious as to how well he'd been able to think on his feet. He wasn't a kid guy, the same way she'd never been the kid woman in any of her social groups.

But this was Jax. Over the past two years, she'd learned to speak his language through trial, error and on-the-spot training.

"Sure, I climb on top of my bed and tell him Santa knows when he's been bad or good." Jax shrugged. "No real elf wants to lose his place on the good list. This guy?" He pointed at the glowing eyes. "He tried to steal toys from Santa and now look at him." He shook his head sadly.

Mira fought a laugh as she evaluated whether Jax's was a strong enough defense.

"If that doesn't work, I call Rob in for backup," Jax added. "No elf would mess with him." He gripped her hand. "Oh, and we gotta get some peppermint to keep by the bed. Bad elves hate peppermint."

Mira met Rob's stare. His lips were curled in that lazy almost smile that never failed to win her over. "I figured I better come up with a reasonable defense in case the kid can't sleep."

Mira appreciated that. "I hope you know how to vanquish elves for good, just in case."

"Give me ten minutes to search the internet when we get home. If anyone knows, it's out there." Rob took her hand and tangled his fingers through hers. "I had a feeling Gina might be as fierce as her sister in that way." Then he moved closer. "'Uncle Rob' has a nice ring when you say it."

This close, Mira could see the warm gleam in his blue eyes. "'Troublemaker.' Did you miss that part?" Licking her lips drew his eyes downward, but Mira cleared her throat. "Because you are."

He shrugged. "I accept that. You could use some good trouble now and then."

Jax's loud groan saved Mira from having to come up with a response. Was he right?

It did sum up her feelings before she'd

found Rob on her doorstep. She'd been bored, ready for…something to shake things up.

Trust her husband to do that.

"What's wrong?" Rob asked before she could. That was amazing, too.

"Not Mistletoe Lane. There are no rides here, no food," Jax whined. Half a second before, he'd been bouncing up and down, ready to punch any bad elves that popped up. Now, he was nearly bent in half under the weight of despair at being faced with the dark path that led back to the front gates. Lights in the shape of candy canes marked the way through the lit displays along the shallow canal of water that reflected their glow.

The rest of Winter Wonderland was about loud, bright fun.

Mistletoe Lane had been built for romance.

And Jax was having none of that.

"This is the shortest way back to the gates," Rob said as he held up the map. "Should we go back the way we came instead?"

Mira bit her lip as she checked her watch.

They had half an hour to get Jax home before Gina called out a search party. Jax's tone and drama were hints that a tired meltdown was impending.

How to head it off…

"How about a ride through Mistletoe Lane?" Rob asked as he squatted. "Hop on. Let's piggyback this mission." When Rob's eyes met hers while he waited, he winked.

That wink melted any remaining worry and irritation she may have had. All that was left was warm heat that reminded her of falling for him the first time around.

He grunted as Jax clambered on. The kid spent half of every family get-together riding someone's back and screaming in their ear. He was an advanced piggyback rider.

"What about your shoulder?" Mira asked as she moved one of Jax's hands off the healing spot. She didn't have to wonder if she remembered where it was.

She would never forget it.

"I might have underestimated exactly how much the kid weighs. Must be the corn dog." Rob bumped her shoulder with his good one. "I've carried heavier packs through a lot worse conditions. Just make it worth my sacrifice." He tipped his head to the side and raised his eyebrows. "Please?"

Mira rolled her eyes at him but followed his lead as they headed off down the path. It was so serene that this might have been another world from the rest of the amusement park. This was the wonderful piece of the wonderland obviously.

Here and there, they encountered couples, but most of the time, all Mira could hear was their footsteps and the music and shouts of a world that might as well have been far, far away. They walked past several decorated scenes: Santa loading his sleigh while his reindeer pranced restlessly, Mrs. Claus and some helpers preparing cookies, snowmen having a snowball fight. Every display was detailed and synchronized to give the illusion of life and movement.

At one point, Rob caught her eye and looked up. Jax had forgotten his complaints. His eyes were wide as he watched. Mira nodded and squeezed Rob's arm to keep them moving.

After they passed the gazebo with multicolored twinkle lights where a photographer waited to capture happy couples, Mira noticed sparkling spots high on a few trees that lined the path.

Rob bent closer. "That's the mistletoe. You owe me so many kisses already." Then he shook his head sadly to mimic Jax.

"Mistletoe doesn't glow," Mira muttered as she stopped directly under one of the spots to study it closer. Leaves. Tiny lights in the shape of berries. She wasn't certain what real mistletoe looked like, but this was pretty close to what she'd seen in the holiday decor section.

He'd stopped to watch her. "Everything here glows. You're glowing right now."

Mira glanced down, mainly to remind herself to breathe, and there was a faint light all over her. He was right.

What would kissing under that mistletoe be like? Magic?

If she waited here long enough, could she find out?

That lazy grin was back as he shook his head. "I made a promise. You'll have to kiss me."

Then he headed away on the path. The real world was getting closer. Already she could see the crowds and hear happy kids. Mistletoe Lane couldn't last forever.

"Mira, can we get a hot chocolate? There was a place right next to the gates, and I didn't throw up after the Spinning Snowball ride." Jax's voice was much more cheerful now, the previous drama wiped away by a piggyback ride and the power of Christmas.

The fact that she'd actually carried him off the Spinning Snowball ride to hold him directly over a trash can because the corn dog was threatening to make a return appearance should help her remember that in the future, rides come first, then food. A valuable lesson.

"To go. Let's get hot chocolates to go. We'll get one for your mommy and daddy, too. How about that?" Mira asked as she helped Rob disentangle Jax. The piggyback ride was over, along with the magic of mistletoe.

Jax nodded wildly, grabbed her hand and started pulling her toward the gates.

As she passed Rob, she reached out with her other hand and managed to snag his so he became a part of the chain.

The way he squeezed her hand in return made her think he'd felt that magic, too.

The receding noise and Jax's renewed excitement made it easier to catch her breath, and soon, they were all loaded into the car with their drinks and headed for her sister's house before she could consider what a kiss under the mistletoe might have meant.

To a couple that was getting a divorce.

The streets passed by as Jax and Rob kept up an easy back-and-forth.

Mira braked abruptly in her sister's driveway as the realization crashed around her shoulders.

She and Rob weren't a cute couple on a date.

Or even a married couple enjoying the romance of a date night.

They'd been separated for nearly two years.

She'd paid a lawyer to draw up the paperwork to dissolve that broken marriage.

And he'd been shot in the shoulder doing a job she didn't want him to do before going home to a house she hated.

So what if he was better with kids than

she'd expected? All the same problems between them still existed.

Her sister was knocking on the window before Mira was able to snap out of it.

"I see my son. He's in one piece. Good job," Gina quipped.

"If he happens to mention bad elves or wakes up in the middle of the night, Rob will be happy to explain the whole story." Mira opened her car door. "We brought you hot chocolate, only lukewarm now."

Gina took the drink carrier. "Bad elves? Do I want to know?"

"They stole from Santa. Now they're stuck in a haunted toy shop. It was sad." Jax hugged his mother's waist. "So much hammering. More broken toys than the bottom of my closet. One tried to take my hammer while I was at Santa's workbench, but Rob blocked him." He mimed a hard shove to the chest. No wonder he was less scared than she'd imagined. Rob had been running interference.

Her sister's loud sniff was one of judgment.

Rob seemed to pick up on that, too. He

held up the car seat. "Where would you like me to put this?"

Mira quickly took the seat and carried it inside the garage. As she slid it on the shelf, she waved to Ty, her sister's husband.

"No problems?" Ty asked.

"Not yet," Mira said cheerfully. "I'll see you guys tomorrow. Tell Dev he's coming with us next year." Dev was Gina's oldest, and he was almost twelve. He would run away from home before he chaperoned his little brother on the baby rides. Still, it was fun to lob the empty threat.

As she made it back to the car, Rob's expression was begging her for an escape. Her sister had him caught in her glare. "Happy birthday, Gina. I hope you enjoyed your date night. Sticky toffee pudding tomorrow."

Gina's shoulders lowered a fraction. "It better be good." Then she glared at Rob one more time before she left to go back inside. Jax was already chattering about all the other things they'd seen and done. Mistletoe Lane featured prominently in his recitation.

"You might have warned me before I

agreed to go into the haunted house that your sister would put me on her most wanted list," Rob said as he got into the passenger seat.

"If it makes you feel any better, you were already on the naughty list," Mira answered as she started the car and reversed out of the driveway.

His grunt made her laugh.

They were quiet as she made the quick trip back to Concord Court.

Once she'd parked, Rob said, "You had your concerns when we started this night. Did I manage to prove myself?"

Mira took the keys out of the ignition. "I expected you to be overwhelmed. I certainly was the first time Jax took me there, but I should have known better. You don't get overwhelmed, do you?"

He sighed. "Sure I do, but it's not loud noises or unfamiliar terrain that includes stick dogs and other weird things I've never heard of. I used to be a kid, although I can't imagine my parents ever agreeing to bring me to a place like that, and Jackson's a cool kid. If he plans military operations as a general the same way he stormed the haunted workshop, you and I will be able to sleep easily in whatever retirement home we're in."

Mira's chuckle was cut short when he traced a finger across her knuckles.

"It's like everything comes into sharper focus when I'm facing the unknown," he added. "Figuring out where dates are stored in the grocery store? That's frustrating. Trying to win back the most important woman in the world? I'm out of my depth." He cleared his throat. "But telling me to find the shortest path on a map? That I can do in my sleep, screaming kids and flashing lights or not."

They had both served in some scary places, but this was the biggest difference between them. Mira had to push forward through the fear, but she had the impression that Rob was energized by it. It was like his superpower kicked in; he got stronger, smarter, better when he was surrounded by chaos.

"Well, Jackson was impressed," Mira said, eyeing the townhouse. Putting some space between them would make it easier to breathe. Breathing might help her remember why falling under his spell again was the wrong thing to do.

"Good, but I was hoping to impress you." She could feel the pull between them as she unlocked her front door. The urge to lean back into his arms and rest against his chest was strong.

She needed a reminder of all the things that were broken between them and quickly.

Inside her place, to give herself something to do, she switched on each of her favorite Christmas decorations.

"Tell me about Christmas in Oklahoma. What kind of celebrations were your parents into?" Mira asked as she dropped into her comfy chair. Having this chance to talk was sweet, but realizing how little she knew of his life before the army bothered her. They'd dated in a hurry, married in a rush and spent most of their time apart. "Where did you go to have your picture taken with Santa?"

He frowned as he considered her question. "I'm not sure. The mall? I don't remember too many, but there is one of me clutching my little sister's hand as she tried to flee." He eased back into the sofa. "All of our celebrations were at church. My dad was always all business, farm business, that is. It's hard work. We didn't do a lot of extra stuff for fun. Mom came to the school shows, and we never missed Christmas Eve service but..." He shrugged.

"Have you gotten your sister's Christmas card this year?" Mira asked. All she knew about his family was that there had been an argument and he'd kept his distance ever since, but his little sister left the door open.

"Patty sent the card. Her kids had Santa subdued in a headlock, but he didn't seem to mind much." Rob shifted a pillow behind him. "Her boy is smart. It's my clever niece Santa has to watch out for. Reminds me of her mother that way."

Mira wanted to jump in and ask a hundred questions. He'd just admitted more to her than he had when she'd originally asked why he didn't go home. "I didn't know executing wrestling moves on Santa was a thing kids do. We were lucky that Jackson made his feelings clear with a yawn." The kid had personality. He'd registered his boredom at being forced into hanging with the other babies at Santa's Photo Shoppe. Mira hadn't wasted another second and managed to get her sister's birthday present—their souvenir photo—from the second shot the photographer took after Rob convinced the guy it was necessary.

They made a good team.

Letting go the chance to dig deeper, she recognized how sweet his laugh sounded. Did she hear relief? Maybe, but this time he hadn't avoided her question. He'd replied even though it was painful.

Because she mattered more than the pain? Mira clenched a hand to her stomach at the sudden pain there.

"Do you wonder why we never discussed kids, Rob? I mean, we got married in a heartbeat, but even afterward, we never talked about it."

He scratched his chin, the scrape of stubble on his skin a powerful reminder of all the other times they'd ended the day together like this, the two of them, talking.

"Honestly, Mira, I've never thought much about whether I wanted kids. Selfish or not, I always liked being on my own. Then, when you came along, I was so happy to have found you." Rob braced his hands on his knees. "If it was important to you, sure, we could have talked about kids. I might not have understood how much fun it is to take an excited kid to mail his letter to Santa before tonight, but I would have done anything I could to make you happy."

Except find a safer, boring job.

Mira wanted to say it, but that was old ground. Tonight there was an opportunity to break new ground and find out something she'd never known about him.

"I guess, maybe… I never thought about it, either." Mira watched the lights dance across the ceiling. She'd left the overhead ones off, so only Christmas decorations illuminated the room. This was her favorite way to end the day. Having him here made it better. Loneliness might creep around the edges of her satisfaction sometimes, but tonight, there was none of that. "Until I was living here in Miami and meeting my sisters' kids, I didn't consider the point much. For the first year, I sort of held my nephews at arm's length because I didn't know how to talk to them. Then I nearly lost Jax at Santa's Mailbox, shouted at him as if I were his overworked mother, and we crossed over the line from strangers to devoted family. Everything has been easier since then."

"Is that something you want to do, after the divorce? Find a guy who's ready for kids?"

Mira frowned because she'd never considered that, either.

"I think…" Mira stopped to formulate her answer because it mattered. She wasn't sure what she would say, but she knew it was important. "If I decided to date again, I want the kind of relationship where I know more than how you load the dishwasher or the way your face lights up when you talk about successful night raids or even how sweet your kisses are." She sighed. "That's the part that hurts. Those kisses could make the whole world right."

Then she covered her face with her hands. Admitting it had been a bad idea, but there in the small living room, with him watching her, she'd had to say it all.

At first, the silence made her wonder if he was holding his breath. Was she? She had to breathe.

Then he scrubbed a hand through his hair. "I get it. We dated and married in a hurry, thanks to the plans of the United States government. Lots of people do the same, get married before a deployment or new orders come in, and they have to figure out how to make things work after the wedding."

"And lots of people don't figure it out, Rob," Mira added quietly.

Then he offered his warmest smile and the tension building between them seemed to disappear. "We aren't like lots of other people, Mira. You know that."

She had to laugh. It hurt but it was comforting at the same time. "Right. Lots of people don't climb mountains on their second date or go ax-throwing to celebrate their one-month anniversary."

"Or make it all the way down Mistletoe Lane without a single kiss or successfully navigate an amusement park with a six-year-old and avoid a tantrum." Rob pointed a finger at her. "You gotta admit it. Together, we're unbeatable."

They were impressive.

"We could even manage to corral your sister's kids for the family photo, couldn't we?" Mira asked.

He studied her face. "You and me in Oklahoma?"

Mira waited for him to add something else, but his frown made her wonder if it was the first time he'd ever considered that scenario. Would having her by his side make it easier to go home? Whatever the problems were, it had to be better to bring backup.

But she wasn't going to Oklahoma. She wasn't going to be the fixer who patched the rift in his family. They were getting a divorce.

"If I quit the job, left Atlanta and moved here, would you reconsider the divorce?" Rob shifted back as if he was bracing for her answer.

It was so tempting to say yes. He'd given her everything she wanted. How could she say no?

Then she remembered how often she felt swamped with guilt in the early days when he'd talked about how hard it was to settle into civilian life. She'd still been in Djibouti when Rob returned stateside, and finding another job had been his obsession. Work had always been how he'd measured himself. Listening to him struggle without being there to help had hurt. He'd been so happy with what he'd achieved being in the military and he'd given up that happiness because she'd asked him to. She'd made her decision to retire at her first opportunity, and she'd wanted them to be together, building their new lives and careers.

Then she'd made them both miserable by demanding more.

Telling herself he'd finally become content and adjusted had made it easier to live with the guilt. Blaming the job in Atlanta was also easier than admitting any of her own failure.

But she owed it to them both not to make the same mistakes over and over.

"Rob, I… I don't want to play hypothetical games. At this point, I want the divorce. That way, you can make your own decision about what's best for your future and I can, too." How awful that felt.

His silence was new. In the past, he'd reassured her, sort of the same way he had about having kids. If she wanted it, he did, too. Tonight he was silent.

"I'm going to go upstairs, take a shower

to wash off some of Santa's wonder." Mira stood slowly.

"Okay. Good night, then." The resignation in his voice was another blow that she had to absorb.

Suddenly, with the reminder of those kisses she'd be losing with a signature and how he'd watched her under the lights of Mistletoe Lane flooding her mind, she stepped closer to him and squeezed his hand. Mira was certain that was all she'd intended and she would have happily gone upstairs, comforted with the knowledge that she was doing the right thing for both of them in spite of the heartache.

But she met his stare.

Then she bent closer to him, his warmth, the strength of his arms so tempting.

Pressing her lips to his was natural, like seeing home after a long time away, but then his kiss changed. Heated. His hand slid under the fall of her hair to squeeze her nape while his thumb brushed her jawline. And the amazing spark that had always flickered between them was alight.

Before she gave in to the temptation to slide onto his lap, Mira broke the kiss and forced herself to take two huge steps away from him.

Rob's low raspy chuckle tickled down her spine.

"You made it worth waiting for, that kiss," he said.

Mira inhaled slowly and tried to exhale quietly. "Thank you for your help with Jax. I had fun."

"Me, too."

She'd reached the stairs when he asked, "Are we running in the morning?"

With one hand clenched on the railing, Mira again considered keeping her distance. She couldn't let herself get in the habit of running with him every day. When he went away, it would be a daily reminder of this loss.

But she couldn't say no. "At sunrise."

"Meet you at sunrise, then," he said softly and she had to jog up to the top of the stairs and lock herself in her bedroom before she answered the call for another kiss.

CHAPTER EIGHT

ROB REALIZED HE had lost track of how many hours he'd been trying to fall asleep when he heard his own sigh. Replaying the earlier events of the evening hadn't revealed any new clues on how to change Mira's mind. He wanted to focus on the kiss or how she'd stared at him from under the glowing mistletoe, but what he kept coming back to was his question.

He'd asked the one thing that he'd been trying not to during the long drive from Atlanta. Would moving to Miami change his wife's mind?

Even asking the question made him wonder if he was prepared to do that, to give up everything a second time, for her.

His whole life, there had been work to depend on. Even when he and his father had been at odds, chores still had to be done, hay had to be brought in, livestock fed. The cold shoulder had slowly melted. His father had always appreciated a person who pulled their weight.

He'd put the time and effort in to make a place on the special ops team in Atlanta, and he was making progress beyond that. Could he go all the way back to the beginning again?

If Rob were at home in Atlanta, he'd get up, run on the treadmill, take a shower or tackle the laundry, anything to get himself out of his own head. If he was thinking too much, a physical task was the solution.

But here, he had a wife upstairs who would notice any of those solutions.

Waking Mira up might lead to more conversation, and to be honest, he didn't want to get any closer to hearing her say, "No, I wouldn't stay married to you even if you gave up your job, moved to Miami and found other work…"

Unless she had the answer to "Other work"? He was not interested in poking that bruise tonight.

Or if she gave him the even shorter answer: "I don't love you anymore."

If Mira made it that far, there would be

no more reason to fight. He'd sign those papers and hit the road. Licking his wounds in his big empty house would be easier than on Mira's cushy couch with holiday cheer all around, his wife within kissing distance but a world away, too.

"Get up, you chicken," he muttered to himself as he swung his legs off the couch to sit up straight. His paperback was on the coffee table. He could read.

Or walk around. His thinking was entirely too loud in his head that night for words, spoken or written.

Rob took Mira's key ring off the hook and made sure to lock up before he paused in the quiet parking lot. A drive? That might help.

But he had the urge to move, so he shoved his hands in his pockets and wandered toward the office where the running group had met. As he got closer, he could hear the murmur of voices. Was that the pool area? People out at this time of night couldn't be up to anything good.

Moving carefully to keep his footsteps silent, Rob eased closer to the fence.

Sean was sitting with his work boots propped up on the table, while another one of the guys from the group handed him a bottle. Beer? A beer would hit the spot.

The need for stealth gone, Rob resumed his normal pace and both men turned to face him. A third guy leaned out of the heavy shadow at the corner of the table.

"Well, now, I thought we were going to have to cancel the party since nobody else showed up, but it just got interesting," Sean said as he waved a bottle in Rob's direction. "Come in. The water's fine."

Rob read the pool rules posted prominently as he opened and closed the wrought iron gate. "Looks like the water's closed."

Sean nodded. "That's why you keep your voice down and clean up after yourself." He pointed. "Or else Reyna Montero will make us both regret it."

Rob eased down into a chair and took the cold bottle. It had a twist cap. Because it was water, not beer. He tried to tell himself the healthier choice was for the best, but beer would have hit the spot. "Is she in charge here?"

The other guy Rob hadn't met yet said, "Nope, Reyna is Brisa's sister, but Sean is very good at keeping her happy."

Rob nodded as he took a sip of water. It might not help him sleep, but it cut through some of his funk.

"Sean you know, and you met Jason on the morning run. I'm Wade," the other guy said. "You're Mira's soon-to-be ex-husband. I was the blind date."

Rob studied the man. "And now you're with Brisa, who's in charge of Concord Court?"

Sean chuckled. "You got it in one."

Rob stretched in his chair, happy that the muscles in his shoulder relaxed now that he was away from the contortions to fit on the couch. He was healing quickly. Not even a rambunctious six-year-old in a piggyback had caused a twinge.

"Guess news travels fast around here," he said. Had they been talking about him or Mira or him *and* Mira before he'd walked up?

"Sean was catching me up before Mira got here." Wade frowned. "Except she's not coming tonight?"

"No idea," Rob replied. "I was going around in circles trying to sleep and I didn't want to wake her up if she was more successful, so I decided to get out. Is this by invitation only or can anyone join?"

"We don't take attendance, but anybody who might be having trouble in the middle of the night can come join us. Like you and Mira, we're all military. Sometimes the memories make midnight tough." Sean moved his feet off the table. "Mira's always pulled us together, gently smacked our heads verbally when we needed it. She's the heart of the group." His voice was hard. He was giving Rob another warning.

Wade added, "We're going to miss her when she leaves Concord Court."

"I understand what that feels like." Rob studied the sky. It was clear enough to spot dim stars. "Missing Mira." He shook his head. "Right now, I live in a house where I pictured Mira and me making a home, working jobs that we'd like and be good at, and instead, I'm wondering if this is the last time I'll ever see her. I'm already missing her while I'm struggling to keep her."

The other men were unexpectedly silent.

"You sit here and drink water every night? Ever get wild and go for beer?" Rob asked as he tilted the bottle up to his lips.

"Not when I'm around. I'm sober and my friends support me," Wade said.

"Oh, I'm sorry." Rob coughed. "I didn't think before I spoke."

Everyone was silent as they absorbed that.

"I did not expect that, Bowman," Sean said quietly. "I had you pegged for the guy who made the rules and expected everyone to fall in line."

Rob answered truthfully, "I have been. In the past. I guess Atlanta's proof of that." He wasn't going to add anything more, but he wanted someone to understand. If he talked long enough, maybe things would be clear enough to him. "Mira wanted out of the military, and I wanted her. That's it. I didn't have a plan. I didn't have this second career that I'd planned out in my head like she did. All my life, I've understood two things. A man is as good as his work and he takes care of his family." It was as easy to picture his father saying those things as if they'd been transported into the middle of a sunny Oklahoma pasture. "I wanted life with Mira, so I got out, but then there's nothing but wide-open space, you know?"

He glanced at the guys but didn't wait for them to speak. "I've had chores or a job since I was big enough to drive a tractor or put out feed, baling hay in the summer for neighbors. And yet, I'm not meant for life in Oklahoma, so I joined the army. I was a good soldier. I was military police, so what am I going to do here? Get a job with a police force. To do the right thing for Mira, I took the best of what was available to me. Big city. Lots of opportunity for her to find a school she loves, not too far from her family and exactly far enough from mine. Every choice I made was logical."

Rob now waited for them to answer, embarrassed that he'd admitted as much as he had. What was happening? Something had loosened his lips. He was telling Mira about his family and these guys about…way too much. "It's not like I hadn't put any thought into these options, you know?"

Sean sniffed. "Did you talk about any of this with Mira?"

Rob fiddled with the cap of his water bottle as he considered that question. When the answer came crashing down over his head, he cursed under his breath.

"I didn't think so. So, you shouldered the responsibility, did the best with what you had, and set about building a nice, secure little spot for Mira…one that she had no input on." Sean grunted. "Makes perfect sense to me. That's how I know you did the wrong thing."

Wade chuckled and it was easier to relax after that. Rob would have said he'd done the only thing he could.

But sitting there in a dark corner beside the pool, he realized he'd skipped the most important step two years ago.

"It's not like she did a lot of talking to me, either. Not about how important it was to be close to her family." Rob closed his eyes. "I guess I should have asked her."

This time, both men laughed, but it was one of sympathy, not ridicule. "Either one of you messed up this big?"

When they were both quiet, Rob knew the answer.

Jason braced his elbows on the table. "You have come to the right place. We know messing up. Losing my leg had once convinced me life was over. That was so wrong."

Rob braced his elbows on his knees. "Yeah? So what happened?"

Jason held a hand over his heart. "This place happened. And I met a girl. My whole life changed. She brings the adventure, the rush I used to get, and now my job has me convinced that what I do matters. Every time I help somebody get a job or try a new career, I'm sure I have the best job in the world." Then he thumped Rob's injured shoulder, which caused a small twinge. "And if you need a new job after you manage to convince your wife not to divorce you, I might be able to assist with that. I'm a career coach."

Rob studied the guy who drank from his water bottle, not a single concern about his life or world written on his face, and wondered what brought him out to the pool area. Other questions tumbled in his mind, the loudest being "What else can I do?"

"Okay, okay," Jason said as he made the "keep it down" motion. "No need to think that loudly at me." He narrowed his eyes. "Police experience. Military experience." He tapped his fingers on the table. "Off the top of my head, reaching for out-of-the-box ideas that do not include jeopardizing your safety on a daily basis…" Then he straightened. "I was thinking instructor, police academy or private security, but what about overseeing emergency response? Miami is the home of an agency that provides oversight and coordination for all military and local, state and federal civilian first responders for Florida and the southeastern coast… Natural disaster response, pandemics, large-scale criminal investigations, terrorism, war, basically any threat that requires multiagency response is coordinated through centers like the one here in Miami."

Rob considered that and Jason added, "The state is looking to hire officers that sound a little like internal affairs to me. These folks ensure all the strategies and responses meet policy, with the goal of protecting civil liberties. The new guy in charge, he hammers hard on transparency and accountability with the communities served. There's been some trouble with that and he's cleaning house of bad actors. The guy's former army." Jason raised his eyebrows. "Might give you a leg up there."

Rob could understand how his experience lined up perfectly. As military police, he'd learned to investigate his fellow soldiers objectively. "How would I go about getting a job like that? I don't have a degree or…"

Jason twisted his bottle in a circle. "Not sure about that, so we'll need to do some research as soon as possible." He grinned. "We can do this, no problem."

Sean grunted. "First, you have to make sure this is what you want. We don't start a project like this, inevitably involve the Montero sisters for a guy who's going to fade away if he doesn't get what he wants, not when it comes down to my best friend's happiness anyway."

That made sense. This what-if job Jason was describing… Well, Rob could see the potential and feel that weird trickle of restless energy that he'd learned to trust whenever he was on to something. "I'd like to find out more about this type of work," he murmured.

"Sounds like a guy who might be interested in making a job change," Jason said. The satisfaction was clear in his voice. "I have a real knack for this 'job counseling' thing Reyna pointed me toward."

Rob wanted to ask more questions about Reyna and Brisa and Concord Court and Mira and this group, but his biggest problem remained.

How did he convince Mira to give them another shot?

Uprooting his life again without any guarantee of winning her over... It didn't make sense.

"Okay. If we agree there might be choices for me here in Miami, there's still the problem of my Atlanta mistake. Either one of you have any suggestions on how to recover?" Rob asked.

"The problem is that Mira is the one who always straightens out our knots," Sean said, "but we can't go to her for help this time."

When that was all he had to say and the other guys added nothing, Rob was resigned to fumbling along on his own.

"I've asked her, if I quit and moved to Miami, whether we could give this another shot," Rob said, feeling anxious. "She didn't have an answer. What if there's nothing to recover anymore?"

Sean held his arms out to the sides, a wide stretch. "Wade, did Mira have any trouble telling you that she wasn't interested in dating you?"

Rob turned so fast to watch the other guy answer that his neck hurt.

Wade shook his head. "No. She was blunt, honest, no sugarcoating. If I were fragile, it would have been a real problem."

Sean leaned toward Rob. "He means if he hadn't been half in love with Brisa already but too slow on the pickup to know, it might have hurt his feelings."

"Do you have a point, Sean?" Wade asked before leaning over toward Rob. "The guy rambles. We tolerate it because sometimes he finds the right path. You'll learn to pull him back from time to time."

"My point," Sean interrupted, "is that if the answer was no, she wouldn't want to give this another shot even after you quit your job and moved to Miami..." He raised his eyebrows, waiting for Rob to fill in the blank.

"Then she would have said that." Rob inhaled slowly. All night, as he'd stared up at the ceiling, he'd been stuck on what if the answer was no.

But Sean was saying that it wasn't.

The answer might not be "Yes," not yet, but it wasn't "No."

So he still had a chance.

His grin felt good.

"Of course, you have to ask yourself if that's something you'd be willing to do," Sean added. "You're the one who put it out there, moving here, I mean, as an option."

Rob hadn't considered it before he'd asked Mira the question.

And since then, he hadn't thought of anything else.

"If she asked, I would. A year ago? I might have been too frustrated but now, with this real threat of losing her, I would quit and move immediately." Rob sighed. "But she's never going to ask. I've spent our whole relationship trying to read her mind because she doesn't need or want any help. Mira goes her own way, and if I want to keep up, I follow or I jump out in front."

Until he admitted that out loud, he hadn't realized how frustrated that made him.

All four of them said nothing.

"If I wake up Reyna to get her help, we'll be in trouble because we aren't supposed to be here." Sean hummed. "Brisa? Neither one of them has a lot of experience working through these love problems. We basically had to convince them to let go and fall for us." Sean held out both arms. "And I'm a real catch, so you know Reyna had some things to iron out."

Jason's grumble was the only answer.

"Brisa told me to look at things a different way, that that's what she had to do to clean up her mess." Rob was speculating, no longer worrying about what the others were thinking, but they'd sort of reached the point where there were no wrong answers... Because there were no answers at all. "Like the difference between buying the best dress and the right dress." He thought that's what the story had illustrated.

The guys were quiet as they considered that.

"But they're not the same dress," Jason said slowly. "Right?"

That answer he knew. "Right."

"I have the most experience translating Brisa. So…" Wade said carefully, as if he were solving a math problem in his head. "Brisa has to be on the right track. She's smart like that, but the dress thing throws me. Looking at this from another perspective… What if you take Mira out of the equation? You can't know the answer to your question about whether you have a shot if you're here in Miami. Instead, what if you figure out if you can be happy in Miami, with or without her."

Sean studied the stars. Jason tilted his head to the side. Wade took a heavy swig of water as if that hypothesis had taken it out of him.

Rob realized he was waiting patiently for one of them to answer the question, but he was the only one who could.

"I'm not happy in Atlanta without her. Why would I be any happier here without her?" Rob asked.

Then he realized he couldn't name three other men on the face of the planet whom he'd discuss relationship trouble with. Those he'd served with in the army were scattered all over, and none of his coworkers on the Atlanta Police Department inspired sharing.

Not like this, anyway.

Meanwhile, this trio had navigated choppy waters already.

"What if you made the question smaller? Atlanta versus Concord Court. Could you be happy here? The rules? Go to school for your second career or find a job. That's it. If you wanted to move to Concord Court, there's a job counselor here. There's a connection to the local university. They might be able to help you find something that you love that doesn't scare Mira. Might not work out, but you'd be better off in the long run if you give yourself the chance." Sean stood slowly. "And that will add time to the clock. If she's not saying no, you're still in the game."

Except he'd made her a deal. The buzzer would sound on Christmas Day. There wasn't enough time to figure out everything that quickly.

"Walking away from another career is tough," Wade said. "For me, that was my constant. I was a surgeon before and after, and I still felt lost some days. Don't quit and move unless you answer a few of those questions first."

Rob admitted it felt good to share. Dividing the weight meant he was carrying less of a burden about what to do next, and he appreciated it. Appreciated these guys and their willingness to listen. They'd clearly all been through a lot.

"Okay, my plan A was to charm her and convince her we belong together *somewhere*. That's all I've got. It's weak, but it should buy enough time for me to explore plan B, which is mainly a collection of questions right now. Who am I if I'm not a cop? And can I be happy here, even without Mira?" Rob realized it still left things undecided, but he had a direction now.

"Thanks for the talk," Rob said. "I needed help."

Sean collected the empties. "You did. We were the same. It took most of us longer to realize that, too."

That was almost a compliment from the guy Rob knew would be the hardest to win over.

"I didn't believe it when former buddies warned me how hard it was going to be when I left the service," Rob murmured. "I went from having all this support and pretty rigid structure into the world where I had nothing. I was too uncomfortable with the uncertainty. I wanted progress, so I made big decisions fast. I regret it now."

Wade rose from his seat. "I know what you mean. I was sure I had everything figured out. I had a job lined up and everything else was about to fall into place… except I had a daughter to get reacquainted with and a home to build. Simple was not all that easy. I could have done it, but I'm glad I didn't have to try without Concord Court. Think about talking to Brisa about a spot here." He shrugged. "If you decide to give Miami a try."

Jason offered him his hand. "I'll help with the job piece any way I can. Once you make up your mind, give me a call and we'll get started."

The emotions that settled over him as all three men turned to go were a surprise. Gratitude was at the top of the list. They were Mira's friends but they had made room for him at the table.

He was still fighting his way into that spot with his coworkers in Atlanta.

"Will you be here in the morning?" Rob

asked as he stepped through the gate. He might be able to sleep now. Understanding that Mira hadn't said no was encouragement. Believing that there were other possibilities for his work and knowing he could get help to find them… That was a game changer.

"Yep, ready to run. You know, to pay me back for all this excellent advice, you could convince your wife that marathons are silly ideas. Only nerds run that far." Sean carefully slipped his chair back under the table and judged it to make sure it was properly placed. Reyna must be a stickler about the pool rules.

"I'll do my best," Rob said.

When he pulled the keys out of his pocket to unlock Mira's front door, Rob decided that it might be nice to run a marathon, an accomplishment.

Did that make him a nerd? Who cared?

If Mira wanted it, Rob was on board.

He'd find some other way to pay Sean back for the advice.

CHAPTER NINE

MIRA STUDIED ROB out of the corner of her eye as she removed the carefully packed sticky toffee pudding from the back seat of the car. He hadn't offered to pack it safely or suggest where to put it on the floorboard for maximum protection. There had been no complaints from him about her insistence on driving *again*. She'd also gotten the impression that if she'd told him that she would prefer that he stay at her apartment and skip her sister's birthday party, he might have agreed.

Rob was on his best behavior.

Every single bit of that was weird.

The oddness had started from the minute they'd stepped outside to meet Sean and the rest of the group for their sunrise run. Now that it was the two of them, somebody had to say *something*.

"You okay?" she asked as she closed the

door. When he held out his arms for the pan she'd carefully wrapped for transport, Mira handed it over. It was easy enough to cooperate when he wasn't challenging her over nothing and everything. "You've been awfully quiet this morning."

He pursed his lips and tipped his head to the side, a cute display of how hard he was thinking. "Well, I supported your extra-long run and explained how much I'd love to finish a marathon one day."

Mira nodded. "Right. That's weird."

He chuckled. "I didn't know I wanted to do it until you said you wanted to, but that only means it never occurred to me. You have good ideas." He met her suspicious stare and blinked innocently.

Was he *trying* to confuse her or doing it naturally?

"That reminds me. Why was Sean so mad when you said that?" Mira asked. "Did he say something about a deal? That the two of you had a deal? And Jason laughed until he had to sit down. What was the joke?" It made no sense. They didn't know each other, and she was nearly certain Sean would send Rob back to Atlanta in the trunk of an economy-size car if he hoped he could get away with it.

Rob frowned. "I'm sure I don't know."

Mira crossed her arms. She wouldn't lose this small advantage. Her family would find them soon, and distract them both. Getting answers now was her only chance.

"I couldn't sleep last night. I didn't want to wake you up, so I decided to go for a walk. Sean, Jason and Wade were at the pool and they gave me some good advice. Maybe he thought from that I would owe him one." Rob shrugged.

As she pictured the four of them meeting around their usual table in the off-limits, after-hours pool area, Mira had so many questions, but the ticking clock meant she had to narrow down her options.

"So this isn't some kind of silent treatment? A way to use reverse psychology to bring me around to your way of thinking by...being polite?" Mira asked. That would be new and unexpected. Bossy and insistent had always been his preferred way of winning a fight.

Since that was her move, too, they'd butted heads.

"You don't have to act so shocked. Old dogs can learn new tricks," Rob said before adding, "and I'm more seasoned than old." He tipped his head back and viewed the brilliant blue sky. They'd driven inland, toward Homestead, and it was a beautiful day to celebrate with her family. He'd taken her suggestion and dressed in layers, jeans, a T-shirt and sweatshirt, all topped off by the elf hat. She'd done the same, but without the hat. Rob was dressed to fit in.

Normally, it was easy to imagine how the whole day would go because her family had done a version of this get-together ever since her parents had chosen southern Florida for retirement.

But Rob was here. That would shake up everything.

"This is me realizing that I've made some mistakes. This is me deciding to keep my mouth closed and my ears open more." He stepped closer until his running shoes bumped hers. "This is me, the guy who desperately wants you to be able to say yes to the question I asked you last night." His gaze was locked onto hers and the memory of their kisses like a spark between them.

Mira refused to give in. "Don't ask me the question again, Rob. I made the mistake of asking you once to give up the career you loved. I won't be responsible for that a second time." Mira had spent a good part of her night tossing and turning while she tried to find the right answer to whether she'd tear up the divorce papers if he'd quit the job and move to Miami. She could have everything she wanted, right? But it would feel terrible. Wrong.

So she still had no answer. Talking it out with friends might have helped.

But she realized that if she had tried to sneak past her sleeping husband the night before, she would have discovered him at her table by the pool in her townhome complex with her friends who were giving him advice about her.

Why did that almost seem like a clue that Rob might not be on the wrong path if he did what she would never ask him to do? Was she going in circles?

"My head hurts and it's all your fault," Mira said with a sigh.

"I know the feeling," he answered and

dipped his chin. "Sure do wish I could kiss it and make it feel better."

Mira rolled her eyes and shifted away as Jax came hurtling around the side of her parents' ranch house. "MiraMiraMira!"

She laughed. She had to. Things between her and Rob were tense, but her family never failed to offer a soft landing.

"After we eat, Grumpy says I get to pick my own team this year. You'll be on it, right?" Jax grabbed her right hand and jumped up and down.

Mira nodded to match his rhythm. "Of course I will, yes, yes, yes!"

Then he was screaming and running back into the sprawling green space behind the house.

"Teams?" Rob asked.

"Don't worry. You don't have to play." Mira's lips twitched as she said it. She knew he'd find it impossible not to play, but Rob had no understanding of how cutthroat her family's competitions could be. Flag football was the tradition for Gina's birthday celebration, but it didn't matter if it was cricket or soccer or badminton or darts, everyone played to win.

Whenever her father, now forever nick-named Grumpy by his grandchildren, received new orders and the Peters family moved, they took with them and added to a network of friends and acquaintances who contributed new holiday recipes and customs, including games for all the kids. All those new friends? They learned every Peters played to win.

Rob would figure that out on his own.

"It's been a while, so remember… My mother is charmed by good manners. My father loves interesting facts. He's a teacher, therapist and lawyer at heart, so avoid arguments if you can. You will lose." Mira wasn't sure why it seemed important to help Rob. Her parents had already formed their opinions, especially given this separation. Today wouldn't change them much. "The food? It's going to be international. Everyone has their favorites from the countries we were stationed in growing up and my mother loves to cook. Stay away from my sisters. They will do their best to question you over…" She shrugged. It was impossible to put into words. No matter how many times she told her family that Rob wasn't to blame, they ignored the message.

Her parents should have been more understanding of him and their situation. They knew how quickly orders could come and require relocation. When she and Rob were faced with trying to be in love over long distance, they'd done what lots of other military couples did. They got married before they were ready. Now, with time and space, it looked like a mistake, but either they were both at fault for that or neither of them was at fault.

"If things feel a little…cool in the atmosphere…" What? What could he do?

"Don't worry, Mira. I can thaw a cold reception." He waggled his eyebrows. "I'm good at talking my way out of tight spots."

"Just for today, stop overthinking. That's what I want to do, too." Rob put his arm around her waist. It felt right. Reassuring. "Try to forget everything else except enjoying this day with your family. You missed too many while you were in the service to let this day go by easily."

Since Rob was as competitive as she was, Mira was surprised to hear the sweet sentiment coming from him. He was good at making plans, assessing conditions and pressing his luck to advance his cause. He could do that here.

But there was no calculation in his eyes. He meant it.

"Look at you with the good advice. I promise I'll try to switch off. We can return to untangling everything tomorrow." Surprising them both, she slipped her arms around his waist. The hug they shared was quick because Mira forced herself to step back, although she wanted to carry on where she was.

"Do you know why dogs run in circles?" he asked and murmured, "Like my brain." Then he raised his eyebrows.

She wasn't going to do it.

She wasn't going to give him the satisfaction.

Then he bumped her shoulder. "C'mon. You know you want to."

Mira huffed out an impatient breath. "Fine. Why do dogs run in circles?" she grumbled.

"Because it's too hard to run in squares." His bland expression as he awaited her reaction was too much. The giggle was out before she could stop it.

"That's honestly the worst kind of charming," she said under her breath, "and the most effective." She turned on a heel and headed for safety. Her big, loud family would force some space between them and buy her some breathing room.

ROB SWALLOWED THE smile that wanted to bloom when he deciphered what she'd said as she'd marched away. Whatever the worst kind of charming might be, Mira had to be referring to him when she'd said it.

It was good to know he was charming, that he was hitting the mark. He was putting maximum effort into it. There had to be a return. Her giggle was like hitting a jackpot.

During their sunrise run, as he'd kept up the pace as the anchor of the group again, Rob had realized panic had led him down the wrong path with Mira. Something about her had always shaken him from his careful approach to life. Life in the military police had never been easy, not once. Investigating the men and women he served alongside had always come with two different pulls.

He wanted to serve his position well, do a good job, but he respected the sense of duty and loyalty of those very same soldiers.

Facts. Data. That had been his rescue on every case.

And life in the civilian police force had required the same.

But Mira… She didn't fit the patterns he knew.

The surprise he felt every time she said yes had knocked him off-kilter. Every time he'd approached her, whether it was their first date, their first kiss, that wedding proposal… He'd wondered if this would be the time she would say no and mean it.

His ability to charm her had held at each stage.

Getting that set of divorce papers in the mail had blown up his process entirely.

So, while running, he'd made the decision to return to his old ways, to observe, gather information and then construct a solid case. He also had Brisa's advice to look at things from a different perspective, which he liked, and Sean's reminder that no answer didn't mean "No."

Even more important, he had the deadline looming…

It would be difficult, but it seemed that all signs pointed to, "Yes, Rob, try this."

So, here he was, holding a sticky toffee pudding that contained dates that were a kind of fruit that did not always live in the produce section, while he watched her walk away. He knew where to find dates in the grocery store. How did that help his case? No idea, but it was a fact and right now he'd take all he could get.

He was definitely open to learning new things.

Mira had noticed the change.

Rob couldn't tell exactly how that made her feel, but knowing that she was in tune with him was satisfying.

Just before she disappeared into the backyard, she glanced over her shoulder at him. Her long hair blew across her face and she brushed it away. Graceful. Beautiful.

"You going to stand there all afternoon?" she yelled before shaking her head. "Jax, please go get Rob."

He could hear the little boy whirling around the corner so Rob knew he better move. Jax stopped abruptly beside him. "Show me where the desserts go, kid."

When he reached the back of the house, he could see the audience had been notified he was about to appear on stage. Everyone was watching him.

And there was a lot more everyone than he'd ever encountered at one of his own family gatherings. Mira's younger sisters were easy to pick out. They looked so much like her. Some of the men had to be husbands, fathers to the younger boys Jackson led in a weird combination of a march and Simon Says around the grassy area. There was a white-haired older couple seated in the shade of an awning. Rob guessed they were Mira's mother's parents.

Before he could ask her to make the introductions, a short guy with a fringe of graying blond hair and big bushy mustache popped up in front of him. Mira's father. They'd talked to each other over video calls after he and Mira had gotten married.

Marrying his daughter without warning anyone hadn't pleased John Peters, and unfortunately, the relationship had gone downhill from there.

"Mr. Peters. It's good to see you again, sir." Rob set the sticky toffee pudding down and held out his hand. Her father stared hard into his face for an uncomfortable eternity. When her father finally shook it, Rob forced himself to relax his shoulders. He'd expected this to be difficult. It looked like he was right but maybe it wasn't hopeless.

"I never expected to meet you in person at all. Even if I forget the fact that you married Mira without introducing yourself to her family, you waited long enough to visit her in Miami," her father said. His expression suggested he hadn't been that upset about never meeting Rob in person. "Alisha, they're finally here. Let's eat!" Mira's father yelled and turned away from Rob.

Rob glanced over at Mira, who shrugged. "I did warn you. The crowd here will be biased."

Biased, sure, but what had she told them about the situation? On a scale from one to taking candy from babies, how bad was his reputation?

Whatever. The damage was done. He had a birthday party and a beautiful afternoon to make progress on repairing it. Everyone would have only positive comments after he left today… That was the new goal.

"Can you introduce me to your grand-parents?" Rob asked. He'd take every bit of this in stride if it could be done. Generally, old people loved him. He could work from the easiest to the hardest in the group. He needed time to determine whether that was Mira's father…or her mother.

Mira tucked her hand around his arm, which immediately made the next steps easier.

"Nan, Pop, this is my…husband, Rob," Mira said as she pointed to him. Was she afraid they'd mistake him for any other strange man who didn't belong in the back-yard?

Her grandfather stood slowly, his eyes narrowing as he studied Rob. When he opened his mouth, Rob braced for impact.

"Thank you for your service," her grand-father said and shook his hand. "All veter-ans receive twenty-five percent off monthly rent at any All American Storage facility." Then he pointed his finger. "Don't you let me find out about you going anywhere else, young man."

Rob knew his mouth was hanging open but it had been such an unexpected conversational opener that it took him a minute. "Thank you, sir, that's good to know. I'm considering making a move to Miami, and I may need some temporary storage."

He didn't check to see Mira's opinion of that but he could feel the warmth of her stare.

"Better late than never, I suppose," Mira's grandmother said. She didn't stand, but her presence was definitely felt.

The urge to fidget under her stare was growing.

"Nan, don't scare him off, please," a woman said from behind Rob. "That is quite clearly my job." Mira's mother had come out to put something down on the food table. As she brushed off her hands, a long braid with strands of gray swung over her shoulder. "My mother is one tough customer, Rob. Now you will know where I get it from."

Her lips curled, but her eyes were serious.

Manners. Mira had reminded him her mother loved good manners.

He hoped whatever etiquette his mother

had managed to cram into his head was up to the challenge.

"Ma'am, thank you for having me today. It's terribly impolite to crash a party, but I wanted to meet the rest of my family." Rob met her stare, determined not to blink. Claiming them as family was bold, and boldness always had the potential to backfire. "Is there anything I can help you with in the kitchen?"

A small frown appeared on her forehead before she straightened. "No. All that remains is to make sure that Mira's offering is here." She pointed at the pan and glanced at her daughter. "This is it?"

Mira very visibly swallowed. "Yes, Mom, Rob and I made it yesterday."

Her mother tipped her head back as she studied her daughter. "You have not taken a bite out of it, have you?"

Mira blinked slowly. As if she was gathering her patience.

The question seemed out of place. Even boys raised in barns like him knew better than to take a bite out of the birthday cake before the party. Mira grumbled, "I haven't done that since I was a kid."

When he realized he'd been privy to tales of Mira's bad behavior, Rob kept his mouth shut but he knew amusement was written all over his face. Mira attempted to step on his foot but he moved quickly out of reach.

"Seventeen is no child," her mother said as she moved off to yell for the kids to come make their plates.

"One time and they never let you live it down," Mira stated and frowned up at Rob. "You aren't laughing at me, are you?"

"Not at you, no." Her lips twitched and he let his smile bloom. "Laughing with you."

"Not laughing, funny guy. You've met Gina. Well, she deserved it. I took a bite of her special birthday treat because she ruined my favorite jacket, which she took without my permission. Payback was justified. At seventeen, my choices were limited." She indicated her mother by pointing with her chin. "Good try, offering to help in the kitchen."

"Manners. You said she would be impressed by manners." Rob watched the families form as moms and dads came to help the kids fill plates and settle at the kids' table under a tree to the side of the yard. "This place is great for big family gatherings."

"I always wondered what kind of place my dad would go for when he was finally done with jobs all over the world." Mira nodded. "This is pretty perfect for them. My dad's parents are gone, but Miami is where my mom and dad grew up. From all the places they'd seen, they decided to come back home, but no one was surprised when they picked a spot this far out of the city. Close to my grandparents, but not too close and lots of space. My dad likes collections." She pointed at a red shed near the house. "This is the first addition. My sisters and I call it Expansion Phase One. There will be more. My mother doesn't complain as long as he keeps all his treasures out of her house."

"That must have been hard living the air force life. Plenty of moves. Lots of packing." Rob followed her lead and got into line to fill a plate.

"When I was a kid, my dad was always buying things. His excitement was contagious." Mira shrugged. "Then he started a collection for each of us girls, too, and my mother got…fussy." She wrinkled her nose. "That's where the snow globes started. Packing and moving was hard enough, but add glass globes filled with water. I'm glad to have them, but not as glad as I am that I'm the only one who can force me to move again."

Her eyes darted to his. Rob could derail their progress by reminding her that they should make these decisions together.

Or not.

"What did everyone else get? You have snow globes. Let me guess… Gina got shot glasses, Kris got those little collectible spoons and Naomi—"

"They're all Christmas related. All of my girls love the holiday," Mira's father said. He drew out the last syllable until it was mildly threatening. Then he marched away.

So, add another strike. Surely, he had three strikes for an out to end the inning at this point.

Gina stuck her head between them. "Shot glasses could be fun. Instead, I have buildings for the world's most eclectic snow village." She pointed. "Kris has to deal with dolls." She stuck her tongue out and her tone was distinctly "Can you even imagine?"

"And Naomi?" Rob asked, hoping to get a point with the sisters because he knew who was missing.

"Ornaments," Gina answered, "because she's always been the lucky one." Then she moved away to snatch a football out of mid-air before it could hit the drinks table.

"We're glad he's closer to Pop's storage places now. That discount comes in handy," Mira added.

Rob considered that. "Your grandfather charges your father rent for his storage?"

Her eyebrows rose. "Are you kidding me? My dad is one of his best customers. Always pays on time. If my father builds collections for all his grandkids, Pop will be able to stop taking nonfamily customers altogether, just collect monthly checks from us." Her smile was wicked. It made his heart ache that he couldn't drop a quick kiss on her lips. She began to study all the dishes on the table. "Take whatever you want but be sure to clean your plate." She waited for him to acknowledge her direction, so he saluted.

He also realized that when Mira had said everyone's favorites, she hadn't exaggerated.

There was a fragrant curry in the center of the table, a sausage dish next to it and a variety of potato sides as well as a giant salad, and several kinds of vegetables.

"Mom picked up recipes everywhere we were stationed. Every meal has options. The family cookbook is huge. Have Mira show it to you," Kris said, handing him a plate. "Try the curry. Love the curry. That will get you points with both my mother and my grandmother." She patted him on the back, which was a much warmer reception than he'd expected. Kris was his new favorite sister-in-law.

Rob followed her suggestion and was glad he had. After meekly trailing Mira to a picnic table with an open bench that would hold them both, he worked his way through every helping he'd chosen. Every single one of them was excellent.

He tried to imagine what his father, who'd turned a suspicious eye on every casserole as being too fancy, might think. His mother was a good cook, but Alisha Peters had mastered truly international cuisine.

"How often do you eat like this?" Rob asked as he scooped up the last bite of curry.

"Every chance I get. I also demand leftovers come home with me," Mira answered, her chin pressed close to his shoulder. "Jealous?" Her eyes twinkled as she stared up at him.

That face, those eyes, the husky tone of her voice… The family party faded away, and he might as well have been falling for her all over again. Mira was no flirt. She was used to working with military guys and knew how to handle them, but when she did let a guy know that she was interested, she was irresistible.

Rob could see the minute she realized what she was doing. Shadows appeared in her eyes before she stared down at her own empty plate.

It had been sweet while it lasted. Rob refused to lose any of his faith in what was between them. If he was remembering, she had to be, too. He took a quick sip of water and realized they had an audience.

When Mira's mother studied his plate with narrow eyes, he was able to show her he'd cleaned it completely. "Everything was delicious, Mrs. Peters. That curry? You could serve that in a restaurant."

He watched Mira's mother exchange a look with her own mother. He couldn't read it, but eventually she turned back to him and nodded. "I'm glad you enjoyed it. For the next occasion, you will have to let me know your favorite meal. Perhaps I have the recipe."

Next occasion? That had to be a good sign.

Mira's mom then pointed at his plate and the men instantly mobilized. Rob stretched back in his chair until he realized all the guys were clearing the table. He jumped up and grabbed two of the side dishes to carry inside. Mira's mother was manning the left-over station. She sniffed when he handed her both bowls, but Rob hoped he wasn't imagining the upward curve of her lips.

Mira's father was elbows-deep in suds.

"Can I help with the dishes, sir?" Rob volunteered as he picked up the dish towel on the counter.

Her father peered at him over the top of his fogged-up glasses and wordlessly handed him a platter to dry. "Stack everything up. Alisha likes to put everything away herself."

"Can't lose my salad bowls for an entire year that way," Alisha Peters said before snapping the towel she held at her husband.

"One time and they never let you forget it," Mira's father grumbled. Rob smiled. He and his daughter had said the same thing in nearly identical tones.

Chores had been part of most of his waking hours while he was growing up. It was natural to step into the rhythm in the kitchen. The more he thought about it, the more clearly he could see the remnants of military precision in how the Peters all worked. Chores were evenly delegated. No one needed a lot of direction because they'd immediately assumed their roles.

Rob glanced out the window to see that Mira and her sisters were moving chairs out to the grassy area. Nan and Pop had taken a spot near the Expansion Phase One red shed.

"Her mother's easier to impress than I am, soldier," her father muttered as he turned off the water and wiped down the sink. "Kitchen duty is one thing. How are your offensive skills?"

Rob dried his hands as he struggled for an answer.

"Football first, then dessert," Mira's mother called out and stepped out the back door, a collection of what looked like bandannas in her hand.

Rob followed the crowd out onto the patio as Mira's father spoke up. "Oldest player versus youngest player. That's the way we've always done it. This year, Jackson's stepping up to captain his own team." Rob watched as Jackson claimed his spot next to his grandfather, his shoulders thrown back as if he planned to conquer the world. "We flip a coin to decide who chooses first. We added Jackson, so Rob's been drafted to the players to even out the number. Mom is the referee." He pointed at his wife. Mira's mother twirled a whistle on a string.

Mira leaned over to say quietly, "Don't expect a fair fight. My mother doesn't care about the rules, but she likes to blow the whistle."

Rob nodded. It had been a long time since he'd played flag football, and he was certain he'd never played it this way. It would be nice to do something to impress Mira's father. If he could have picked any activity, football would have been his choice.

After the coin toss, Jackson yelled in excitement. "Auntie Mira is on my team!"

Rob hid a grin as her father groaned. "Best player out here." His shoulders slumped as he pointed weakly at Rob. "I'll take the newbie. At least he has size." From his tone, he might as well have been saying, "Might as well take the biggest loser on the field."

"Dad, his shoulder is healing, so be careful," Mira said as she grinned at Rob from her place at Jackson's side. "Not sure he should be catching *or* throwing."

Rob met his father-in-law's disgruntled stare.

"Could have warned me about that before I picked you, soldier," her father muttered.

"I'm ready to catch and throw if you are, sir," Rob answered. "Mira can put me back together if necessary." No way was he going to let a twinge keep him from showing what he could do. Now that he could see her grinning in anticipation, he was lost all over again. Mira Peters might run circles around him because she could, but every second would be a joy.

She was comfortable with the home-field advantage, but he was going to shake that up.

After the teams of five were chosen, Rob felt good about his father-in-law's chances. Jackson had chosen Mira, his mother, his father and one of his cousins. That left Mira's father with Rob, Dev, who was the oldest of the kids, and Kris and her husband, whose name was Raul. Rob repeated it to himself a few times, hoping that would make the name stick.

At their first huddle, Mira's father said, "Faking. Cheating. Any dirty trick you can think of. It's all welcome here." Kris and Raul both nodded firmly. "Kris has always been our second-best arm. She's quarterback, but we'll be running sneak plays, too. Dev here is fast. He'll receive." Mira's father thumped the kid on the shoulder. "Rob? Tell us what you can do." He crossed his arms over his chest, prepared to be disappointed.

Rob had been one of the best quarterbacks in Oklahoma at one time. Should he say that here or surprise them? "I can throw." His shoulder might slow things down a bit, but once it was warmed up, he'd be fine. "I can also catch, and I'm faster than Mira." Sometimes. When he had to be. No one better tell her that he'd said that.

Mira's father narrowed his eyes. "Nobody will know what to expect. Let's start you out with the ball, throw or run as you can but make it to the end zone." Before Rob could ask any questions, her father clapped his hands and their referee was blowing the whistle.

"Line up." Mira's mother pointed at an imaginary scrimmage line. "No intentional contact involving my grandsons, Dev, Oscar or Jax. If anyone injures my precious boys, you better keep running. Flags are tackles. When your flag is gone, you are done." She handed out the bandannas and watched them all tuck them in their waistbands. "First team to ten touchdowns wins unless it takes too long and then I will give you a ten-minute warning because I don't have all day for this."

Rob watched everyone nod and met Mira's stare from across the line of scrimmage.

"Looks like we're matched up, Rob. You ready for me?" she asked, the glitter in her eyes familiar. She'd challenged him the same way more than once.

If they were running together, he'd have jumped out to an early start and battled her comeback for every mile. Here? He was going to watch each move Mira made. It would take a minute to learn her patterns so he could anticipate them, but he would.

A slow nod was his best answer. She'd always been a much better trash talker than he'd been.

"I guess we'll see," Mira said and then dropped her head, ready to run as soon as the ball snapped.

It was on from that point. This family did not hesitate. They didn't pull any punches for visitors when the football was on the field and his flag disappeared about two seconds into the first play, sidelining him and allowing him to watch Mira streak to the end zone with the ball she'd caught with two hands.

The gleam in her eyes as she trotted back

to him was hot, so sexy that it might as well have been the two of them alone. "Looks like I got your attention." She twirled the bandanna and then offered it to him. "You gotta play harder than that, hotshot."

He took one end of the bandanna and pulled until he could grasp her hand. "I might lose some battles, baby, but you're reminding me what's at stake in this war." He pressed a hard kiss to her lips and watched her emotions flash across her face. Surprise. Interest. Confusion. Then she realized everyone on the field and off was waiting for them to rejoin the game.

Mira cleared her throat. "We both know who's going to win."

Rob took his place across from her. Ready for the next play, he said, "In the end, we both will."

Her eyes met his for a split second. Then the ball was in play and they were racing down the field. Rob had never played such a hard game of flag football in his life. Had even real high school football games involved this much running?

Rob caught his breath as he stopped to study the scoreboard. Pop held one set of numbers, Nan was responsible for the others, but she was relaxed in her chair, snoozing. One of the little kids had been propping up numbers as ordered.

"Tied score. One more play. I want dessert," Mira's mother announced and she blew her whistle. "Let's go!"

"Last shot, soldier," Mira's father said to him. "If you're going to shine, now's the time."

Mira laughed silently as Rob bent to face off against her. When the ball snapped, he moved in to press a kiss on her lips and then ran around her while she stared after him. He was laughing as her father threw him the ball. The plan had been for him to receive it while everyone scrambled to run interference. That worked, except Mira was left out of the tangle and she was racing toward him.

He cut back once to avoid Jackson, who immediately tripped and fell. Rob slowed to make sure the kid was fine, but the sight of Mira closing the distance between them reminded him he had a game to win.

His hesitation gave Jackson enough time to recover.

Rob was only steps from the end zone when he glanced over his shoulder. Surely he was due a gloating smile at Mira. Instead, he caught sight of an intense determination in Jackson's face, and before he could change direction, the kid had launched himself through the air as if he'd been shot from a cannon, head down, aimed right for Rob's abdomen.

Catching the kid was the only self-defense either one of them had. Rob dropped the ball and grabbed the kid as Jackson's head made contact. They both landed in a hard bounce in the grass.

Then, after the seconds it took for him to gather his wits, all Rob could hear was Mira's delighted giggles as she ran the full length of the field back to her end zone to score the winning point.

Jackson had immediately bounded away to join her celebration.

Rob decided he would take as much time as he needed to recover his breath and his dignity.

"Didn't I warn you dirty tricks would be coming?" Mira's father admonished as his head blocked out a piece of the clear blue sky above Rob.

"Cheating in the last play is kind of family tradition," Dev said as he stared down at Rob. "Next year, you'll know."

It was nice they were assuming he'd live. As Rob stretched out his arms and legs, he decided they might be correct.

The rest of his team bent over him. They stared with concern until the whistle blew. "Dessert!" Mira's mom hollered and all his supporters scattered. She stood over him. "Nice catch. Not a scratch on the kid." Her smile was genuine as she walked away.

Since the dessert line would be long, Rob closed his eyes.

"Did I kill him?" Jackson asked.

"He'll be fine," Mira answered. "Why don't you go and make him a plate? One of everything."

Before Rob could argue that he might never hold down solid foods again, the kid was gone.

"Not sure how you think a man who has taken a first-grader to the abdomen can clear a plate full of desserts," he said and cracked an eye open to stare at his wife.

Winning suited her.

So did a fast-paced, mean game of flag football with her devious family.

"I told you to sit this one out," she said as she stretched out beside him, her head propped on her elbow, "but you never listen."

He never listened.

Rob wondered if she'd been holding that back for a while. Did it fit here? No, not really, but it might work in other places in their relationship.

"I listened, but your dad asked." He sighed. "And I wanted to win."

She ran a hand over his shoulder. "Should I check to make sure you're okay? No blood?"

Rob considered her offer. Having his wife's hands on his skin was tempting.

Stripping out of his shirt while her family watched was less so.

"Nah, I caught the kid. No pain then. It's mending." Rob turned to face her. "Happy?"

She nodded. "Everyone's having a good time."

Her slow smile was better than scoring

the winning touchdown. "I'm glad you came today. My family needed to meet you."

Even if they were getting a divorce? Rob thought it but didn't want to remind her.

A plate appeared above his head. "One of everything," Jax said proudly.

Rob groaned as he sat up. "Thanks."

"It's the least I could do," Jax said with a grin. "When we play baseball, I want you on my team."

Rob raised his eyebrows at Mira. "Baseball?"

"The kids get to choose what we play on their birthdays," Mira said as she stood and offered him her hand.

Rob took it but rolled up gracefully from the grass. He would have pretended it was that easy even if it killed him. The faint ache through his arms and shoulders was proof he was still alive.

Jax was dancing from one foot to the other as the plate heaped with sweets bounced in his hands.

"Okay, but I'm better at football," Rob said. Jax's face fell dramatically.

The kid sighed heavily as he gave Rob the plate. "A deal's a deal, I guess." His shoulders were slumped as he trotted back across the grass. Obviously, he'd figured on a more impressive performance on the baseball diamond.

"And to think I almost played college football," Rob muttered as he stood alongside his wife.

Her grin was adorable. "That doesn't hold up for Peters flag football. You probably played by the rules."

"Always." Rob was caught by the way happiness glowed from Mira. In all the time he'd spent with her, he'd seen a variety of emotions on her face, but nothing as pure and sweet as this.

"Sometimes, in the real world, you gotta learn when to bend the rules to win." She tapped her chin. "Such as breaking a promise not to kiss a person, especially when it distracts your opponent perfectly."

"Am I covered by the 'cheating is encouraged' and 'anything goes' rules of Peters flag football?" he asked. Kissing her had been the right thing to do, he was sure of it.

"Can't argue with good gameplay," Mira said as she towed him back to her family.

Rob endured all the insults and teasing with good humor, glad when her father came up and clapped his hand on Rob's back. "Good catch. The kid weighs a ton. You saved my back this year."

Apparently, catching a first-grader was a common play in Peters flag football and he'd passed one of their key tests.

That felt good. Mira handed him a fork and he dug into the mound of desserts on his plate.

He'd clear it to impress her mother.

And then he'd get to ride home with the woman who beat him on the football field.

Had life ever been any sweeter?

CHAPTER TEN

AFTER MAKING THE morning run with her soon-to-be-ex-husband and eating breakfast with her soon-to-be-ex-husband and packing up a few moving boxes with her soon-to-be-ex-husband, Mira was happy to take a few minutes to catch her breath and walk over to Concord Court's office. Something in her relationship with Rob had shifted while they'd been stretched out in the grass after flag football and she needed it to shift back immediately.

Mira had seen Rob in a brand-new light and she couldn't seem to dismiss the image or the thought.

When they'd been dating and even married and trying to keep up long distance, the time she'd spent with Rob had either been in familiar base surroundings or places that were new to both of them when they'd traveled together. Spending an afternoon with her family, watching how Rob fit in as if he'd always been there...

Well, it was shaking her confidence in her decision to quit him.

And that was before their upcoming get-away to Key West.

After a small detour to her new house to unload several boxes to make room for more packing, they were going away together. Exploring new locales with him had always been amazing and fun and romantic.

Rob hadn't called this trip *romantic*.

But there was almost no way that Key West itself could be anything other than romantic, especially with her ex-husband at her side.

"Calling him ex-husband when he hasn't signed the divorce papers yet is a weak defense, Mira," she told herself as she opened the door to Concord Court's office. She clamped a hand over her stomach and tried to ignore how it had twisted into a knot.

Brisa, Reyna and Sean were gathered around the large well-crafted wood desk that dominated the space. All three of them turned in her direction.

"Am I interrupting?" Mira asked. Maybe

this was a bad idea. She'd come with a reasonable excuse to talk to her friends, but if she were honest with herself, a pep talk would be welcome.

Sean was her best friend. He was obligated by Best Fiend Code to dislike her ex-husband on her behalf. Mira was hoping his dislike might prop hers up. He wouldn't let her down.

"Interrupting? No. We need to call a timeout on this discussion before one of us loses our temper." Brisa smiled exaggeratedly at Reyna, who crossed her arms over her chest. "A little disagreement about the budget for our New Year's Eve party."

Mira planted her hands on her hips. "A party? As soon as I leave, you guys start throwing more parties? I think I'm hurt." Was she? Maybe a little.

"Fourth of July was successful. Got a ton of positive feedback. For this one, I'm extending invitations to the veterans' groups that refer residents to us." Brisa tangled her fingers together. "It will help us expand our outreach into the veterans' community here in south Florida. More support for the small businesses we're launching. Better word-of-mouth among the men and women who could benefit from our programs."

"And there'll be extra shine for the Montero name, so you know their father will be pleased," Sean added, "and it'll generate good publicity, which will make fundraising easier. Win-win-win." He draped an arm over Reyna's shoulders. "You have to spend money to make money, honey."

Reyna scoffed. "There's no way this will make money and it doesn't have to." She snapped her fingers. "This is the time we find a local restaurant to do the catering, support a veteran or at least a neighbor." She whirled around to type something in the computer, then started jotting down things in a stuffed notebook.

"Did you need something, Mira?" Brisa asked as she stepped away from the desk. "And I won't listen to a word about you missing this party. We're going to open it up to all our alumni, too. Sean's already on board to pick up Charlie and his date from the rehabilitation facility for the evening. You have to come. Who doesn't love an occasion to dress up?"

Charlie had been a resident at Concord

Court until it became clear that he needed more help than the bridge facility could offer. He'd moved not too far away, with Sean's help, and every story Mira heard about him at the nightly group meeting around the pool confirmed it had been the best decision Charlie, Reyna and Sean could have made. A happy ending for the old guy who told the wildest tales.

"Hey, I'm not a fancy-party-dress wearer, Brisa. We discussed that when you wanted to send me on a blind date to the swankiest restaurant in town, but I love a happily-ever-after story. I wouldn't miss seeing Charlie," Mira said. "I came in to ask if you could keep an eye on my place for the next few days. Rob and I are going out of town."

Sean's immediate scowl was reassuring.

Brisa blinked, her look expectant. "Details. We'd like more details." The corners of her lips curled in delight. "Are you two on the verge of giving happily-ever-after another shot yourselves?" Brisa clasped her hands over her heart and did a dance of excitement.

It was cute. Too bad Mira had to dash her hopes.

"When Rob arrived, his plan was to take me on a getaway to remind me of how much we enjoyed spending time together." If he'd known how effective navigating a family birthday party at her parents' house would have been, he might have saved on the time and money for Key West. Mira wasn't going to tell him that. It was still clear that she belonged in Miami.

She refused to think about his question anymore. She would never ask him to give up something as important as his job again. How could she be so clear about what she wanted for the second stage of her career and ask him to give up his own?

Was working SWAT in Atlanta his dream? Mira frowned as she realized she'd never asked.

"Where are you two headed?" Reyna joined her sister in front of the desk.

"And are you in danger of forgetting about the divorce and moving to Atlanta?" Sean demanded. Of the three of them, he looked the most worried.

"No way. I'm not in any danger. I agreed I'd do this in order to get his promise to sign the papers, so we could take care of the divorce the easy way. We'll be back before Christmas Eve. Rob will sign the papers the next day and go home. I'll finish packing and my friend Wade and his moving team will make sure I'm in my new home by New Year's Day. That's the right way to start the New Year." Mira pretended to brush her hands together and reminded herself of all the reasons she knew this was the best solution for her and Rob.

Mira was satisfied with almost every bit of her life in Miami.

As a single woman, she'd have the chance to find the last missing piece.

Rob deserved that freedom, too. He could pursue his career dreams and find a good woman who didn't lose sleep over the memories and new worries every night.

It would mean happily-ever-after for both of them.

"This trip to Key West…" Mira shook her head. "I've fought the urge to argue my way out of it, but he's kept every promise he made since he got here."

Brisa wrapped her arm around Mira's shoulders. "Whatcha scared of?"

That the other two people glared at Brisa

made Mira laugh but her pride wanted a solid argument. Instead, she went with the truth. "Honestly? I'm scared I'll remember how bad it hurt in the early days, after I left Rob to come here, and I'll…" Weaken. Forget the promise she'd made to herself to find the life she'd dreamed of now that she had a second shot. She was so close to having it all.

When both women nodded to show they knew exactly what she meant and no further explanation was needed, Mira understood. It was almost like falling in love so hard that the threat of forgetting herself was real.

But Mira didn't want to believe it was actually…that fear that was holding her back.

Fearing for Rob's life while he took on dangerous jobs? That was logical. It might even be unselfish, caring more for him than he did for himself.

Being afraid of losing herself…

That was selfish.

There was no avoiding that.

It might even be cowardly, too.

"I'll be happy to keep an eye on your place," Reyna said.

"Do you need me to get your mail?" Brisa asked. "Just a few days you said?"

"No, the mail is fine." Mira had done what she came here to do. Why wasn't she leaving? Everyone was waiting for her to leave.

Finally, Sean huffed out an irritated breath. "Go on your trip. Remember why you married the guy in the first place. You need to realize how much you're leaving behind if you give all this up." Then he crossed his arms over his chest. His glare indicated he didn't enjoy coming down on Rob's side. "What? They've been separated for a long time. If there's nothing there now, this trip will show it."

"But what if there is something there?" Brisa asked before clapping her hands. "Sean, you romantic! I love this!"

When Brisa grinned, he shrugged. "Someone in this room has to be the romantic. Might as well be me. I can't say I'm a fan of the guy, but…" He nodded. "I understand exactly where he's coming from. Falling in love isn't easy. Once you've done it, you owe it to yourself to fight for it. That's all he's doing."

And she wasn't? Sean didn't say it. Mira wasn't even sure that she was following the thought to its rightful conclusion but it was true. She hadn't fought very hard.

"Key West should help you answer his question," Sean stated. Mira opened her mouth but she wasn't sure what to say. That one meeting around the pool must have been something for both Rob and Sean.

Rob had told the guys he'd asked if she'd give them another chance if he gave everything up in Atlanta and settled in Miami.

He'd also obviously told them she wouldn't answer.

"He deserves to know where you stand, even if it's hard for you both," Sean said softly.

It hurt to hear that, but Sean was right.

When had she become such a coward?

Mira had to face this head-on because it was an important decision. It was a hard decision. For those reasons, she couldn't back down or run away again.

Ready for any distraction from the worrying itch that she might possibly have bailed on Atlanta and Rob, Mira said, "I'll catch up with everybody when we get back from Key West."

Then she executed a precise about-face and marched for the door.

When she made it back to the townhome, Rob was loading up his duffel and her small suitcase in the cramped back seat of his truck. Her boxes were taking up most of the space. They'd already negotiated loudly about who would be driving.

Giving in had been easy enough, although Mira had put up a solid fight.

When he'd sweetened the pot by offering to move a load of boxes to her new house on the way…

Well, it was easier to give in gracefully.

"Anything else to go?" Mira asked as she stepped up to close the door.

"Nope, let's hit the road." Rob moved to open the passenger side door. Mira raised her eyebrows at him as she slid inside. This wasn't like them, either.

"I'm used to getting my own doors, Rob." She crossed her legs and tried to ignore how it felt when he watched her movements.

"I know, but I enjoy taking care of you." He closed the door quietly and entered on his side of the truck. As he started the engine, he said, "Let's play a game. Hit me with the explanation of why you don't need me to take care of you."

Mira bit her lip.

"Sounds like you might have heard it before," she answered, the creeping feeling that she might have delivered the lecture the first night she'd met him at the bar in Djibouti.

And a few more times since then.

His slow grin was confirmation. "I like to listen to you talk."

Her reluctant chuckle escaped before she'd decided to let it go. "Because I can take care of myself. I'm self-taught. Years of fighting for my place are impossible to forget, I guess. Even when I don't have to prove myself, it's this automatic urge. Gotta be tough and independent and strong. Sometimes I'm not careful, though, and people get caught in my sights."

He nodded. "I get it."

Mira thumped her head on the headrest. How many times had her automatic defenses kicked in when Rob hadn't deserved it? "Can I give you a blanket apology for whenever you were innocent, collateral damage that didn't deserve defensive artillery?"

Rob laughed as he made the turn she indicated. She better pay attention or they'd miss the last turn. "No apology necessary. I'm sure I deserved far worse than I got. I'm glad you fight, Mira."

"Take this left." She squeezed the tip of her nose to push back the tears. Had anyone ever told her that?

He stopped in the driveway of the house she pointed out. "Not tears."

Rob's voice held the same horror she'd heard from the Court guys at one of their midnight sessions.

"Nope." Mira cleared her throat. "Just… gratitude." The urge to hop out of the truck to avoid more conversation was hard to fight, but she paused. "When you showed up, I was afraid we were going to lose us. Things would get angry or sad. You've been as sweet to me as you always were, even with the divorce papers in hand. I'm really glad. If we changed who we are as people…" That would break her heart, but she couldn't admit that out loud. He deserved time to fulfill his own dreams.

After he got out of the vehicle, lowered the tailgate and pulled out two boxes, he said, "Even mad and afraid, I will always love you, Mira. Whether you're right next to me or a thousand miles away." He frowned. "And if we can't make it and I find someone new to love and you do, too, it wouldn't matter how far away I was. If you needed me, I would be there. Before I loved you, I liked you. All of you." He motioned with his chin. "Grab a box and show me your house."

Mira had two choices. The first was the most appealing, but heartbroken sobs at the kindest thing any man could say to her would upset them both.

So she decided to go with pretending. She'd forget big decisions and pretend this day and this trip were fun adventures to take with a good buddy, a best friend. That's what Rob had been before.

Rob was right. No matter what happened, she would always call him a friend.

This could be the last time they were together like this. The hard knot in her stomach returned, this time for a different reason.

Had she ever imagined a lifetime where she never saw Rob again? Not the ex-husband who had to go his own way and would like to pull her along, but the friend she would always love.

Pretending. In that moment, it was her only choice.

She would pretend that "goodbye" was forever away.

To make it through, Mira would have to pretend broken hearts weren't real, or at least, not as real as friendships that outlasted them.

CHAPTER ELEVEN

ROB SHIFTED THE boxes he'd grabbed and studied the outside of Mira's house. On a scale of architectural styles, his taste and hers might not be poles apart, but they weren't close, either.

He'd gone with new construction in a planned subdivision with a brick facade that would last, even if it was nearly identical to the houses on either side. His priorities had been solid construction, careful investment and plenty of space. He and Mira had been forced into cramped housing for their entire careers, places built with true governmental efficiency. He'd wanted the best he could afford for Mira.

What had she chosen for herself?

"What do you call this...style?" he asked, careful to keep confusion out of his voice.

He might as well have been honest because Mira read between the lines.

"Personality. Let's call it that. It blends many different eras and styles." Mira pulled keys out of her pocket and unlocked the front door. Around to the side, Rob spotted a detached garage.

He bit back the advice that welled up immediately.

Yes, she would have been much safer with an attached garage that allowed her to park, lower a garage door and then enter the house directly.

Like the house he'd chosen for them.

But Mira knew that.

"The original house was built in the fifties. You can see the influence of the mid-century modern back here," she said as she led him into the kitchen. Everything was very…square and plain, but giant windows looked out on the tiny backyard. Sunshine poured in. Rob had to admit that was nice. "Then a new family moved in and kids started coming and rooms were built onto the side. Those have a more…modern feel, if by *modern* you mean the eighties. Lots of glass blocks."

Mira put her box down and motioned for him to follow her. Rob stuck his head into the added bedrooms. They were nothing special, but the space would be good for snow globe storage, no doubt.

"Two bathrooms, pink tile in the original and light blue in the en suite." Mira gestured toward the master bedroom. The windows from the original house continued in there and on one of the walls, built-in bookcases created a cozy nook with a narrow window. It reminded him of her favorite chair at her Concord place and the bookshelves holding her collection. "No closet to brag about."

Rob rubbed his forehead. The different pages they'd been on while choosing homes... Wow.

"I know. It's overwhelming. Let me show you why I love it." Mira led him outside. There was an external door in the bedroom. He hated that. "I know it's a security problem, Rob. You're thinking so loud that I can hear it. I'll install an alarm, cameras on both doors, and I might get a dog." She shrugged. "My dad's imagining a Doberman, German shepherd, something with a terrifying bark and brilliant white teeth."

Relieved that she planned to improve security, Rob stepped out on the shaded patio. "And what kind of dog are you imagining?" They'd never talked about dogs, either. Rob liked dogs but moving so often would have been even more challenging with a pet.

"Oldest dog in the shelter, possibly two seniors. I haven't decided how far to press my luck yet. Sean has a great program going where he takes shelter dogs and sets them up with fosters who train them to act as service dogs for veterans. I've fostered a couple, learned about training. I want to have my own, but I never had a chance to figure that out. My mother is anti-pet hair, so we never had one growing up. I have decided to show her the error of her ways."

Rob smiled because she expected him to, but he realized it hurt to listen to all her plans that didn't include him or his hope to save their marriage.

Mira held her arms out. "This is why I picked this place. Well, this and being under ten minutes to Concord Court. I don't want to leave my new family completely."

While he considered how she was attached to her friends at Concord Court and didn't want to be too far away, but had had no problem decamping Atlanta without giving him a shot at changing her mind, Rob studied the garden. Someone who'd lived here before had done good work.

"An orange tree!" Mira pointed excitedly. "A lemon tree! In my backyard. And see this?" She stood between two posts in the ground. "The hammock in the garage? It goes right here. There are beds for a few vegetables. I won't go too far. And the garage? It's lined with rosebushes." She clasped her hands together, as if that was the only thing that might contain her glee. "I'm going to plant things and watch them grow!"

Rob couldn't imagine getting that wound up over a garden. As a kid, he'd learned vegetable gardens were hard work, but he could admit it was nice to have some space of your own to play. "Do you know anything about growing vegetables or roses?"

She tilted her head to the side as if she was confused by the question. "How hard can it be? I'll do some research."

Mira would figure it all out. He had no doubt about that.

"Let's finish unloading." She exited

through the gate and went back around to the driveway where he was parked.

On their third and final trip, she said, "You think it's silly, don't you? You would never choose a quirky house just to get your hands on the garden."

What did it matter how he answered now? She'd made her decision and she was happy with it. Disagreeing with her choice wouldn't accomplish anything.

But he wanted to understand.

"Spacious attached garage. Walk-in closets in every bedroom. New kitchen and bathrooms. A pantry big enough to dance in." Rob ticked off the Atlanta house's selling features. "And a yard where you could plant anything you want." She would have to since it was bare of anything but spotty grass that came with new builds. The fresh slate had seemed promising, but almost three years later, he hadn't improved it at all. Not a single rosebush or orange tree.

Mira folded her arms over her middle, as though she was protecting herself. "When I walked in there, all I could think of was all the featureless places I'd been forced to add life to in the past. Even Concord Court.

Once my stuff is out of there, it could be an average apartment in any city. This place… The first time I saw it, I knew it was mine. I fit here." She dropped her head into her hands. "Does that make any sense?"

That was not a feeling he'd ever experienced, not about a place, but her joy in every feature she pointed out was convincing.

"I'm glad you found a place you love. Dogs are a great addition, and you should be able to grow anything back there. You have nice sunny spots." Rob smiled. "I can picture you swinging in the hammock while you grade papers."

"Me, too!" she agreed.

Rob waited for her to lock up the door. It was time to head out on the trip he'd planned to win her back. Why didn't he feel more confident? He'd made exactly the wrong decisions on the post-military career he thought would fit his expectations and Mira's for himself. He'd also chosen so poorly on the house he'd wanted to present to her like a gift when she made it home.

What if Mira was absolutely correct about the divorce, too?

Sadness hit immediately, but he couldn't let her see it.

If this was the last trip he took with Mira Peters, he was going to appreciate and enjoy every minute.

There would be time to be sad later.

AFTER A COUPLE of hours on the road, Mira needed a break. Something had changed while they'd discussed her new place. Rob was quiet. Too quiet.

"Want to stop for food?" Mira asked as she pointed out the sign. "Famous Key Largo is coming up." She read the billboard. "Seafood and sea view. We both love that."

Rob took the turn off the two-lane highway. "Famous Key Largo… Because of the song? And Bogie and Bacall?" He hummed and slowed down as the short road opened to a large, empty parking lot.

Mira vaguely recognized the tune, but wasn't sure what he was talking about. "Because of the movie? Starring Bogie and Bacall?" She studied the facade of the restaurant. "Well. If we wanted to eat inside an overgrown tiki hut, we have arrived."

Food had been a great suggestion. This

place? The beat-up facade and the splotchy, fake thatched roof that was supposed to create the atmosphere of the island getaway didn't inspire confidence.

"Yeah, and the crowd has dwindled some, so our timing is perfect." Rob parked next to the three cars lining the front of the restaurant. "Come on. It's the middle of the afternoon. I bet the place picks up at night. If we judged places by the buildings they were in, we'd have never found that pub in London."

He was right. The place served the best fish and chips but from the outside, she'd been afraid they'd found the hideout for Britain's most dangerous biker gang. After they made it out of there with happy stomachs and zero punches thrown, they'd returned the next day for dinner.

Mira swallowed her suggestion that they look around Key Largo for better, busier options. It was easy to follow him.

As Rob held open the door to the restaurant, he said, "The song was about the movie that featured Bogie and Bacall in Key Largo. Never heard it?"

Mira trailed the sunny girl who waved

them out to the deck with a wide grin. "Bill-boards don't lie! We've got seafood and a sea view. Pick your table and I'll grab some menus and two lemonades." She held up a hand to stop a reply. "Don't argue. The lemonade is the right choice."

Mira raised her eyebrows at Rob and chose a table next to the railing. Brilliant white umbrellas covered each table, the sea breeze an awesome plus. It was perfect.

The beach in front of the restaurant was nearly empty, leaving them with a view of expansive water.

After the waitress set two cold glasses of lemonade between them, Mira decided to go with the flow. Normally, she'd also ask for water but when in Key Largo… The first sip of her drink was so cold and sweet and right. Had she ever had such an amazing drink?

Rob laughed at her expression. It had to be pure bliss on her face. Then he sipped some more and nodded.

The waitress returned with the menus. "Can I get you an appetizer while you look?"

Without hesitation, Rob said, "Bring us

whatever goes best with the lemonade that you knew we needed before we did. We trust you."

Mira agreed.

"Mama didn't raise no fool. Sampler platters coming up!" She whirled away. "And keep the lemonade coming."

Mira braced her elbows on the table. "Back to the song. I can't place it."

Rob frowned. "Are you kidding me? When I was a kid, my mother would play the local country station and the DJ must have put on that song every single night. It had to be his favorite. If my dad had come in from the barn by that time, he'd two-step her around the kitchen." He settled back in his chair. "I haven't thought of that in a long time. I listened to that station whenever I could over the internet, when I was overseas, but it's been a while." Then he hummed a bit and sang the pieces he could remember of a song about a couple who'd fallen in love like Bogie and Bacall but were facing the end.

The lyrics brought her right back to sitting across from the man she loved and the man she was about to divorce. Rob cleared his throat awkwardly, and Mira was sure they were both glad when the sampler plates showed up.

Mira didn't want to live with the tension for the whole trip. "I'll trade you my shrimp for your oysters." He hated oysters.

Rob handed his oysters over. "Keep your shrimp. Plenty of food here."

"Fair is fair," Mira sang as she plopped her shrimp on his plate. She kept one, as a kind of commission, and ate it before he could argue. His chuckle made it easier to breathe.

"You don't talk much about Oklahoma. The only stories I can remember are ones your sister told me." Mira stared out at the sea. Next to the ocean, it seemed easier to talk about things that might matter. "Like when you chased her around the house."

"She should have helped me bring in the green beans like my mother told her to." He shrugged. "It was easy enough to live in my house. Just do what Mama and Daddy said, no backtalk. Perfect preparation for life in the army, if you think about it." He smiled. "It's almost like they were right there with me every day, except there were fewer chores for Uncle Sam."

Mira sipped her lemonade. "I know you told me you don't go home often. Argued with your mother, right?" Since Mira and her mother were so close, it was hard to imagine one argument being enough to cause such distance.

"She wanted me to come home, take over, after my father died." Rob studied the ocean. Mira waited, hopeful he would confide more. "I couldn't. That time, I couldn't follow their orders. She was fine, the farm was fine, they had my sister and her husband who knew what they were doing. But it wasn't for me anymore. I'm not sure Oklahoma is home anymore, but I'm still in touch with my sister. We talk about once a week."

Mira watched him eat and wondered if he was done with the topic.

He finally met her stare. "When you told me about how your family lived, and that you moved, and how you and your sisters would rule every new school by the end of the second week, how much fun your dad could be with the exploring every time you landed in a new spot…" His expression was intense and vulnerable all at the same time, and her heart ached for him. "I couldn't imagine growing up like that. With that big, open love. For my parents, for my whole family, there was work…and the occasional two-step around the kitchen, which I hadn't thought about until we stopped in Key Largo."

Knowing his background made some things clearer.

Rob did hard things without complaining because that's what he'd learned.

He had to work to find value in himself because that's what he'd learned.

Whether he knew it or not, he was a kitchen two-stepper, too, because he'd learned that, as well.

That was the piece of Rob she loved the most, the one he didn't know he had.

"Spending time with my family must have been overwhelming for you. Everyone gives orders, and obedience is almost never expected," Mira said softly. They were so different. Without the army and the air force and a shared base in Africa, they would have never met. That was sad.

"No one in Oklahoma would allow such blatant cheating at football, flag or otherwise," he drawled. "Football is a way of life there." He took a few bites. "But it was nice to see you as part of the family, your sisters around you. Makes me wish we'd done this the old-fashioned way with a big splashy wedding where our families would annoy each other and we'd wish we'd eloped. Your dad would definitely like me more."

He was right. "My dad is sweet, a little goofy with the way he loves every single holiday and custom, but it's about tradition with him. He likes knowing how things are connected. It's weird. Neither of my parents is old-fashioned. Kris shaved all of her hair off when she was seventeen, and they rolled with that. Anyone we brought around was welcome. I think he sees being there, meeting our friends or dates or husbands, as part of his job, something the dad does to keep his family safe. Sort of like your dad's rough-and-tumble approach. I can't imagine my mom or dad ever allowing distance to come between us because they'd be failing at their job."

If Rob's parents had loved him the way

he deserved, they would have pursued him. Mira believed that.

The fact that he'd pursued her instead of sticking with what he knew...

Mira gulped the last of her lemonade to ease the lump in her throat. Their efficient waitress darted over to refill the glass before Mira set it back on the table.

Rob picked up his glass and tapped her lemonade. "Stopping in famous Key Largo was a great suggestion. To the brightest wife in the world."

Mira hesitated but drank to his toast. This trip was going to make everything so much harder, but that danger couldn't stop her or hopefully him from enjoying every second. They finished their lunch and Rob paid while she followed the railing back to the truck.

Then he reversed out of the parking spot and headed for the highway.

"Tell me about the Atlanta force." Mira hoped it would remind her of every nightmare she'd imagined he would face. That might help put that distance back between them. Metaphorically speaking.

"So you can remember why you hate it?

No way. Let's find a new job for me here." He scrunched up his face. "Although, I can't surf and my swimming is only passable. Landlocked Oklahoma didn't prepare me for the ocean, but I would look exceptionally good in red trunks, so lifeguard is at the top of my list."

Mira shook her head. "You're pretty unqualified on the guarding part of that job, and that seems important."

Rob fiddled with the radio and landed on the classic rock station that Mira preferred.

It bothered her that she didn't know if he was making that choice because he liked the music, too, or because he knew she did.

"Fine, not a lifeguard. How about car salesman or…" He tapped his fingers on the steering wheel. Maybe he did enjoy the music. "Waiter?"

The image of Rob dumping a tray over the head of some finicky guy who needed his silverware turned a certain way flashed through her mind. "You aren't great with people."

His immediate frown made her laugh again. "Excuse me?"

"Like, the public, those kinds of people.

One-on-one, you're okay, but lots of people making demands… I don't see it." Mira watched him closely.

"Okay, you toss some ideas out. Let me shoot them down. I'm good at shooting," he said and his grin faded.

He'd reminded himself of their problems.

"Guess you'll have to be a policeman, then." Mira smiled. "Good news, you already know how to do that!"

He tightened his hands on the steering wheel, but he didn't argue.

The radio helped. "This is your song. Hit it." Rob cranked up the volume and waited for her to sing along before he joined in. They were both terrible singers, but in the cab of that truck, no one cared. They had a beautiful sunny day, wide-open road, good music and good company.

In that instant, it was so easy to be happy and to believe in love.

Mira decided to stay in that moment. Worrying about the future and regretting the past could be done later when she couldn't sleep. That afternoon it was time to live.

CHAPTER TWELVE

DRIVING TO KEY WEST with Mira was the perfect road trip. Singing badly with her to the radio reminded him of the first time they made breakfast together in Djibouti. He loved all music, but Mira had a taste for '70s rock, so all of their cooking had also included disco moves, occasional drum solos and air guitar riffs. So many memories were stirred up of this happy, sunshiny woman.

Loading her suitcase in the back seat had tempted him to remind her of the time the airline had lost her luggage when she'd visited him in Germany right after their whirlwind marriage. She'd worn his shirts and the same pair of jeans for the entire weekend.

Even the pit stop they'd made for the restroom and refueling with snacks for the road brought back memories of how honey-roasted peanuts would not work for Mira. Only plain salted would do.

The visit to the house she'd chosen for herself and their lunch conversation... Taken together, Rob had started to wonder how well they knew each other. All the dating conversations, getting-to-know-you moments where they would trade favorite color, season, movie and song or tell their most embarrassing high school stories or share the parts of their childhoods they might like to change if they had kids of their own...and whether either of them wanted kids at all... They'd missed so much as they'd sped through the dating phase, with all its own ups and downs, to jump into a long-distance marriage.

Falling for each other had been easy and instant, but they still didn't know each other.

It was no wonder learning to live together was going to take some serious work.

There were still big missing pieces, but he could pull up the memory of every minute he'd spent with Mira. He'd always been big on the details. She was a part of him.

Her reaction to the place he'd chosen for their Key West stay confirmed his hunch.

He had changed. He had been listening.

As soon as he'd parked, she'd squealed, "Is that a parrot? A real parrot?" Then she'd jumped out to investigate. He thought they were both relieved to discover that the life-sized red-and-blue bird perched on the small porch's railing was made of wood, even if it was painted to fool the eye. Mira's hands were still clasped together, but she'd stopped clapping.

"Welcome to The Hideaway," he said as he entered the code he'd been texted into the keypad. The quiet snick of the lock was reassuring, too. His smooth plans would have a serious wrinkle if they were locked out of their rental. Finding even one available rental property for this week had been a struggle. The fact that it was perfect for Mira, if not quite within his original budget, was icing on the cake.

When she slowly came to a stop to stand in the center of the wide-open space that made up the living room and kitchen, her mouth gaping open, he contained his victory dance.

"It looks like Santa's workshop exploded in here." She turned to take in the shelves of

Christmas decor that lined the room, broken only by three large square glass windows and French doors leading out to a patio. "I love it. I gotta show my dad." She yanked her phone out of her jeans and dialed.

"Hello?" her father said loudly.

Rob could see what appeared to be her father's chin on Mira's screen.

"Dad, it's video, so pull the phone away from your face and speak in a normal tone." Mira waited patiently. Rob stifled a grin. He was almost certain she'd had to say something similar when they'd called to tell her parents they'd gotten married.

Eventually, her father figured it out. "I told you we need to practice this more." He shook his head. "Alisha, come talk to your daughter. She's arrived safely in Key West, even though she is much later than the computer told you she would be when you checked the directions from Miami to Key West." He bugged his eyes out as if to say, "Your mother was worried, but I knew better."

There was a dizzy jumble but eventually her parents figured out how to appear correctly on the screen.

"Good trip?" her mother asked. "I am glad to know you are there safely. I will be sure to let Nan and Pop know, as well."

"Mom, it is safe. Or, was safe. I'm safe, Rob's safe—" Mira motioned vaguely at him. "If you wanted to know what time I expected to get here, you should have asked me. And instead of worrying Nan, you should have called me on my cell phone. You know I have one because I am calling you from it right now."

"I didn't want to bother you." Her mother huffed out a breath as if she couldn't imagine being that rude.

"Easy drive," Rob said. "We moved some of Mira's boxes to her new place and I wanted the complete tour. Then we stopped for lunch. I'm sorry it took longer than expected." When Mira glanced at him, he wondered if he was supposed to make himself scarce. He crossed his arms over his chest. He wanted to hear this conversation.

"Did you warn her about that garage and the door in the bedroom going outside? Safety issues, both of them," her father stated. Rob wondered if being called in to be on her dad's side meant he'd made some progress in redeeming himself.

"I tried, but—"

"My daughter interrupted you to tell you about the cameras and the dogs and her smart plans to look out for herself, I guess. I'm telling you, I will be down to inspect." Her father pointed at the phone and shook his finger.

Mira's lips firmed into a thin line while she paused. Her parents eventually figured out how to get both of them on the screen again while she reclaimed her patience.

"I had to show you this place Rob found, Daddy. You'd love it." Mira turned her phone and did another slow circle to get all the decor in. "Look at all this!"

Exclamations were her answer until she turned the phone back around.

"Could it be any more perfect?" she asked. He waited for her to look at him so he could shake his head no in agreement, but she didn't.

"Too many pirates," her mother muttered. Rob studied the shelves. For a Santa scene, there were more pirates and mermaids than he'd expect. He found four different scalawags holding large knives and wearing black scarves along with their red-and-green clothing.

Should he point them out or not?

"That's what makes it perfect. It's Key West," her father said deliberately as if Mira's mother was missing the joke. "Pirates make better sense than a big man in a red furry suit. Nice and warm, good ships for sailing."

Her one-shouldered shrug suggested she wasn't bothered by his answer.

"There's a small private pool outside and a rooftop deck that looks down over Duval Street where there will be a parade tomorrow," Rob continued. "I've booked us on a catamaran for an exciting excursion that you can't get anywhere else, and I've made reservations for a private table on the water that you are going to love." It was supposed to have the best seat in Key West for the Christmas boat parade and if it didn't, his bank account had been hammered for no good reason.

The way her eyes lit up at his list of excursions reminded him that he had done his best. Mira would love every minute.

"Good thing I brought the only cocktail dress I own. I expected you'd want to go big," she murmured. Going big. She'd suggested he was doing that every time he picked a place with linen tablecloths and sommeliers. He loved seeing her dressed up. Whether she was murdering the Eagles with the windows rolled down in the passenger side of his truck or dressed in her finest, Mira was eye-catching.

"Fine. You should get on with it all, then," her mother said before narrowing her eyes. "Mira, give the phone to your husband. I wish to speak to him briefly."

Mira opened her mouth to argue, but finally handed over the phone. This time, her eyes met his and there was an apology there…along with a gleam of humor. She would spare him this if she could, but since she couldn't, she would enjoy his predicament.

It was the most beautiful she'd ever been, there surrounded by over-the-top Christmas decor with her parents looking and listening in.

Rob took the phone and told himself to be brave. "Yes, ma'am?"

Mira's mother gave him a hard stare but her father tipped up his chin. That looked like approval.

"My daughter is worth every special thing you have planned." Her mother waited for him to agree. Was that approval, as well? If not, it was something close. "But do not believe that you can move her away from her family. Not now, after we've finally gotten her back." Mira's mother tsked. "I know a thing or two about her, and I will pull out the big guns if I am forced to."

Then her lips spread in a wide grin.

"Yes, ma'am. I understand." Each of them wanted Mira to make her home with them.

Losing her felt more inevitable than ever, but he was going to bet on the enjoyment they'd always found together.

All he had to do was convince her to give him a chance, to wait on the divorce until he could quit Atlanta, find a new job here and sell the house and locate someplace to stay... Rob shoved aside the thought of the number of things that would have to be done before he could live in Miami.

Worrying about the future would rob this special trip of all the magic.

He was determined to bring Mira some magic.

"Go and get food. Her sunny mood disappears when she's hungry. It's a family trait," her father said somewhat grudgingly as Rob handed the phone back to Mira.

When she was in control again, Mira rolled her eyes. "Happens to most humans."

"You might be too late," her father shouted as Mira smirked. "Bring me a souvenir. I want a pirate or one of those unique mermaid fellas."

"Love you both. I'll let you know when I get back to Miami." Mira ended the call.

Rob bent to pick up her suitcase. "Choose the bedroom you want and I'll put your bag in it. Then we can go explore if you're ready. The place has three. There should be one on this floor—" Rob muttered as he wandered down the short hallway and pointed into the room there "—and two upstairs. I think they have views."

Mira gestured for him to go up, so Rob moved on to the second floor. There were two generous bedrooms and a bathroom to share. On this level, all the decor was still related to the sea. Santa might rule over the living room, but that was it. The bedrooms were focused on tranquil waves and seashells. The view was of tropical foliage, but one room had a peekaboo view of water in the distance. "You take this one."

Rob set her suitcase down and then tossed his duffel on the bed in the other bedroom.

Mira stared out the window for a second, before turning back to him.

He couldn't read her expression. "Every thing okay?" He ran a hand through his hair. He didn't know where they would stay if she hated the view. "This whole town is full up until Christmas."

"No more rooms in any more inns? Is that what you're saying? That fits Christmas." Her lips twitched, so he grinned... Then he got her small joke. "I never guessed so many people would want to be away from home for the holiday. For the most part, I was okay with being away from my family on important days, like missing a birthday celebration or whatever, but missing Christmas at home, which was wherever my parents were stationed before they moved back to Miami... That could bring me pretty low. Make me do things like accept a drink from a stranger in a bar who used a terrible joke instead of a terrible pickup line."

Rob had thought his pickup strategy inspired, mainly because it worked with a tough customer like Mira, but he hadn't tried it before her or since, so he might not be the best judge.

"Lots of sunshine. Sand. Water warm enough to still enjoy. I guess that's enough to draw a crowd," he said, "and Key West doesn't do Christmas like everyone else. Lucky people like us can have both, Christmas here and then at home with our families." Her family, anyway.

"This place is good, Rob, a one of a kind all the way around." She squeezed his arm.

"Not very traditional. I'll figure something else out, if you want," he added. He would. He'd build them their own hut on the beach if that's what she wanted.

"This place is absolutely perfect for me." She inhaled slowly. "Almost as if you planned every minute of this trip on what would please me, instead of what you would enjoy. Santa pirates don't seem your style."

Rob felt sheepish. "To be fair, I didn't see the pirates until your mother pointed them out. Still, given the choice between something that I know you'll love and something that suits my minimalism, I'll pick you every single time."

Mira sighed. "Ugh. No more giving up what you want for me. That's…" She held her arms out in frustration.

Rob stepped closer to take her hand. He wanted to kiss her. Desperately.

But he was going to keep his word.

"You don't get it, Peters." He waited for her to open her eyes and then said, "Nothing makes me happier than seeing that pleasure, that glow, on your face. The way your eyes light up. Your bottom lip, how it curves. Stick me in a soulless chain hotel, fine, but if I can choose a place that lights you up like this, one hundred times out of one hundred, I know what I want."

She bit her lip. "Why doesn't it bother you that I'm not the same? That I pick me over you and you pick me over you. That's not right." Mira closed her eyes. "Selfish."

Rob realized she was calling herself selfish, this woman who was voluntarily standing in a high school classroom to teach

science when she could do almost anything else.

"Food. I'm picking the food that I want."
Rob grinned as she opened one suspicious
eye. "Promise. Forget unpacking for now. I
want to explore."

"You're going to do it again, pick the perfect place for me," she muttered and nodded, "but in this we agree. After riding for
so long, I'm ready to walk. Let's see some
sights."

They stopped in one of the shops on
Duval Street and bought a map and two
bottles of water. When they were back out
on the sidewalk, they dodged a few groups
of tourists and paused in the shade of a tree
with bright red blooms.

Rob wanted to remind her that he was
supposed to be choosing, but she was frown-
ing down at the map, studying what would
be her preferences instead. He'd never visited Key West before, but it was exactly as
he'd imagined in some places and different
in others. There were fewer souvenir shops
and more art galleries and about as many
bars as he'd expected. An open-air trolley

bus trundled past them and Rob could hear the tour guide talking.

"...you might know Ernest Hemingway and Jimmy Buffet made homes here in the Conch Republic, but there's a long list of celebrated authors and artists including poets Robert Frost and Wallace Stevens, writer Judy Blume and even..."

Did he want to hear the rest of the names? Maybe. Was that the most touristy tourist thing in the world? It was close to it, if not.

He had time for things like that now.

"Put the map away. I want to ride that trolley," he said as Mira checked the cross street. When she whirled around to stare at him, he shrugged. "I can read the sign from here. It's hop on and off, so we can get the lay of the land first, then spend more time where we want. Plus, I need someone to tell me the name of this tree." He pointed at the blooms. "It's now one of my favorites."

Mira's lips curled as she folded the map and slipped it into her jeans pocket. "You have favorite trees?" When he held his hand out, she tangled their fingers together. "This I've got to hear."

Relieved that she was going to follow him

in this, Rob started toward the kiosk where the trolley stopped to find out if they could buy tickets. "Number one is easy." From the corner of his eye, he slid her a glance. "Palm tree has to be number one."

"Well, you're in the right place now. Lots of palm trees," Mira said and blinked at him, daring him to go on with whatever he was cooking up.

"Ask me why the palm tree is my favorite." Rob squeezed her fingers and felt the familiar rush when she tipped her chin up and refused. She was going to make him work. He would wait her out.

A few seconds later, her gusty sigh was his reward. "Why is a palm tree your favorite tree?" Then she smacked her forehead as if she couldn't believe she was going along with him.

"Because I can hold it right here in my hand." He pulled her hand up and tapped her palm, so happy to have a reason to tug her close. Mira fake frowned so broadly he had to chuckle. Then she pressed a quick kiss on his lips that knocked him back on his heels. Before he could recover, she was leading the way.

"I guess that makes my favorite tree chemistry. Because I'm a scientist. Get it? Chemis-tree? Terrible jokes. Just really bad." Then she pointed at one of the trees he'd wondered about. "Royal poinciana. Put that as number two on your list. That's the name. Biology teacher. I know a thing or two about Florida flora and fauna."

Of course she did.

"Welcome. Y'all are just in time. Trolley pulling up right now. Two tickets?" the older gentleman in the shade of the kiosk asked. He pulled his straw hat off and stirred his hair with it like a fan until Rob offered his credit card. "See anything you'd like to explore, hop off and catch the next trolley. When you make it back here, you've seen the show." He slid tickets across to them and then waved a hand as the trolley came to a stop.

Mira climbed up the steps and took a window seat. As Rob slid in next to her, a breeze sent her hair tickling across his shoulder. That made it easier to slip his arm behind her.

When she relaxed into his side, Rob knew he'd made the right choice. All they had to do was be together and take this ride wherever it went. Easy.

"Afternoon, folks, you've joined us on the leg of this tour that will take us past Hemingway's house. You'll be able to see the wall Hemingway built himself to keep the crowds out, with help from his friend, Captain Sloppy Russell. It's a little crooked, suggesting Hemingway was also under the influence of his favorite libation." The tour guide paused. "Which was? Anybody know?"

Rob and Mira grinned at each other. They had no idea. Maybe a tree question would be coming next.

"Mojito," someone yelled from the back of the trolley. The tour guide clapped silently.

"Good guess." He bent his head. "Wrong, so wrong, but good guess. Gin and tonic. Papa liked his drinks like he liked his writing…true and simple. But do you know where they love a good mojito?" The tour guide moved to the left side of the trolley. "Cuba! Where it was invented. We're coming up on the southernmost point in the United States, this concrete buoy you can almost see behind the throngs of people having their pictures taken with it. What does that have to do with mojitos, you may well ask?" He held out his hands. "Well, right here we're about ninety miles from Cuba, where they serve very good mojitos, not that Hemingway would care."

Mira bent close to whisper. "This is so cheesy. I love it. You knew I would."

Rob wrapped his arm more tightly around her. "This guy is speaking my language. I love it more because you're here with me."

Her eyes met his, and whatever else had happened in the past or might come next, he knew that in that moment, they were on the same page. They were connected and perfectly content.

Not because they were in Miami or in Atlanta or on a military base in Djibouti, but because they were together, both doing something they loved.

That was the piece they were missing.

And if he was being honest with himself, he was the challenge. Mira knew her mind and her heart. She'd planned to make her dream come true, while he'd…floundered.

He'd wanted to make her his dream, but that wasn't fair to Mira.

"At the next stop, let's do some souvenir shopping." Mira frowned up at him. "Is that okay?"

Rob nodded. "I want to buy your dad one of those mermen. We could start a new collection for him. Every time we go somewhere new, we can pick him up a different ornament unique to the place."

Mira giggled. "You're saying that as some kind of threat, but he'd love it. My mother on the other hand…"

"Whatever works." Rob could easily imagine giggling in souvenir shops all over the world with Mira, on the hunt for the next starring bit of her father's collection. Unless he was on the wrong track, he had a lot of work to do to make that happen.

But he'd never been afraid of work.

It was still possible for them to fit long term but asking her to do the hard part was impossible. It was good he had experience with planning and logistics.

He was going to need it.

CHAPTER THIRTEEN

A SEA BREEZE slipped under the brim of Mira's floppy straw hat, but she managed to catch the accessory before it was lost over the side of the *Key West Wonder*. The impressive sixty-five-foot catamaran was scheduled to take them and about forty other people on an "extreme water adventure."

At least, that's what the brochure that Rob had handed her before they'd left The Hideaway said. She dropped it inside the huge tote he'd insisted on buying the day before. Asking for details ahead of time had been a waste of time on her part. Her husband, the romantic, had been determined that the surprise was an important part of the fun.

"Good thing you gave me the list of what we were supposed to bring for this, given all our time to prepare," Mira said drily as her husband dropped down on the padded bench next to her.

"A swimsuit and towels." Rob shrugged. "All the rest is extra. They're going to feed us, give us drinks, entertain us and provide coral-safe sunscreen. What else is there?" He stretched his arms out along the railing. His cocky grin was adorable, even if the planner in her would have appreciated a bit more notice that morning.

"One of us might need something for seasickness." And it wasn't going to be her. Rob had surprised them both by turning green on the short boat ride they'd taken together in London. "Did you think of that?"

He held up a hand, put one finger under the band around his wrist and popped it. "Bought this on the advice of the girl who sold me the tickets for the tour. It controls motion sickness without the drowsiness. I have taken care of everything." He bumped her shoulder. "Admit it."

Instead of agreeing, Mira raised her sunglasses to peer around. "You said they'd feed us. When? Where?"

With perfect timing, one of the crew stopped with a tray of drinks. "As soon as we're underway, the captain will address everyone and we'll get the show started, ma'am. In the meantime, can I offer you a mimosa? Or we have water and tea if you prefer."

Rob cleared his throat as if to say "I told you so" without the actual words, so Mira smiled up at the young man with the tray. "A mimosa would be perfect. Thank you." She took the champagne flute and sipped it modestly until the crew member had moved on.

"You surprised me with this 'extreme' adventure. I expected a quick tour, and then we'd have our feet on dry land. Water's not really your thing." Extreme water? Definitely not for him. Mira turned to face Rob.

"It is not, but you and I, we only do extreme. Give us a choice between a Sunday stroll and extreme, and we don't hesitate." He rolled his shoulders. "I can swim. I just prefer pools. No oceans in Oklahoma."

Before Mira could remind him that he'd squeezed his eyes closed when they'd watched the ridiculous movie where some guy had to cut his way out of a shark's stomach with a chainsaw, the captain said,

"Good morning and welcome aboard the *Key West Wonder*. If I or my crew can do anything to make this tour better, please do not hesitate to let us know. We are serving breakfast on the deck below.

"The band will be playing any minute now. On our way out from Key West, I'm hoping we'll see some curious dolphins. When you move below deck, check out the glass-bottomed observation areas. The waters here are filled with unique fish, birds, and this crew will be able to answer your questions."

Mira fought the urge to grin at Rob. The excitement was almost overwhelming. If someone had tried to build the perfect tour for an adventure junkie who was also a biology teacher with a big appetite for breakfast food, they couldn't have done better. It was difficult to pretend to be cool as she sat there.

When Rob's hand slipped under her hair to stroke her shoulder and nape, she shivered and leaned into him. Playing it cool was silly anyway. This was the perfect day with the perfect company.

"We've got a quick trip out to where we'll

drop anchor, ladies and gentlemen. Jet Skis, kayaks, an amusement park in the water with climbing and slides, snorkeling in the reef…" The captain paused as the music below started. "We've got it. For those of you who prefer your water more relaxing than energetic, we've also got shaded lounge chairs on the starboard side, the perfect spot for another mimosa and a nap. We'll wake you up for the dolphins." Faint laughter floated up. "For now, have a good breakfast and enjoy the scenery."

When he stepped away from the bridge, it was easier to hear music drifting up from the level below them.

"Can you find us a lounge? I'll get breakfast," Rob said with his eyebrows raised, as if he was waiting for her okay. Since it was a flawless plan, Mira nodded. "And another mimosa."

They launched into action, no other words needed. Mira smiled at the slow stream of people who were moving carefully around the catamaran and located starboard more easily than she expected. The lounges lined one side, the cushions wide and deep enough for two people. She'd just dropped her floppy hat inside the tote when Rob paused next to her, a heaping plate of breakfast sandwiches, fruit and two mimosas clutched in his hands.

"My hero. I almost starved." Mira gave him a smile as she accepted the food and waited for him to sit next to her. When they were settled, she wondered how she'd ever force herself out of such a great spot. It was cool in the shade, the breeze stirred her hair, and they had enough food for at least an hour.

"Can't have that." He sighed as he leaned back. "This is nice. I did good."

The satisfaction in his voice was too cute. Mira laughed. "You did. This is amazing." She shook her head. "But don't you hate it, this boat out in the middle of the big water?"

Rob dropped his sunglasses on the cushion and offered her a grape. "No place I'd rather be than right here next to you, even if we are doomed to a watery grave at some point today."

The shocked stare of the elderly woman who'd taken the lounge next to theirs caught his attention. "It's a joke, ma'am. Inside joke, that's all." She didn't seem reassured at Rob's words, and he cringed when he turned back to face Mira.

She smothered her giggles with a bite of her breakfast sandwich.

"Except for frightening the other passengers," Mira said as she leaned close to his ear, "you have done so well with this trip. I love it. Thank you."

His eyes were gleaming with satisfaction as he settled into the lounge. "What should we do first? Snorkel? Kayak? The climbing tower has hand and footholds like a rock-climbing wall. That was what convinced me you had to do this."

Mira was struck again at how well Rob knew her, and how important her opinion was to the decisions he made.

"Folks, I never expected to see them this early in the trip, but we've got some curious dolphins. Move to the starboard side and look out in front of the catamaran," the captain announced over the loudspeaker.

Rob jumped up and offered her his hand so they could move closer to the railing. There, in the distance, she could see fins as the dolphins surfaced in the water. The boat moved and the dolphins leaped out front, disappeared for a minute and returned as their audience gasped and cheered. Mira pulled her phone out of her pocket to take video. Biology teachers could use dolphin footage to liven up a classroom.

When the dolphins tired of their game, she and Rob returned to their comfy lounge. She still had her phone in her hand. "Let's take a selfie. I don't want to forget this day."

He took her phone and stretched his arm out. Mira shoved her sunglasses into her hair and relaxed into his side as Rob pulled her close. "Smile." Mira didn't need the reminder. She was pretty sure she'd been smiling since the first mimosa. When he had the picture, Rob texted it to himself. "I want a reminder, too."

They were quiet as they resumed eating the breakfast Rob had assembled.

"What do we want to do today? Snorkeling, for sure. And the climbing tower thing. Gotta do those." Mira wasn't sure where her shyness was coming from. For some reason, sitting next to him like this had started to remind her of an awkward first date.

"Good plan," Rob said as he stretched

out next to her and tangled his fingers through hers.

Mira copied his pose. If he was relaxed, so was she. "What's number one on your list?"

He turned his head. At this near distance, it was easy to see his eyes. That had always been her best clue about his emotions. Happiness. Contentment. That's what she could see. "This is number one on my list." He held up their joined hands.

All the questions she intended to ask him about Oklahoma, his job, life in Atlanta… They were important, but not as important as those eyes. "How did you sleep last night?"

He paused to study her face. "Like a baby, actually. Kind of unexpected. It's been a long time since that happened. You?"

"Same. I guess your crushing my hopes of smuggling one of Hemingway's cats out of his museum took it out of you." Mira watched his eyes crinkle when he smiled in response.

"Your future geriatric dog security team would not appreciate having a boss like that." Rob trailed his thumb over her fingers.

"I was going to give the cat to you." Mira blinked innocently at him. "You wouldn't say no, would you?"

"Never. Any gift from you I'm keeping." Rob wrinkled his nose. "But I didn't want to miss this day because of having to bail you out of the Key West jailhouse."

"Smart." Mira wasn't sure what else to say to keep the conversation going.

Then she realized that was the nerves talking and there was no need for that. She and Rob had always been okay with comfortable silence. "Wake me up in fifteen. I want to go see the glass bottom part of the boat next. You can stay here. I'll tell you all about the sea monsters swimming under us. I will definitely not say anything about the watery grave, though."

He squeezed her hand.

Neither of them slept.

It was too perfect to miss a single second.

ROB HAD BEEN telling himself that the ocean was nothing but an oversize lake since he'd booked this tour, but watching his wife step up to the open edge of the boat was not easy. In a lake, he might be able to get them both to shore if he had to. Here? He had to trust other people and believe that sharks preferred water where there was less excited screaming. Even the older lady who'd been offended by the watery grave joke had given a whoop of delight as she'd gone over the side.

His grim determination to enjoy himself was the exception here.

The way Mira turned to beam at him before jumping feetfirst into the ocean was cute, but his first reaction was panic. She popped back up with a gorgeous expression on her face, and even at this distance, he could tell she was enjoying his hesitation.

"Sir, are you going in?" the crew member next to him asked. Rob realized he was holding up progress.

"Yep." Rob's tone was annoyed, but that didn't stop the kid from flashing him a grin.

"Nothing to worry about down there, but it is a lot of water. Would you like a life jacket?" he asked.

Since his worry was more about what was in the water with him than the actual swimming, Rob stepped forward bristling and waited for the splash. Cold water covered him, a shock that caught his breath, but faded by the time he kicked up to the surface.

Mira swam alongside him. "Good job."

Rob swiped his hair back and glanced around. "Where to first? Climbing wall?"

She nodded wildly. "Definitely second. First…"

Rob waited while Mira moved to him. She was a natural in the water. He'd never found anything she was ungraceful at. Her hands slipped over his shoulders and she floated next to him. Rob was immediately distracted from the image in his head of a great white shark circling the deep, and hungry for a man in red swim trunks.

"My brave husband. I love adventures with you." Mira pressed her lips to his, an easy kiss, one they'd shared often and was sweeter because of it.

Before he could react, decide to try for a second one, she turned away. "Last one to the climbing tower is a landlubber." Sunlight sparkled over her skin as she swam hard for the inflatable tower.

Rob had to laugh. He was drowning under the love that washed over him when he heard satisfaction, love, admiration in her voice. That was his whole goal: to put that look in her eyes, that warmth in her tone.

She'd given it to him and swam on, pursuing her goals while he...

Well, he was treading water.

"I'm winning," Mira called out about the same time Rob felt the shivery sensation of something swimming near him, under him, or was perhaps thinking about it.

Determined to at least be a moving target, Rob followed his wife as quickly as he could. He'd climb the tower, give the creature time to pick some other snack out of the water.

He'd come back to thinking about how long he'd been treading water, stuck in the same holding pattern in his own life, later.

CHAPTER FOURTEEN

MIRA WATCHED ROB CLOSELY. She was trying to make sure he didn't know she was watching him. It had been a long, wonderful, wild day that he'd chosen because he'd known she would love it. Unfortunately, he'd hated it. Or at least, if the emotion wasn't quite that strong, she knew he was glad the whole thing was o-v-e-r.

When he sipped from the cold bottle of beer that had been dangling from his fingers for at least two minutes, she was sure he wasn't asleep, but he hadn't spoken. They had come out to watch the sunset from the tiny, perfect roof deck, him with a beer, her with a lemonade that was in no way Key Largo quality.

"After you finish that, you might want to try water. It's easy to get dehydrated while you're in the water. Counterintuitive, but true." Mira propped her feet up on the railing and ignored the twinge in her biceps. That soreness was how she knew she'd had fun on the five-hour excursion they'd had that day.

"No more water," Rob insisted before glancing at her, one corner of his mouth curved up.

The excursion that he had not enjoyed in the least.

"Spending time on the boat was nice." Mira grinned. "Actually, every single minute of the day was awesome. Snorkeling along the reef. Climbing those amazing inflatable slides out there in the middle of nowhere that dump you right into the water. That guy who was doing flips off the one you climbed with the rope? That was amazing. Not bright, but very athletic."

Rob grunted and rubbed his shoulder.

"Did you enjoy the one that had the handhold and footholds that you climb like a rock wall?" Mira had. "That was the biggest leap into water I've ever taken."

He nodded.

Mira knew that because she was staring without letting him know. She'd been doing it all day, studying him out of the corner of her eye or from under eyelashes.

That's how she knew his shoulder was bothering him now when he'd been perfectly fine before the catamaran trip.

That was something she hadn't known existed before this trip, but as soon as she'd seen the enormous, inflated slides, she'd had to try every single one.

Her husband knew about her love of climbing. The fact that he'd kept up as she'd chosen each new handhold or foothold reminded her of their second date. He'd invited her to join some friends who were hiking the Goda Mountains, one of the precious green spots in Djibouti.

And he'd been annoyed, in a cute way, at how easily she'd made the hike.

Mira had been overwhelmed and grateful to have the chance to leave the base and the city to explore somewhere so few people got to visit. It had been easy to ignore his fake irritation then.

Here…

She was tired of waiting for him to admit he was hurting. "Are you ever going to tell me how badly your shoulder hurts? I have ibuprofen." Then she stared at him over her glass of lemonade. "I could help."

"Another wife might have offered me a couple of those with a bottle of water instead of poking at me." Then he propped his feet up beside hers. "Could I have a couple of pills and some water, please, Doctor?"

Mira patted his leg. "Not so hard to do. Back in a second." She was digging through her purse when she realized he was right. He'd done similar for her before, guessed what she needed and just…done it.

And not because she asked.

That was the kind of guy he was. That's what taking care of her looked like to him.

To her, it was either irritatingly sweet or annoyingly bossy, depending on her own mood.

But that was how he loved her.

Had she ever figured out how to show him the same kind of love?

Mira returned with the painkillers and two bottles of water. He'd finished his beer and was stretched out with his head on the back of the chair, staring up at the night sky. It was still early, no stars this close to the lights of Duval, but the quieter street was nice.

"You're so unselfish with me, Rob." Mira gave him the pills and plopped down in her chair, disappointed in herself again. It had been so easy to blame him for all the things that had broken their marriage, but the closer she looked, the better she understood her own weakness.

"Why do you sound so disappointed?" he asked as he took the bottle from her and washed down the pills.

She sighed. "Admitting I'm not perfect is disappointing."

He chuckled loudly and downed the contents of the bottle.

Mira held out the second bottle of water. "Drink this one, too. You might have a headache tomorrow from so much sun. This should help."

Rob didn't argue but scooted down in the chair and stretched his legs. "You had a good day. That's all I wanted."

"I had a once-in-a-lifetime day. Didn't know places like that existed. So much fun." Mira turned and drew her legs up in the chair. Why was she pretending not to watch him? Rob needed to understand that she saw him. "Although the way you climbed that rope to get up to the top of that slide was impressive. Was the view good? You stayed up there a while. I dunked right back in the water."

He turned his head to meet her stare, their faces so close. "I felt something brush my leg while I was swimming. I had to get out of that water the quickest way I could." His slow smile bloomed as she giggled.

"It was a fish, Rob. You weren't in any life-threatening danger." Mira brushed his hair away from his forehead. A little sunburned, but nothing too bad.

"Saw *Jaws* at a formative age." He pressed his face into her hand. "I was almost certain it wasn't a shark but I had to make sure. If it had been a shark, I would have been in the water to save you."

"Right. We're both lucky it wasn't a shark. You would have been sad when it ate me, and you would have had an excellent view from the top of that slide." Mira knew she was falling for him. All the sun and time with Rob… She was too close to melting into a gooey mess for the man on the verge of falling asleep with his cheek cradled in her palm.

"All I need is you happy. Would I have chosen something on land? Yes. There are fewer sharks on land, although here in Florida, I'm not sure that number is zero." He blinked. "Why are you talking about selfishness? I made all the plans. You didn't make any demands."

Mira traced her fingers through his hair. "I don't do the same for you, though. I convince you to leave the service so we can be happy…and then, I don't stay. What kind of woman does that?"

Saying it out loud was hard, but the guilt was growing heavy to carry.

Rob kissed her palm. "There's my favorite tree again." Then he inhaled slowly. "If we want to, we can discuss how there's enough blame to go around. I can admit I'm closed off, bossy and sort of expected you to get smart and move on from me the first time you beat me up those mountains in Djibouti. If I'm not the man, not the biggest and strongest to protect and care for you, how could someone like you stay with me?"

Mira blinked back the tears that surprised

her. He'd never said anything like that to her before.

"I got it wrong, Mira. *Protecting* and *caring* are the wrong words for building a world and expecting you to fit in it." He held her gaze. "But never believe that being unselfish with you was a sacrifice for me. I never understood wanting anything or anyone until you rolled your eyes at me in that bar, until you challenged me on that hike or on our first run or the time we entered the trivia contest in that London pub. Each time you succeed, I love you more. I want to give you more.

"Yeah, that's got to be annoying. Smothering. Being someone's everything in the world has to be exhausting. Tell me how putting you in that position is anything but selfish."

Mira bit her lip, afraid anything she might say would stop this flow of words. They might constitute more honest emotional truth than he'd ever given her before.

"Thank you for the ibuprofen and the water and your promise to believe that I would have saved you from that imaginary shark if you'd needed it. Today was for you. Tomorrow night is for me. You, in a fancy dress and a whole lot of romance." He stood slowly. "I'm also going to be selfish right now and head downstairs to take a hot shower and have nightmares about sharks chomping through inflatable slides to eat me…and you, of course." He paused to give her time to avoid the kiss she could feel in the air between them.

His lips were warm and sweet against hers. The way his hand smoothed across her cheek and down the sensitive skin of her neck raised goose bumps and good memories.

Then he stepped back. "Broke my promise. Sorry, not sorry." He gave her forehead a quick peck and then disappeared inside.

The desire to follow him was strong. So strong. She'd missed his kisses.

His arms around her. How his voice turned husky at the end of the day.

Rob was close enough to touch.

He would never tell her no, not about more kisses, not about anything.

If she asked him to give up everything again and move, he would do it.

The uncomfortable weight of realizing

how much he'd already given her and how much more she would take if she weren't careful…

Right. That kept her in her chair. Mira stared up at the night sky and wished the support group from Concord Court's pool area was there to talk her through this.

She wouldn't be sleeping tonight. All the choices and what-ifs and lost chances were tumbling through her mind, all set for some heavy-duty consideration. Mira wrapped her arms around her knees and wondered if she had a hope of finding solutions on her own.

Until she had some answers to her growing number of questions, she would stay up here on the roof. Away from Rob.

Because one unselfish thing she owed him was not to make this situation any harder because of her own doubts. He would get some rest.

Mira would keep her distance.

CHAPTER FIFTEEN

AFTER THEIR ADVENTUROUS excursion day, filled with sun and sand and possible sharks, Rob was relieved Mira had been content with a day of sightseeing. Or she'd seemed to be and he had resolved to stop trying so hard to read her mind and anticipate her needs. Hearing her say she was selfish had been a wake-up call. If what he was doing made her feel bad, he'd change what he was doing.

After sleeping late, which for both of them was barely after sunrise, they'd gone for a run on the beach. Rob had been certain he didn't need anything else to be happy with his life, just sunshine, the ocean and Mira. Then she'd convinced him to stop at one of the restaurants along Duval for brunch and his perspective changed again.

The place's name was in French, so he had no idea what it was called.

The front door had been guarded by a beady-eyed rooster.

And Rob had been able to redeem himself after the shark scare of the day before, because Mira had asked him to rescue her. Actually, she'd said something like "Do something about that" and pointed at the chicken.

His first "Beat it, buddy" had gotten no response, so he'd added an aggressive hand wave. With one superior "bok" the chicken had stalked off.

"Obviously speaks French. Had to put some body movement to it," he'd drawled before opening the door in a grand gesture. Her cheeky grin as she brushed past him had been the cherry on top of a perfect morning.

Dark shadows under Mira's eyes had convinced him she'd been struggling to sleep, probably overthinking. That had been his problem most nights. Although, after all their recent excitement, as soon as his head hit the pillow the night before, he'd been out.

It was nice to have an easy start to the

day, Mira's smile and a good meal, even if he'd had to face off against a chicken.

Then he'd enjoyed crepes better than the ones he'd eaten in Paris and started to worry that the day would go downhill.

But it hadn't. Everything had been smooth between them. Had they ever communicated as well as they did under the magic of Key West?

Even bickering over the correct souvenirs to take back to Mira's parents and nephews had been enjoyable, not tense. Ditching her long enough to pick up a gift for her had taken some planning and misdirection, but he'd managed it.

Now that it was time for dinner and the most romantic piece of his entire Key West strategy, Rob was nervous. The pressure had returned with a vengeance.

"You look so beautiful this evening," Rob said as he squeezed the hand Mira had slipped into his. "I'm glad you went with the comfortable shoes instead of the heels. This walk to Mallory Square is longer than I remembered." Because his nerves were strung tight.

He was going to ask her the question

again at some point tonight, fully prepared to hear her say, "Yes, quit your job and move to Miami." His case would never be stronger than it was right here. They belonged together. She had to understand that, right?

"It's not so bad. I know you miss the heels," Mira said as she raised her eyebrows because he'd been pretty vocal approving the black stilettos, "but these sandals go with the dress better, and now we can take the long way home. We haven't seen much of Key West under the stars. It's our last night, so we better make it count."

"Good suggestion," Rob murmured, content to walk wherever she wanted, her shoulder brushing against his and the ocean breeze stirring her hair, leaving behind the sweet smell of her perfume. He should find out what it was called. "What kind of perfume do you wear?"

Mira snorted and he would swear his heart twinged, like an inexperienced teenager with his first girlfriend. "That is eau de shampoo. The bottle has pink flowers on the front. Does that help?"

Rob grinned. "Why am I not surprised?"

"You should have seen all the bottles of this and that which Kris had when we were growing up." Mira sighed. "I liked fussing with makeup, but I could never get into perfume. Every scent gave me a headache."

In Mallory Square, foot traffic picked up and the parking lot was filled. Rob wondered if making a reservation at an expensive restaurant had been the way to go. Mira loved people watching and the crowd out here was growing, but he was glad to have one of the big decisions already made. He led Mira into the stand-alone establishment right on the edge of the water.

Instead of blending into the fishing village theme, Sunset stood out, a boxy glass building lit from within at the moment. As soon as the sun set, they would dim the lights for the parade. Once the host sat them at their table along the southern edge of the building, Rob realized they would be able to watch the sunset and the parade with no obstructions.

He should give his credit card a kiss the next time he saw it.

"Would you like to start off the evening

with our featured sauvignon blanc?" asked the first suited waiter to stop at their table.

Since all he and Mira knew about wine was how to drink it, they were comfortable accepting recommendations. With one quick nod, dinner was underway. Every recommendation was taken, and every choice was good, so they were able to enjoy the slow setting of the sun with the soothing murmur of low conversations taking place around them. As it darkened outside, the lights lowered, leaving only the gleam of table candlelight.

And Mira Peters set against the backdrop of the night sky and the reflection of flickering lights was…magic. He wouldn't wait anymore. He was going to ask her to give him a full second shot. He'd move to Miami into her "quirky" house and they could figure out his next career together.

Yes, he was relying on her for help, but he'd learned an important lesson with the Atlanta failure. To get it right, they had to make decisions together.

Before he could get the words out, a ripple of excitement spread through the restaurant.

"Oh, my, would you look at that?" Mira asked, her voice a mixture of awe and wonder like a six-year-old on Christmas morning. A large boat… Ship? He wasn't sure whether it should properly be called a boat or ship, but it was sailing through the water toward them and lit from the tip of the mast and from one end to the other in red lights. The words "Sun. Sand. Santa" were outlined in white. A giant Santa Claus was perched in the center and was waving, with a forest of palm trees lit in white lights surrounding him.

"More of your favorite tree," Mira said as she squeezed his fingers. Her eyes were bright and her happy grin was wide. "I've never seen anything like this. I love it. Can you even imagine how my dad would flip?" She made grabbing motions. "My phone. I want to take some pictures to show him."

The woman had no trouble making her wishes known sometimes.

Like when she'd told him she wasn't carrying a purse for the evening because it didn't go with her dress.

Or when she'd informed him that he'd have to carry her phone and her lipstick because she couldn't possibly go out without them.

He exhaled slowly as he slipped her phone into her hands. "Good thing I have pockets."

"Yeah." She turned back to the window, completely missing his teasing.

Or ignoring it.

Either way, that was pretty cute.

That had to be a sign of true love.

For the rest of the parade, Rob divided his time between watching Mira and watching the boats. Every cartoon character appeared in some fashion, all of the reindeers multiple times with Rudolph being the favorite, and the man of the hour, Santa, fished, surfed, waved and danced in a variety of outfits including board shorts and scuba diving gear. It was impossible not to enjoy every single minute.

The final boat was as beautiful as the others had been fun. Brilliant blue lights were strung from the mast, forming a triangular ray of light topped by the large star at the top.

Compared with the rest of the parade, it was moving and simple.

It reminded Rob of the Christmas Eve services his family had attended faithfully in small-town Oklahoma. He pulled out his own phone and snapped a picture. The idea that his mother would have loved to see it wouldn't go away.

The whole restaurant was still until the star faded into the distance. The lights slowly came up and it was easy to see Mira brushing under her eyes, as if she'd been crying. When she realized he was watching, she waved her hands in front of her face to hide. "Don't look. I'm being a girl."

"A beautiful girl. I'm glad I got to share that with you." He held up his phone. "I took a picture. Thought my mother might enjoy it."

How her eyebrows shot up and immediately lowered suggested Mira understood that his doing so was a big deal but she wasn't going to make it any bigger.

"I'm not sure why I've been thinking of her and home a lot on this trip. Being with your family, and even the friends you've made at Concord Court... Well, it's clear how nice it can be to have that support, especially when you're starting over." If he lost Mira, he'd be truly alone wherever he ended up. For the first time in a long time, that was clear to him. That had to be why he was feeling the pull of his own family. What he might do about it was less clear.

Rob scooted his chair back and offered her his arm. "The long way home?"

"Don't you need to pay?" Mira asked, her voice lowered. Did she think they were going to dine and dash?

He leaned closer. "It's all on the card I gave them for the reservation."

She whistled. "Aren't we fancy? Living like high rollers."

Her teasing settled him, smoothing his emotional turbulence and bringing him back to his plan: ask the question, get the answer he wanted, win.

When they stepped outside, a cool breeze caught them both. Mira shivered, so he immediately removed his suit coat and draped it over her shoulders. That was the benefit of fancy nights out, room for old-school chivalry thanks to beautiful dresses that didn't allow for things like purses or clunky coats. Did anyone do that anymore? It felt good to have the chance.

Mira said, "Mostly, I have a hard time picturing you growing up on a farm in Oklahoma. Sweet gestures like this remind me."

When she said it, something clicked in his mind. Taking Mira home to show her where he'd grown up was the perfect excuse to go back to Keen, to talk to his mother about more than what he'd been doing at work or what the ladies at church were raising money for. Mira would make that visit easy.

"Something about this trip has made it clear to me that I'd like to show it to you some time." Rob glanced down at her. "Where I grew up. You could meet my mom and my sister in person, not just over a phone call. I'd like to see if I still recognize the place. A lot can change in four years."

Mira didn't answer immediately. That wasn't a good sign.

They walked farther down the oceanfront before turning toward Duval Street.

"You're going to ask me to make the decision for both of us, aren't you?" she said softly. "I told you I wouldn't do that, but you're going to put it between us again."

Rob shoved his hands in his pockets and forced himself to breathe slowly. Now was the time to keep a firm grip on his emotions. He might not have another shot. "As I see it, there is only one decision to be made. I want to be married to you. I've offered to do the only thing I know to do." He inhaled again and released the long breath. "At this point, only you can decide if that's good enough."

Mira tipped her head back with a groan. "Seriously, Rob?"

Since he had no answer for that, Rob waited.

"I see I'm not alone in the selfish department," Mira said before she tilted her head to the side, "although in a competition, asking you to leave the service puts me way ahead on that scoreboard."

He was going to keep his mouth shut and his ears open.

He could hear his mother in his memories giving him that advice.

"I can't make your decision for you, Rob. I should never have tried that in the first place, pushing you to do what I wanted even though I knew you would have trouble. I'm sorry. Have I apologized for that? Even if so, I'll do it again. I'm sorry. The guilt keeps me up sometimes, because I know how important work is to you." Before he could tell her to let that go, she held up a hand for him to wait. "Almost since my first deployment, I knew that someday I was going to get out of the military and become a science teacher. Tell me what you dreamed about."

Rob wanted to have a good answer to that, but nothing came, so he told her, "I didn't have any dreams until I met you, Mira." Her snort wasn't cute this time. "I mean it. Now I can dream of playing baseball against you while Jax ties my shoestrings together or us making it back to Mistletoe Lane, where I'm free to kiss you without a chaperone stuck to my back. We're going to run a marathon. We'll study how to grow rosebushes and I'll do my best to talk you out of planting a garden every summer and I will lose every summer. How in the world could I dream those things until I met you?"

Rob stopped, ready for her answer, but Mira kept walking. When he managed to catch up to her, tears were rolling down her face. "That's beautiful and sweet and I can see every one of those things."

"Then tear up the papers." Relief settled across his shoulders. This was all going to be fine.

"I can also picture you grimly going to a job…somewhere that is not the police department to keep me happy. I see you hating the struggle to find a good profession that's worthy of you and your skills that also satisfies your selfish wife." Mira angrily wiped her tears away. "And it's easy to imagine how frustration and disappointment might build up over all those forced choices and losing every argument. But you would never leave, would you? You would never quit that job to go back to what you love. You would never rip out the vegetable beds and toss the seeds. Because of me. You're too…" She wrinkled her nose. "This has to be the silliest thing I've ever said out loud, but you're too generous to me. We never learned to fight. We didn't have to because I always win, on purpose, right, Rob?"

She covered her face with her hands. "The one time it would have been so much easier on us both if you'd followed my instructions, signed the papers and put them in the envelope." She laughed but it wasn't because she was amused. He could tell that easily.

They walked silently until they were outside of The Hideaway, the large wooden parrot waiting for them on the porch.

"Is that the best no you have, then?" he asked. He wasn't going to make this simple for her.

Mira pulled his jacket tightly around her shoulders. "When I first arrived at Concord Court, I had visits with the therapist Reyna had found to work with veterans. She served, and she understands the struggle of coming home better than a lot of people would."

Mira cleared her throat. Was she going to ask him to visit this therapist? Rob braced his hands on his hips, impatient to tell her he'd go by himself or they could go together.

"I couldn't sleep. I have these nightmares." Mira frowned. "I've had a version of the same dream for years, the memory of trying to stop a kid from bleeding out while we were in the air. After I met you, the dream changed." She fidgeted with the collar of his jacket. "When we're together, I sleep well. Then, while we were long-distance, I'd struggle for a couple of nights and even out, but when we were in Atlanta…" She met his stare. "Every night, the dream would come and I'd watch you bleed out in front of me. Sometimes it was the back of the helicopter, but sometimes it was you as a cop. While I was awake, Atlanta was lonely. When I went to sleep, it was…"

"Painful." Rob rubbed his forehead. "That's what it would be for me to watch that."

"Yeah. It gets stressful to even think about sleeping, and life is… It's too hard without sleep, you know?" She slipped out of his jacket. "Since I've been in Miami, the doctor has helped, the informal group therapy has helped, running every day has helped, being with my family has helped…"

"And being away from me has helped." Rob watched her tilt her face up. Tears added a glitter to her eyes, but the sadness was impossible to miss. "Why didn't you tell me any of this?"

Mira shook her head. "I was fooling myself, telling myself that you deserved a chance to follow your own dream, when it's clear I've cared less for your dreams than my own. I can't say what would happen if you moved to Miami because I don't know. The dreams might stop or they might get worse. We might be happy or we might make each other miserable. I don't know. I can't answer your question, never mind won't."

She wiped the tears off her face, and he realized he was making them both miserable.

That was nothing new for him, but Mira had been happy before he'd asked her to play out this scenario for him. Rob knew the right answer for her.

"I guess there's not much reason to wait until Christmas Day, then. When we get back to Miami tomorrow, I can sign the papers and leave for Atlanta. You have plenty to get done between the holiday and the move." Was he going to give up that easily?

Then he realized driving from Atlanta to Miami, winning over her family and planning this getaway hadn't been any small effort. As far as grand gestures go, he'd done everything he could.

This divorce was going to hurt, but he'd tried. He couldn't regret the effort.

"I wanted to bring you to church with my family on Christmas Eve and I wanted you to see the way Jackson opens gifts and I don't want to say goodbye to you yet." Mira straightened her shoulders. "But you deserve the time and the freedom to figure out what you want to do with this part of your life without me pulling the strings. The divorce is going to give you that freedom."

She said it as if she was repeating it for her own benefit.

"With no guilt for either of us," he added.

She nodded and stepped up on the porch. He realized she had no keys because she carried no purse to ruin the lines of her dress, so he opened the front door and stepped out of the way.

Mira hurried inside and he sat down on the steps to think.

He'd never imagined what came after No. In his head, Yes was the only choice.

One thing was certain.

The drive back to Miami was going to hurt, but after he dropped his soon-to-be-ex-wife off, he'd be facing the long road back to Atlanta, where he'd celebrate Christmas all on his own. That would hurt worse.

Rob closed his eyes as he pulled out his phone to check the time. Not quite nine o'clock, still early for Key West and even earlier in Oklahoma.

For some reason, when he tried to conjure a friendly face, only his sister came to mind immediately. Patty usually called him to catch up on Sunday afternoons. Would she answer if he called at this time?

"Never know till you try." Rob hit her number.

The video call rang once before Patty filled the screen. "What's the matter? What's wrong?" she asked breathlessly and shoved her long blond braid over her shoulder.

Before he could answer, his niece and nephew stuck their heads in front of Patty's. "Who is it? What's wrong?" someone asked from off-screen. Had to be his mother.

"Nothing's wrong. Can't a man call his sister to talk without the world turning it into an international incident?" Rob asked. His niece was the first to vanish from view.

"Hey, Uncle Rob," his nephew said, "do

you like to read mysteries?" He held up a book, but it was gone before Rob could read the title. Rob and Blake had gotten into several animated conversations about a certain boy wizard because they both loved the books and the movies. "I almost finished this one, and I'm hoping Santa brings the newest one."

"Santa better not forget. You've been a good kid this year." Arms entered the frame and picked up Blake before his brother-in-law wedged himself into the screenshot. "Better tell your sister you're alive and kicking, Rob. She worries." Then Will was gone, too, and Patty was there finally.

"Nothing is wrong." Rob rubbed his forehead and wished he'd come up with a full plan instead of half an idea before he'd made the call. He was in the middle of it now. Jumping was the only option. The parachute better appear on the way down. "I know it's short notice, but I was hoping someone might have time on Christmas Eve to make the drive to Oklahoma City to pick me up from the airport. I'd like to come home for a few days."

The stunned silence that met his request wasn't reassuring.

Plan B, then. "Or, how about this. I'll rent a car and—"

"I'll pick you up. Text me your flight information," his brother-in-law said firmly from off camera.

Rob had the uncomfortable suspicion that he was messing up their plans.

And his mother still hadn't spoken.

"No, I don't mind making the drive. That way you won't have to change your day up and—"

"Text me your flight information," his brother-in-law said more firmly. "I'll be there."

Uncomfortable, Rob decided to try one more time. "You've got cows to feed and—"

The blur on the screen took a minute for him to adjust to, but his mother's face then came into focus. "If Will can't make it, I'll come get you myself. You okay to sleep on the couch?" She moved closer to the camera, too close and stepped back. "Never mind that. I'll go stay with the neighbors and—"

"The couch will be fine," Patty, Will and

Rob all said at the same time. His mother chuckled.

"All right. No need to yell at an old lady." She patted her hair. "May have to find out if I can get a fresh set and style at the Kut and Kurl. It's not every day Rob comes home."

Rob wasn't sure what to say to that. There was still a valley between them, but his mother was acting as if everything was okay. Did that mean it was?

"If you'll excuse me, this is my phone. My brother called me on my phone to talk to me," Patty said. Everything was a blur again until she closed a door and he immediately recognized the scene.

"Be careful. Someone will lock you in that bathroom again." Rob grinned as he watched her take a seat on the side of the tub.

"Doubtful. You're the only nerd who would try that." She sighed. "Besides, it wouldn't last long. This is the only working bathroom in the house right now. Will decided to put new tile in the master for me for Christmas." She brightened. "Now he'll have help."

Rob knew she was talking about him. His

practical DIY experience was slim at best. "I'll be happy to do whatever I can to help out around there, as long as you're sure it's not too big a mess for your holiday to have me dropping in out of the blue."

She frowned. "What are you really worried about?"

Rob cleared his throat. "Mama told me not to call that place home after Daddy's funeral."

"Well," Patty said slowly, "don't hold your breath for an apology because the word *sorry* is not in the woman's vocabulary, although, I don't believe she ever meant you to stay away. More likely, she was using the same strategy that was always successful to get you to fall in line when you were a kid. You never wanted to hurt anyone else, so you'd twist yourself into knots, even for your bratty little sister. Honestly, things are so good here right now, I'd say roll with it."

Patty pulled the phone closer to her face. "If you want to come home, please come home. I'd love to see you."

Rob nodded. "Me, too."

Her grin spread broadly. "Good." Then she wrinkled her nose. "Should I prepare a spot for Mira, too, or…" Rob had told Patty he was going down to Miami. He hadn't mentioned the divorce papers.

It didn't escape him that his sister had immediately zeroed in on the one thing that might cause him to come running home on Christmas, though.

He shook his head. "Nope, it's just me."

Patty tipped her chin up. "Can't wait to hug you, big brother. Book your flight and then send us all the details. It's last-minute, but I might be able to drum up a full Keen, Oklahoma, parade to escort you home."

Rob rolled his eyes. "With Mama and her fresh new hairdo in the lead car. Please don't."

"Okay, my gift to you, I will not do that." Then she waggled her eyebrows, promising another sort of shenanigans that would be payback for something he'd done as a kid.

Which was fine. He could deal with that.

"See you Christmas Eve." They hung up and he stared up at the sky. He'd made the right call. Literally. That conversation alone had lightened the grief weighing on his shoulders.

"You can't go home again," he whispered,

but no matter how the place had changed, his family was going to welcome him. He wasn't sure where this investigation of what his life was going to be after Mira would go, but home seemed a good place to start.

CHAPTER SIXTEEN

MIRA WORRIED THAT she was making the biggest mistake of her life. She ignored her bed and sat in her favorite overstuffed chair between her favorite bookcases, and divided her time between checking the clock, checking her phone and turning the globe upside down to watch the glittery water upend the cheerful shark in the Santa hat. It was the perfect gift to remind her of Rob scurrying up the rope on the slide to escape the imaginary shark in Key West and the funny, dry, sheepish way her manly man had admitted it to her. When the time reached midnight, Mira stood. She wasn't sure anyone would be at the pool in the earliest hour of Christmas Eve, but she could use the company. After she placed the snow globe down carefully on the signed stack of divorce papers, she left to find out.

When Mira made it to the pool, she saw

the whole gang waiting for her. She had to fight back tears.

Of course her Concord Court family was waiting for her.

"Knew you would need to talk tonight," Sean said as he swung open the gate. "Heard Rob left, so I called out the big guns." He pointed at Brisa and Reyna.

"Oh, no," Brisa said from her spot next to Wade. "I was rooting for you both."

Brisa and Reyna immediately wrapped their arms around Mira. Normally, she might shrug them off, pretend that she was absolutely fine, but nothing about the day had been normal.

The long drive home had been terribly polite, so many "please" and "thanks" exchanged.

Until they'd arrived back at her townhome. There, instead of unloading his duffel, Rob had picked up her bag, carried it to her door and waited for her to let him in. After scanning the divorce papers, he'd signed them, paused when he seemed to notice her open bag with the snow globe inside and left.

No more negotiations for more time or

questions about what would make her happy or even information on when he'd talk to her again.

Because they didn't have anything else to talk about.

The pain was crushing, worse than when she'd come back from Atlanta two years ago because this was the end. Leaving Atlanta had been a pause, but this was final. Over and out. Mira crossed her arms tightly to hold it all in.

"Is he already gone?" Reyna asked. She sat in Sean's lap. His grumbles were cute, but Mira was in no mood to smile. Not yet.

"Yeah, in a hurry to get back to Atlanta I guess," Mira said, although she knew it was as much for her comfort as his timetable. He was making things easier for her. "He signed the papers before he went, so... mission accomplished." Mira sank into the chair Reyna had freed up.

"But it doesn't feel like you imagined it would, does it?" Wade asked. Of all the people at the table, he probably understood that the best. He and his ex-wife were good friends raising their daughter together, much happier now than they'd been together, but they'd had to learn to live as a divorced couple. "It takes time, but you're going to be okay." He squeezed her shoulder and that was too much. The tears started and Mira couldn't control them anymore. The awkward, troubled silence at the table might have made her smile on another day.

"I know it's the right decision." Mira sniffed. "He deserves to realize his dream life, whatever he wants. He's such a good cop, like smart and conscientious and the kind of person you want to show up when you need help." She winced. "He should still be in the army, and whatever he wants to do now… He can't do that as long as he's rearranging his life to suit me."

Everyone remained quiet. Mira wondered if they disagreed with her. At this point, quiet was better.

Jason cleared his throat. Everyone turned to look at him. "I mean, not to argue, but…" He ran his fingers through his hair. "Isn't that kind of what marriage is? Rearranging lives so they go together." Then he held up his hands in surrender. "Sorry. I do job counseling, not *counseling* counseling."

Mira flopped back in her chair. "That's

what has been going around and around in my head. We love each other. I know he loves me. I do. He's a good man, has a good heart, gets me like no one ever has." Mira gulped. "But I was afraid to go to bed tonight because…" This was so hard. She'd never told anyone this. Imagining saying it out loud made her nauseous. What if these people she trusted above all else told her she was making a mistake? What if they thought she was a coward, too? "We all know how the past sticks with you. Things you want to forget, you can push them way down deep and they'll stay that way, as long as you're awake. I do pretty well awake, but there are times…" She sucked in a deep breath and let it go. "My nightmares are of applying pressure to a bleeding wound in the back of a helo as we attempt a night rescue. This soldier has been hit twice in the chest, and it's…" She held out her hands to remind herself that she wasn't there. Her hands were clean. "I'm losing the battle to save this kid, probably old enough to drink but not much more." Mira inhaled slowly this time. Good. She was going to make it through this, and she had to do it only once. "And then, in the dream, instead of that young face, I see Rob. Pale, so pale, and I know I can't save him. I understand it's only nightmares and not reality, may never be a reality, but I wish I had a way past them."

Mira felt the full force of her fatigue and lamented how little sleep she was going to be getting for a while. "I can run. I can work my body until it's exhausted, and my brain will still betray me. Over and over, Rob is dying and I can't save him. When I was in Atlanta with him and he worked a couple of overnight shifts, with dangerous drug busts he didn't tell me much about, that vision was with me when he wasn't. I had to get some distance."

Sean gripped her arm. "That's awful, Mira. I'm so sorry."

Murmurs around the table echoed his support.

Mira angrily brushed the tears away. "He'll be happy with the job he wants, and eventually, we will both be better off apart than we are together." Did she sound like she was reading a script? She should write it down and repeat it over and over until it was written on her heart.

"I know my presence here is conditional, which makes sense, because I should remind you that you are all breaking the pool rules every time you show up here at this time, but…" Reyna said, and Sean shot her a wry smile. "And I don't want anyone to shoot the messenger…"

Mira smothered a sob. "Just say it, Reyna. I can handle it." She rested her head back against the chair and was struck by the wide dark sky. Reyna was logical and reasonable. Whatever she said would make sense. Mira had a feeling it might bring her to her knees.

"O-kay," Reyna said slowly, "you said that while you two were together, otherwise, everything was good. Does that mean no nightmares?"

Mira closed her eyes. No nightmares had happened while she slept in Rob's arms. It was only the nights they were apart and she had to wait and worry and wonder.

"Oh," Brisa said. Mira realized the sisters were on the same page. She glanced around the table. It was clear none of the men had turned the page yet. "More time with Rob, living through the fear, welcoming him home safe and sound every day might have overcome those nightmares."

"What if I left too soon? What if all I needed was to learn how to live with him through it all, no distance, no wondering where or how he was because he would be coming home to me?" Mira said slowly.

"What if you'd had a therapist and a support group in Atlanta, maybe talk to other spouses who experienced the same fear?" Reyna asked.

"Or what if you'd told Rob about the nightmares and asked for his help instead of running?" Sean smiled as she frowned at him. "Making an educated guess. You didn't tell him then, did you?"

Mira shook her head.

Sean ran his hand up and down Reyna's back. "That's the trouble with all this mental toughness and independence. Sometimes we need each other. Sometimes that is the only answer."

The realization settled inside her, something profound, something she'd never forget. "That's a lesson I've learned here at

Concord Court. Apparently, not as well as I thought."

Mira had had a chance to test that theory, that talking to Rob might have unlocked her recurring nightmares. He'd asked her for another chance. He'd asked for another chance, which would mean his giving everything up all over again and starting all over again. For her.

He would have eliminated the distance between them.

He would have taken another job if she'd required that.

Rob might have been able to eliminate her fear with one or both of those things and he would have tried.

But she hadn't been honest until the end and she'd refused to ask for what she des-- perately wanted: Rob in Miami where she was surrounded by family.

She'd had a chance to test her theory.

Instead, she had divorce papers.

"We can leave for Atlanta tonight. Right now, in fact," Brisa said. "If that's what you want, I'll go with you."

Mira smiled at her. She was the sweetest, most generous friend. "But tomorrow's

Christmas." And she still believed he deserved the chance to figure out what he wanted without his need to please her. He certainly didn't deserve to be persuaded by a confused woman who couldn't make up her mind. "Everyone here shall have a beautiful holiday. I order it. My family will keep me busy today and tomorrow. Then there's packing to finish and moving. Wade is in charge of the plan to get me moved in on New Year's Eve in enough time to dress up for the Court's big party."

Laying out the days ahead steadied her.

"So, you let Rob go?" Sean asked.

Mira studied his face. He was such a close friend and it was crystal clear that he wanted to find a way for her to have everything she wanted.

Whatever her problems were, no one had better friends than she did.

"For now, yes," Mira said. "But be thinking of grand gestures in case I change my mind."

Sean pursed his lips. "Not sure this is the group you want in charge of that. If you'll remember, you had to lead us by the hand every single time."

Mira laughed. She'd done a little guiding when Sean, Wade and Jason had been on course to mess things up. "Sure, but you have backup this time."

Reyna nodded at Sean. "We'll brainstorm grand gestures. You build a signal, some kind of light that we can shine up at the sky whenever the group needs to meet here. But not a bat. That's been done."

Wade grunted. "If you need help, my inventive daughter can craft a proposal and a delivery system that notifies us all when it's time to assemble."

Mira did her best to relax with her friends and tried not to think about where Rob might be that night. Probably somewhere on the road, she assumed. She'd make it through Christmas and settling into her new place and go back to school. At some point, the answer about what to do about her broken heart and the heart she'd broken might come to her.

CHAPTER SEVENTEEN

SPOTTING HIS brother-in-law's truck outside the airport in Oklahoma City was simple. Since it was nearly ten o'clock at night by the time his flight landed from Miami, delayed because of bad weather in Charlotte and then rerouted through Houston because of more bad weather in Chicago, there wasn't much traffic at all.

Rob was spent in every sense of the word. He'd spent his layover shopping for Christmas gifts. The kids were getting fancy headphones. Did they need fancy headphones? No idea. The deluxe cookies and Belgian chocolates he'd picked up were plan B. Finding jewelry had been easy enough for his mother and sister, and Rob had his fingers crossed he'd remembered Will's favorite baseball team correctly.

It was Christmas. He couldn't go home empty-handed.

So it was a huge relief to see the big, bright red dually pickup truck waiting for him. Mud splatters lined the side of the vehicle Rob could see, but then Will's huge grin and stark white cowboy hat blocked the view.

"Robert Monroe Bowman, the third, I presume," Will joked before he wrapped his arms around Rob in a bear hug. No matter how long it had been since Rob had made it home, Will's welcomes hadn't changed.

Will had married Rob's sister right after they'd both graduated college and the guy knew more about raising livestock than one person should. The farm was in the best hands.

"William, I hope you are giving my sister plenty of trouble." Rob pumped Will's hand up and down, falling into their friendly routine.

"Keepin' her on her toes and now I have reinforcements. These children of mine run us all in circles." Will grabbed the duffel Rob had dropped and carried it around to the driver's side. He stowed it in the back seat and claimed his own seat to start the truck. The immediate rumble reminded Rob of home. He hadn't realized that until that second.

"Hop in. It'll be midnight before we make it home. Patty will kill us both if we mess up Santa's delivery window." As soon as Rob had snapped shut his seat belt, Will hit the gas.

"Sorry about the hour. I could have rented a car or even stayed here in OKC until daylight." Rob hated upsetting their plans, whatever they were.

"Nah. Patty's been like a cat with a new toy ever since you called. Can't settle down, always ready to pounce on the next thing on the to-do list. If she seems wound too tight, she is, but she's juggling a lot right now. Everything will be better once she manages to execute the picture-perfect holiday tomorrow, one that unites her fractured family and restores peace unto our land." Will shrugged. "I might be exaggerating, but I…"

Rob sighed. "I get it. This is important to her so cut her some slack because she deserves it. Thanks for the warning."

Was this spur-of-the-moment trip home a mistake? How would it make returning to

Atlanta without Mira any easier? He was only postponing the inevitable.

Still, if he could do anything to repair the break with his family or make his sister's life better, there was no reason to beat himself up for sticking his head in the sand about his divorce. He was doing the right thing. Patty and Will were happy to have him home. It was past time to straighten things out with his mother.

"Country music okay? Bet you don't listen to that much." Will turned the radio on.

"You know they have radio stations in Georgia, right? It's Georgia. I listen to country all the time." Rob tilted his head to the side and waited for Will to laugh.

"Oh, right, I was still imagining you overseas." Will shook his head.

Rob needed a little levity and he knew his brother-in-law would indulge him.

"They have these things called 'satellites' now, capable of beaming the station you listen to while you're out feeding cattle all the way to me in Atlanta or Djibouti or probably to the moon and Mars by now." Rob stretched his legs and was thankful for the extra room in the big truck. He couldn't remember the last time he'd flown economy, but on Christmas Eve, he'd been happy to take the only seat left: middle seat, last row next to the restroom, both flights. Walking all the way back to Miami would be better for his mental health.

"Does that mean you're still listening to Wolfie on Friday nights?" Will asked idly.

There was no way the guy could know he was poking a tender spot with Rob, since Wolfie's sentimental favorite was "Key Largo."

"Sometimes." Rob stared out at the dark landscape. If it was daylight, they'd be speeding past flat green pastures, soft hills and endless interstate ahead.

"Take the boy out of Oklahoma but Oklahoma sticks like that red dirt on your boots." Will grinned at him. "Got a way with words, don't I?"

Rob was glad to be sitting where he was.

Something about nothing changing, even though everything was different, made it easier to believe he was going to be okay.

"You ever think you'd be driving back from OKC at midnight on Christmas Eve?" Rob asked.

Will shrugged, not even attempting to hide a smile. "Blake told me he was going to finish that book you two were discussing last night. Santa couldn't let the kid run out of books, so I stopped at the bookstore on the way to pick you up. With all the delays, I had plenty of time. Got my dear ole mother-in-law a couple books, too. I'm winning tonight. Gonna be a hero in the morning."

Rob smiled. Will was easy to be with. He'd always added oxygen to Rob's family's conversations.

They settled into an easy silence. Rob realized he was half a second from dozing just as Will slowed down to make the turn onto the long lane that led to the farm. Two windows were glowing along the front of the two-story he'd grown up in.

"Keep your voice down when you go in. If the kids wake up, the Santa story will be in danger." Will slid out and closed his door quietly. Rob followed him up the steps to the porch that wrapped around the farmhouse.

Before either one of them could enter, the door swung open. Patty brushed Will aside and threw her arms around Rob's neck. "Finally. I was afraid… Somehow I was afraid you wouldn't make it." Then she clapped her hand over her mouth. "Quiet," she whispered.

Rob nodded and trailed her inside. The layout of the rooms was the same, but everything else had been updated. New furniture. Hardwoods instead of shag carpeting. Even the Christmas tree was in a new spot, framed by the window instead of shoved into the corner.

"This place looks great, Patty Cake," Rob said and then moved on to the kitchen. His mother was standing in front of the sink, a fuzzy pink robe covering her from head to knee. He'd seen her standing there a thousand times.

But the new lines on her face, that her hair had grown a little grayer, it hit him in an instant that she was older.

The twinge in his shoulder as he turned toward her reminded him they were all growing older.

"Mama, you didn't have to wait up." Rob wrapped his arms around her and inhaled the scent of her familiar lotion. "We could have said hello over breakfast."

"I haven't slept since we talked last night. Too excited." When he would have stepped back, she held him tightly. "It's been too long, son."

Rob wanted to ask about her demand that he move home, but there would be time for that later.

"You hungry?" she asked. That was familiar, too.

"No, Mama, I'm just worn out." He led her into the living room, where he noticed the couch had been made up with quilts.

Which reminded him of Mira's couch.

There was a whole lot less Christmas decor here, although the huge tree took over a chunk of the room and blocked part of the television. That never would have been allowed when his father was around. Will was a pushover for his kids, obviously. That made him think of the book run on Christmas Eve. Rob tried to imagine his father driving to Oklahoma City for books on Christmas Eve or at any time for that matter. The image wouldn't form. He'd always had too much to do. If Rob had the chance, he'd ask Will how he managed to find the free time.

Even so, there was no mistaking that Will worked hard, provided for his family and had done his share for the farm's upkeep. He also had time to retile the bathroom for his wife, make unexpected trips to the airport and visit bookstores for his son. It couldn't be easy, but it fit Will perfectly.

"If we don't get to bed soon, we'll be meeting the kids coming down the stairs on the hunt for what Santa left them," Patty said as she plopped down next to Rob on the sofa. She scrubbed her hand through his hair, making it stand up weirdly. If they were still kids, he would have tickle-attacked her. Then she would have squealed and their mother would have to break up the fight. Too much for Christmas Eve or the fact that they were adults now.

"Bathroom's still in the same place?" Rob asked and nodded. "I can show myself to the bathroom and then I'll hit the hay."

His mother and sister each kissed his cheek and then went up the stairs. "Hey, Will, if I can help with the chores in the morning, let me know. At this point, it's mostly muscles, no memory, but I can follow orders."

Will pointed at him. "Might take you up on that. No need to set an alarm. Kids will take care of that."

When everyone had gone, Rob opened his duffel and pulled out his last clean T-shirt and sweats. At some point, laundry was going to become critical. Tonight, only sleep was critical.

As he stretched out on the couch, Rob refused to think about Mira's cozy sofa, Mira's Christmas magic or Mira's divorce papers.

Flying halfway across the country had worn him out, and before he realized he was going to manage it, Rob was asleep.

IT WAS EARLY in the morning, and Rob could feel the weight of someone watching him. He cracked open an eye and realized two someones were watching him. His niece and nephew were both sitting in the armchair across from him, their feet drawn up, eyes locked on him.

"Merry Christmas, Blake and Shelby." Rob stretched. "Has Santa been here?"

Blake answered, "Seems like it."

"There's a dollhouse. I told Santa which

one to get," Shelby said, her hair a fuzzy blond cloud. How old was she now? Four years old?

"Yes, you told Santa, your day care teacher, and me all about it. We've watched every single episode of that show about the time-traveling fairies. 'Mommy, look at that space house' and 'Mommy, if I had the space house, I could get the alien fairy to go with it,'" Patty muttered as she came down the last step. "Will, can you knock on Mama's door? Party's starting."

Rob folded up the quilts as Shelby and Blake launched themselves toward the Christmas tree. The requested dollhouse produced sharp squeals of glee. Blake was as thrilled but at a much lower volume when he unwrapped a new gaming system. "Whoa" was his only comment as he stared at the box.

"That's what I said when I saw the price tag and the long line in the store on Black Friday, but I did it," his mother muttered from her spot beside him on the couch. "Seeing this makes it all worth it."

Rob raised his eyebrows. "You did that?" He never would have guessed his mother would wade into shopping madness for anyone or anything.

She shrugged. "Blake's a sweet kid, doesn't ask for much, so when he does, I go out of my way." Her eyes met his. "He reminds me of you that way."

So many questions popped into his mind, but wrapping paper was flying. Shelby screeched over every gift she opened as long as it wasn't clothing. Rob enjoyed every minute of her enjoyment.

When the wrapping paper stopped flying, he said, "I have a few more gifts, but you'll have to close your eyes to be surprised." The kids immediately covered their eyes with both hands. Shelby crouched down like a jack-in-the-box, ready to spring when it was time.

"Adults, too." Rob waited until the rest of his family cooperated. He placed his gift in front of each person and then dropped down on the sofa, hopeful he'd chosen well. "Open 'em."

Shelby's squeal was immediate. "Kitty cat!"

The way both Patty and Will snapped to attention, as if they were afraid he'd given his niece an actual cat... Rob had to laugh. "Don't panic. They're headphones with kitty cat ears." He took them from his niece and put them on her head. "Carefully tested with limits on how loud they'll go, recommended for kids from ages two to ten." He met his sister's stare and watched her sag with relief.

Patty murmured, "Does this mean Shelby can watch her fairy show without all the rest of us being haunted by that theme song?" His sister blinked. "I love you. I really love you, big brother."

Rob grinned as he turned to Blake. His nephew was quieter than his baby sister, but the happy gleam in his eyes was satisfying. "These will work with my tablet. Thanks, Uncle Rob."

Relieved that he'd stumbled into doing something right, Rob patted Blake's shoulder.

Mom and his sister oohed and aahed over the jewelry and chocolates, and his brother-in-law grinned from ear to ear with his team jersey. Rob was relieved they all seemed pleased with his choices.

That was plenty for him. He didn't need

any presents. The day was already one of the best Christmases he could remember.

"Santa didn't know you were coming here, Uncle Rob. So I bet your presents are at your house, but that's okay, you can play fairies with me. Here..." Shelby held up her new doll. "I'll be the alien fairy, but you can pick any of my old dolls." Her face was firm. She was going to hold him to that.

"Then, you can set up Blake's new system on the TV upstairs. That would be so helpful." His sister grinned widely.

Rob didn't mind and was glad to pitch in, which reminded him...

As if on cue, Will promptly asked him, "Load up the feed truck first? Then fairy duty and electronics troubleshooting." Will's corny smile made Rob chuckle.

He was nodding as he next turned to face his mother. She patted his hand. "You'll need food if you're going to do all that work. Let's go make a big breakfast while the boys are out feeding cattle." She offered Shelby her hand, but the little girl shook her head.

"I'm going with Daddy," Shelby said and held her arms up. Her dad swung her up onto his shoulders. "Okay, baby, we'll get your coat and go. Blake?"

When the boy agreed, Rob thought he saw the same resignation he'd always felt about life on the farm. They all pitched in to load hay onto the feed truck and then crammed into the front seat.

After a short drive into the pasture, they picked up a herd of cows that began trailing behind the truck.

Will stopped. "You kids keep the engine running. Save me if Snowball comes for me."

"That bull still terrorizing people around here?" Rob asked, surprised. He got out of the cab and shut the door.

"That bull will never die. Shelby will be warning her own kids away from it someday," Will said, and he lowered the hay bale.

Rob helped him open it so they could spread the hay. "Not Blake's kids?"

Will shrugged. "Maybe both of them. Place is big enough for both. My brother and his wife have a trailer parked up on the acreage close to the highway to help keep up the fence and feed on that side. Could stand another set of hands if you're thinking about coming home. We have room and you know the ladies would love it." Will used a pitchfork to separate the hay. "We have police and sheriffs here, too."

Rob wadded up the twine he'd pulled from the hay bale. "Growing up, nobody gave me much of a choice except farming, but I never loved it the way you do. I don't fit here the way you do."

Will sighed. "I get that. I do love it, too. Every bit of this life suits me. I can see it in Shelby's eyes, too." He motioned with his head to show him that Shelby had rolled down the window and poked her arm out to pet the closest cow. It looked like Blake might be reading. "No matter how it turns out, whether both my kids want to live here forever or neither of them do, this is what I love. And most of all, I want them to find what makes them happy." His eyes met Rob's. "Not all parents make it that easy, though. If you've found what makes you happy on your own, be proud of that. Don't give it up, either."

Rob tossed the twine in the back of the truck. "What if I haven't found it yet?" The longer he was away from Atlanta, the less he wanted to return.

"Keep looking. Don't quit. That would make you and everyone who loves you miserable." Will pressed a hand over his stomach. "Growls like a bear, but it's my stomach. We better go find breakfast."

Rob was glad to slide back into the warm interior of the truck. Shelby hung on to his shoulder as they slowly bounced back across the pasture. He noted the brand-new barn that had just been built.

At the farmhouse, Will, Shelby and Blake hurried in out of the cold. Walking slowly across the front yard, Rob cataloged other differences since the last time he'd been here. There was a fancy swing set with a fort constructed on the side. No garden. Patty had complained every minute of weeding and picking vegetables, so apparently she'd given that up.

Will and Patty were doing life here exactly as they wanted. It wasn't a prison built of his father's rules and expectations or even crushing work they hated. Will brought in help. Patty skipped the part she hated.

"You hungry? I made biscuits and chocolate gravy," his mother said from her spot on the porch. She'd pulled on her coat over her robe and the rubber boots she'd always worn to work outside.

"Will and Patty are doing a good job here." Rob came along beside her.

"They are." She fidgeted with the buttons of her coat. "Remember how goofy Will was when they got married? I worried, but I can't imagine a better husband or father anywhere."

Was he going to push the issue or let his return home be enough to smooth over the crack between them?

"I shouldn't have asked you to come home. I hurt you all, you, Patty and Will, but I couldn't see making it all work otherwise." She rubbed her hands together as if to generate heat. "I needed to adjust to life without your father. I'd lived with him for more than forty years, a lifetime. I knew you'd go back to doing what you wanted, and I wanted to get things settled, but with time… The perfect answer took some time."

She touched his hand where he'd braced it on the porch railing. "I was doing the best I could, like always. I shouldn't have pushed. I shouldn't have hurt you. I'm glad you came home."

Rob realized Patty had been correct. His mother was never going to say "I'm sorry" in those exact words but that was her message.

"Breakfast. Then you have some dolls and electronics to get to," his mother said with a grin. That would be the last time they talked about her mistake, but that was fine with him.

He'd made some missteps, too.

"Mama, I've been thinking about the way you and Daddy would dance in the kitchen. That doesn't seem like him." Rob realized that was why the song and the memory and the urge to come home had tangled together. It showed him a different side of his dad.

She smiled. "He was the best dancer. Before you came along, we'd go into town on Friday night and dance. Then we had kids and the farm took over." She bent down to catch his gaze. "I don't know what's going on with your wife or what your plans are for the future, but if you want a happy marriage, don't ever let anything rob you of that time together. Not work or kids or the hundred other claims on your hours and minutes. That time together is the only way to remember why you fell in love in the first place."

Patty opened the door and appeared. "Food's getting cold, brother, and the alien fairy grows impatient for your attention." Her smirk suggested she was enjoying the upcoming doll playdate fully. She might even consider it late payback for the time he'd hidden her favorite doll and it had taken over an hour for her to find it.

Their mom went to the kitchen, but he and his sister lingered by the door. "She didn't say it, did she?" Patty asked as she slid her arms around his waist to squeeze tightly. "But you're okay now?"

Rob returned the hug. "No and yes. We're okay."

"Are you any clearer about what to do when you get home?" Patty asked. "Divorce takes time to heal, I know."

Time. There it was again.

It was something he and Mira had never had much of together—long stretches of time in the same place with each other. What if things were different if they did?

The divorce would end one chapter, but what if that wasn't the end of their story?

If he removed the urgency to get it all right immediately, freeing up his decisions, what would he do? Without the pressure, could he find the perfect fit as Will and Patty had? Could he make the life that fit him and Mira?

Before his trip to Miami and Concord Court, it never would have occurred to him to even ask the question. Working the holiday to earn goodwill and bonus points would have been the perfectly logical choice for him.

Instead, he'd fallen even deeper in love with Mira, enjoyed being with her friends and family, reconnected with his own, a source of pain he hadn't even acknowledged, and raised his head to look for better opportunities.

Just like that, the thing that had seemed impossible when he'd packed his bag in Atlanta became inevitable.

His job in Atlanta was a mistake.

He had to fix that. Concord Court would give him time and space to do that without pressure. To find what he could excel at and be content doing. Enjoy it, even.

The divorce would be final, but his chance with Mira wasn't done.

He owed it to her to untangle the questions about what he wanted for his own life, but then they could come up with the right way to do life together. He hoped so, anyway.

And if they couldn't… Well, he would have zero regrets.

On his way in to eat breakfast, Rob pulled out his phone. He was going to have to change his flight plans again. Instead of going back to Miami to get his truck and drive home, he needed to fly directly to Atlanta. He had a job to quit and a house to list.

CHAPTER EIGHTEEN

IT WAS NEW YEAR'S EVE and Mira was doing her absolute best to remember how much she'd missed her family before she'd left the air force and moved to Miami. In this moment they were dancing on her last nerve.

After refusing to answer any questions about Rob and how they'd ended things, mainly because tears were always at the ready, Mira needed space. Unfortunately, the Peters clan was incredibly good at hovering.

Her sisters especially had taken turns giving her supportive and encouraging looks during the Christmas Eve service they'd all attended and the Christmas breakfast at Gina's house that morphed into the Christmas lunch at Kris's house, where they'd finally congregated.

While they were apart, Gina, Kris *and* Naomi, who must have been looped into the family drama at some point, were sending her memes. Funny cats, silly dogs, videos of giggling babies, the one where the Irish family has a bat in their kitchen—Mira had seen them all during the past week.

Mira's mother had insisted on helping Mira pack and her father had insisted on driving her to the lawyer's office to deliver the signed divorce papers. She appreciated the smiles and the help, but taken together, it was too much.

If she didn't get these people out of her new house soon, she was going to lose her cool.

"Mira, come and see how the pink tile is sparkling now. You did not believe it could be done, but I have accomplished this. The grout is immaculate." Her mother was posed in the doorway to the pink bathroom. When Mira didn't move quickly enough to suit her, her mother repeated her order. "Mira, come and look."

It was that tone. It was the constant repetition of her name. "Mira," followed by a question. "Mira," followed by an order. "Mira," shouted from three rooms away with the expectation of immediate response. "Mira," followed by snapping fingers.

"Are you quite all right, Mira?" Her mother had stepped closer.

Before she could reply that the pink tile might be clean, thank you very much, but there was no way it was sparkling, her father held up her phone. "Looks like your security cameras are functional. I've been watching on the app. Ask Sean and Wade what happened to the lamp you had on the nightstand when they come in. They'll think you're psychic. Don't know if the broken pieces will count toward good luck in the New Year, but we'll say they do."

Before she could demand to know what had happened, Wade and Sean appeared with her couch between them. Then all Mira could hear were grunts and muttered curses as they turned the couch every direction before figuring out how to get it through the door.

After that, Mira was quite sure she didn't want to know where the lamp was resting in pieces and considered it gone. Her father smoothed his mustache. "Don't worry. We'll go over to the storage unit and pick out another lamp. Got two new ones at an estate sale last week in Coral Gables. Do not tell your mother." Then he crossed his arms over his chest. "Alisha, come say goodbye. Mira has a party to get ready for. She will call to talk to you about the bathroom tomorrow."

"I don't know why she can't marvel right now," her mother said with a sniff. "She's not busy at the moment."

Mira glanced at the temporary chaos that surrounded her and had to bite her tongue to control her response.

Her father kissed her cheek. "Glad we could help with this move."

Mira braced herself as her mother stepped up. Instead of another admonishment, her mother wrapped her arms around Mira's neck. "I am going to make a special Italian fish soup for my oldest daughter tomorrow, since she refuses to eat black-eyed peas. Fish for luck, as they swim forward." Her mother squeezed her arms. "This year you will move forward, my daughter. We will not look back."

The tears threatened again, but Mira forced a smile. It was easier this time. This was why she was glad to have her family around for her very first heartbreak. They loved her. They irritated her. They would do anything in their power to help her through every one of life's ups and downs.

"Thanks, Mom, I'll take any luck I can get." Mira inhaled slowly. She vowed she wasn't going to cry. She'd done such a good job of pretending to be fine for her family.

Her father was the hardest one to fool. He was watching her too closely.

"Don't forget to open your windows tonight to let all the bad stuff out. Eat twelve grapes, one for every month, and really think about what you want to happen next year." Her father held out his hands as he ticked off every New Year's Day custom he could think of. "Smash a plate in front of the house, just in case the lamp didn't count." His face brightened. "And we'll make sure to bring you a lucky pig tomorrow."

Mira opened her mouth but her mother beat her to the punch. "Where are we going to find a pig, lucky or otherwise, John?"

Mira caught Sean's eye and tried to communicate how much she would like her parents to continue this discussion on their way home.

Her father grinned from ear to ear. "I know I've got one somewhere."

"Dad, has it ever occurred to you to pick one country's customs and stick with it?" Mira asked. "The grapes…that's Spain, right? That one I get. We lived next door to the Franks and I believe the mother was Spanish." He nodded. "But the plates? What country is that from?" She refused to ask about the lucky pig.

"Denmark." He cleared his throat. "I've been holding back. We could add Brazil or Thailand or the tiny island nation of Vanuatu. I can tell you traditions from almost any country you name. Try me." He straightened as if he was ready to give an important address.

"It's another of your father's collections, Mira. This one takes up much less real estate than any of his other prizes, so let him have it." Her mother shook her head. "This knowledge has been gathered over a lifetime." She pressed a kiss to his cheek.

"It also makes me dangerous when my birthday rolls around and it's time for cutthroat trivia." He brushed at his shoulders. "Only person who can challenge me is your mother."

The way their eyes locked as if they were the only people in the room made Mira squirm. Could she ever have a deep-down loving marriage like her parents?

"But do you believe any of these superstitions?" she asked, mostly to break the heavy, silent flirting. Ew.

Her dad blew out a heavy breath and scoffed. "Did you know some of these traditions were adopted for health or safety reasons centuries ago? It's fascinating research."

If Mira didn't put a stop to this, her father would spend all day telling her the fascinating background of one thing that led to another. He had vast stores of "research" to pull from.

"I'm sure the tradition of the lucky pig brought some poor farmer hope for…" Mira shrugged. It didn't matter. Understanding that it was just another of her father's collections made sense. "And it does help with trivia."

Her father tugged her mother closer.

"That's how I met your mother. We were on these cool high school teams that competed at a state academic tournament." He winked. "Which is trivia with a more impressive name. No one could beat me there, either."

"Again, except me," her mother added in a singsong.

"That was sweet. Still is," he murmured.

Mira cleared her throat. "You guys were going, right?" They needed to leave before anything got more awkward.

Her mother nodded. "Mira, if you are too lonely in this new house tonight, please do not hesitate to come home. I'll make up a bed for you."

Mira smiled. Her mother was easy to love, most of the time. "I'm worried about him, Mama. I'll be okay here, but thank you."

Her mother raised her eyebrows. "Worried over him. Yes, I do understand. I am a woman who has four grown children, one of whom has been in extremely dangerous situations in terrible places while I have been stuck at home, worrying." She brushed Mira's hair over her shoulders.

"What I have learned is you must live every day with no regrets. We worry, yes, because bad things may come at any time. The only peace we may have is to love and be loved fully, daughter. If you are lucky, you will have decades to irritate the same man, over and over, and be annoyed in return. I wish that you are lucky enough to be fully loved. Nights can still be long, but days are much fuller that way." She smiled. "If you are lonely, day or night, come to ours. I will show you how I clean a bathroom so you may keep yours sparkling."

Mira didn't roll her eyes, but she could tell her mother knew she wanted to.

"No chance she'll be lonely tonight, Mrs. Peters. We're all going to a party at Concord Court." Sean grinned. "I'll make sure she rings in the New Year properly. I'll count the grapes myself."

Watching her mother intimidate Sean with a stare was fun.

"It is entirely too soon to hope you will meet someone nice at this party," her mother warned her, "but kissing someone new at midnight might be best to shake off the old someone." Then she waved as if to make the comment disappear. "But what do I know? I'm only your mother."

Her father hugged Mira quickly. "Kissing someone at midnight on New Year's Eve sets the tone for the next year, but it's supposed to be someone you love. This year? Stick with the good-luck grapes." Then he placed his hand on her mother's shoulder and urged her toward the door. "We'll call before we come over tomorrow, in case you want to sleep late. Try to get some rest."

When they were gone, the silence vibrated.

Sean waited a full minute before he said, "What a couple. Your parents are unforgettable."

"They are," Mira said as she flopped down on her couch. "How upset will Brisa be if I skip this party tonight?" The last thing she wanted to do was put on a dress and do small talk. A bath. Some food. Twelve grapes off the bunch her mother had delivered that morning because someone would check tomorrow, and some sleep.

Maybe the nightmare would fade from the move, too.

Imagining where Rob was and what he

thought of her now caused the knot in her stomach to tighten and the nightmare to hover on the edge of her consciousness. She'd scheduled a meeting with the Concord Court therapist, but until next week, she was on her own.

"You haven't heard from him this week?" Sean asked. He picked up her legs and dropped down on the couch next to her.

Mira started to point out that he hadn't answered her question about skipping the party, but everyone in the room knew the real problem. Yes, she was tired. It had been a busy day.

But the sadness and disappointment that had been hovering behind her eyes since she'd dropped the divorce papers off was what had depleted her energy.

Time. All she needed was time to adjust. Leaving Rob in Atlanta had been difficult but she'd recovered. This time hurt worse, so it would take longer to heal. But getting back to teaching would help. So would the move.

And so would her friends and this party at Concord Court.

"No word from him. I had hoped he

would let me know when he made it home. Atlanta is a long drive." Mira draped her arm over her face. "But I didn't ask him to let me know and there's no reason for him to try to read my mind now. He's free of that."

Sean groaned.

Mira moved her arm to narrow her eyes at him. She was tired, but not too tired to battle.

"What he means is," Wade said slowly, "you can still change this. If Rob were here, what would you say?"

"Easy." Mira had played through so many conversations that the only difficult part was deciding where to start. "I've missed you. How are you? Can you forgive me? I'm stupid. I made a mistake. Don't hate me. I've missed you. How are you? Are you safe? I don't know what the answer is, but I'm ready to be selfish now. So ready. Quit your job. Move to Miami. Never work again. Be a house husband. Raise our dogs to be fine young men and women. Be with me." Her nose was stinging, she was completely aware of how pitiful she sounded, and she couldn't stop. "If none of that works…" She closed her eyes. "I guess I'd want to negotiate how often my parents can visit us in Atlanta. I would start with weekly and hope to end up at no less than monthly."

When no one laughed at what was a terrible attempt at humor, she stared at Wade.

"What are you doing here, then? You should be on the road to Atlanta to say all that." He kicked his voice up a notch as Sean started to sputter. "We would miss you. Your family would miss you. But this isn't you. You need to say those things to him."

Mira turned to Sean.

He shrugged. "I mean… Okay, maybe."

Mira hesitated. "I want Rob to have time to figure out what he wants. He deserves it. If he finds something he loves, he might make the best decision for himself instead of giving me everything I ask for."

Sean tilted his head back. "You know, Mira, you're one of us, one of the guys. You get us, but the truth is there are things you don't understand about us." He patted her leg. "If Reyna asks me for something and I can give it to her, get it for her, steal or build or bleed for her, I'll do it. Why? I trust her. I know her. Reyna isn't one who makes frivolous requests, manipulates or uses. You aren't, either. Neither is Brisa, so Wade is going to back me up on this. If she asked, you'd move mountains for her. Right?"

Wade wrinkled his nose. "I would give it my best shot, even if it hurt me. I trust her to ask for important things."

"That's love." Sean shook his finger at her. "Rob's a man in love."

Mira blinked back the tears. It was true. She'd seen it in action.

"Why couldn't I do the same for him?" she asked. "Live in Atlanta. That's all he asked. Let him do his job and live in Atlanta. And that was a mountain I couldn't move. Am I not in love? Why couldn't I give him what he needed, even if it hurt me?"

Sean cleared his throat and motioned as if he wanted all eyes on him. "I never expected the tables to have turned like this, but I would like to take advantage of it. If I could have your attention, I'm about to make a stunning revelation that changes the course of true love." He placed his fist over his mouth and cleared his throat.

"Don't make me hurt you. I can do it." Mira raised her foot in a weak threat.

Sean grunted. "Fine. You're robbing me of my triumph but…" He got serious. "He made sacrifices for you. They hurt. Now you're asking why you didn't do the same thing for him?"

Mira nodded and reconsidered turning her threat into action.

"Isn't that what this divorce is? It's hurting you, but you want him to have the freedom to make his own decision about what this part of his life will look like, what will make him happy, without bringing you along. And it is hurting you. We can all see that." Sean pointed at her leg. "Enough to threaten your best friend with violence when he clearly doesn't deserve it."

"New Year's Day… It's supposed to set the tone for the whole year." Mira took a calming breath. "I'll call Rob tomorrow. I want this year to have him in it."

Sean patted her leg before standing and dumping her back on the couch. "Good. Our work here is done. You need plenty of time to get beautiful for tonight's party."

Mira slowly stood and looked at Wade. "Is he saying that the amount of effort it will take to make myself presentable for this party will require possibly...hours?" How insulted should she be? Her heart warmed. She had great friends.

Wade shrugged. "Honestly, the guy's brain is zapped at this point. He made sense right there at the end. He'll be spouting nonsense for days." He put an arm around her shoulders. "What do you need from us before we leave?"

Mira glanced at all the boxes and shook her head. "Everything can wait. I need to start the overhaul to make Sean eat his words immediately. It will take some doing. He's right about that."

Wade laughed. "See you later."

"Soon as you get these boxes unpacked, let's head to the shelter. There's an old golden retriever there named Queso that needs to be sleeping in that sunny spot by the window." Sean's bear hug robbed her of breath, but it was nice, too.

She was still giggling when they left.

Then she turned on her heel and marched into her funky new bedroom. Finding her makeup and her shoes and the dress she wanted to wear would be a treasure hunt among all these boxes, but for the first time in days, she had the energy to accomplish her goal of showing her new family that she was going to be okay.

She had a plan, a way to move forward to try to build something new with Rob starting tomorrow.

The plan, as loose as it was, gave her hope.

That felt good.

CHAPTER NINETEEN

ROB SPUN SLOWLY inside the wide, open space that had been crammed full of Christmas the last time he'd seen it. Mira's townhome was empty. She'd finished her move without him. It was impossible not to be depressed by the room now that he knew what it could look like with someone who'd made it a home.

Brisa closed the last kitchen cabinet. "Sean can get a crew in here to repaint next week if you like. Carpet is in good shape. I'll take a look upstairs, but I'm sure Mira hadn't left any damage. Hmm, Sean? Well, he did help her move, but whatever he broke, he will fix before you move in." She held out a key ring. "If you're up for it." She tilted her head to the side. "I'll be happy to show you another unit, too. A place with zero memories might be easier to call home."

Rob took the key ring and slipped it over one finger. "No, I like knowing what's possible if I put the work into it."

Her eyebrows rose and she jumped up and down. "We're not only talking about the furniture and decor here, are we? If you put the work into it, you and Mira can be together again, too? Please, oh, please be saying that!" Her eyes were locked to his, begging him not to disappoint her.

"I might have meant both, but I was talking about furniture." He propped his hands on his hips. "I'm not in any space to be speeding too far down the road, although it may be a good road. I've quit my job—"

"Jason will help you find a new one. I know he can. I'll text him right now to set up an appointment ASAP." Brisa yanked her phone out of her pocket and sent the text before Rob could tell her he'd already made one for Wednesday. He was also going to check into what was required to join the Miami Police Department. His experience should make that simple, but he could do the police academy if he had to. If he completed all the testing in time, that was his first plan.

He was going to do this the way everyone else did. No more knowing anyone. He'd apply for a job, pass the physical aptitude and background checks, follow every step of the process, no matter how much time it took or rules he had to follow to find the job that fit him. If something else came up while he was doing that, it would be good to have options.

Regardless, there was one thing Rob was certain of. He was a cop. He was a *good* cop. Leaving the force made no sense, but that didn't mean SWAT or Atlanta was right for him.

"This isn't the time to be getting involved with anyone." He waited until she nodded along with him. "So, any blind dates you're thinking of setting me up on can wait."

Brisa frowned. "Wait?" she repeated as if she wasn't certain of the meaning. "I'm no good at that."

Some of the concern that had been itching across his nerves ever since he'd handed in his resignation disappeared. The people here at Concord Court were unlike any others he knew. No matter what else happened, he would not second-guess moving here.

"Don't suppose you know where I can get some cheap furniture? I don't want to buy too much because the moving company will have my stuff here by the end of the month, but it would be nice to have a bed." And a couch and two bookcases that made a nook that might attract his favorite teacher. He didn't say that aloud. He was trying to keep his hopes very, *very* low in regard to Mira. He wasn't moving here because she'd requested it or made him any promises.

That didn't mean that he had no plans to pursue his ex-wife.

He did.

But he wasn't going to let himself rush into making another mistake.

"If you'll come into the office in the morning, I can give you the name of a couple of furniture rental places. Normally, I recommend buying but not if you'll have your own stuff soon." She gripped his arm. "I'm so glad you decided to give us a chance, Rob. Every new person we meet here at Concord Court contributes something new and special to the place we're building. You and Mira… Well, I know you're not alone. Learning to live together again has to be a challenge lots of military families face and we can do a much better job of supporting them. I'll be picking your brain for help with that soon."

Since he and Mira hadn't made it, he wasn't sure how much help he'd be, but her enthusiasm was impossible to resist. He nodded his agreement.

"Does Mira know you're doing this? Have you spoken with her?" Brisa asked.

"No," Rob said as he rubbed his eyes, "I've either been on a plane to Oklahoma or a plane to Atlanta or a plane back to Miami to pick up my abandoned truck in the airport parking lot or making phone calls to set up a real estate agent and moving company or leaving my job without giving any notice. My boss, Booker, tried to be understanding but I don't think he'll be doing me any favors in the future, which is fine with me." He and Book would be okay eventually. The guy might live to work, but he didn't want officers whose hearts weren't in the job, either. That was fair and the right thing.

Rob sighed. "I'm tired. I'm going to get some sleep tonight and then call Mira tomorrow to let her know that I'm in town.

Not to put pressure on her, but to let her know where I am. I hate wondering about how she is. I'll check on her and pretend that she'll care that I've moved into her old townhome tomorrow."

When Brisa laughed, he turned to study her face. It wasn't amusement, but more like the villain's celebratory gloating when a perfect trap has been sprung, but her expression immediately cleared. "I know you need rest, but I was wondering if you'd like to be my guest to this New Year's Eve party we're throwing tonight. Not everyone will be there, because some of our vets aren't big on socialization, but it will be a good time to meet your neighbors." She blinked innocently. "I can introduce you to admissions people at the local university if you like. We'll have friends from the community coming, as well. My father will drop in at some point. He knows everyone in southern Florida, and he can point you in the right direction, whichever direction you want." She leaned closer to him. "All the shrimp you can eat and champagne at midnight." When she stepped back, the gleam in her eyes worried him. There was a catch somewhere, but he wasn't seeing it and he did like shrimp.

"I won't be sleeping anyway, right?" He shrugged. "I assume fireworks to mark the New Year?"

"No, no fireworks at Concord Court. Too many vets have problems with the noise, but we've got something special planned to mark midnight. Please come." She stayed where she was.

As if she was waiting for his agreement.

"I'll be there. I'll bring in my clothes and my sleeping bag and..." He held out his hands. "I guess that's all I have on my agenda for tonight."

He didn't understand what was happening, but Brisa hugged him quickly and practically danced her way out the front door. Rob took one more slow circle around the room and felt comfort settle into his bones. Mira had been here. It had been a home. He could make it one again.

After a quick text to his sister and mother to let them know that he'd been reunited with his truck in Miami and made the trip to Concord Court successfully, Rob unloaded his truck in one trip and then sat down on the floor to make a mental list of all the things he needed to get done before his meeting with Jason, the career counselor.

Before he realized how much time had passed, it was dark outside his bare window.

"Time to meet the neighbors." Rob unpacked his toiletries and decided to shave. His haggard expression from too much travel and a splotchy beard improved with a fresh shave. "Good. Don't want to give Sean any easy jokes." Rob wasn't sure what his reception would be with Mira's group, but he could handle it. He'd won them over once. He could be a friendly neighbor for sure.

His suit coat was the only unwrinkled thing he owned, thanks to hanging in the window of Rob's truck while he'd been crammed in the middle seat for unending flights all over the South, so he slipped it on. New Year's Eve could handle fancier attire, right?

It was nearly ten o'clock by the time he headed for the pool area. Unlimited shrimp was calling his name and he'd pinned all his hopes on finding a beer before the champagne poured. As he stepped out into the courtyard between Concord Court's buildings, he was dazzled. There was no other word that fit for the transformation.

Where the Christmas decorations had consisted of understated wreaths, for New Year's Eve, every surface was lit with bright white lights. The palm trees were strung with lights and twinkling. Strands of bigger, old-fashioned bulbs crisscrossed between the buildings, and there was a movie playing on one wall. "*Forrest Gump*. Need a chair?" Reyna asked from her spot near the buffet table. "I can get someone to bring you one. You haven't missed too much."

Rob shook his head. "No, right now, the only thing I need is shrimp and a lot of it. Possibly a beer if there's one around."

Reyna pursed her lips. "No beer, but we have water and plenty of tea. Grab a plate and make yourself at home." She grinned. "Brisa told me we're going to be neighbors."

"Yeah," Rob said. "Think I need to worry about my reception here?"

Reyna shook her head. "No way. We've missed you this week. All of us. Sean complained about Mira's run yesterday for so long I started to think he meant what he was saying. For some reason he hoped you might be their representative, negotiate for easier terms, if you were with them all the time." She rolled her eyes. "I told him you'd always back Mira up, but he has his heart set on shorter runs someday."

Rob laughed. "He complains to hear himself talk, doesn't he?"

"My ears were ringing. Are you chatting about me?" Sean asked as he slipped his hand around Reyna's waist.

"No, honey," she said and fluttered her eyelashes innocently.

He burst out with a laugh before he met Rob's stare. "Welcome to Concord Court. Our original agreement still stands. Hurt Mira and I'll round up as many folks as I need to make you sorry."

Rob tried to be flattered that Sean thought he might need backup to make good on his promise, but said, "I'm not here for Mira. I'll stay out of her way if that's what she wants. I'm here for me."

Sean dipped his head. "You want me to believe that you, a man who is stupid in love with his ex-wife, has no plans to rekindle that?" He sniffed. "I thought better of you.

Happy to see I was wrong and I can go back to plotting against you."

Rob appreciated Sean's style and his loyalty to Mira.

"I'll talk to Mira tomorrow and take my direction from her. If she's open to…anything, I'll be there. Whatever she wants. Whenever. This life will have enough room for a job I love and a woman I love." Rob tipped his chin up. "And if she's not open to any of that, I won't bother her. I want to know she's okay. That's all."

Sean ran his hand down Reyna's arm. It seemed unconscious, as if that's just what happened when they were close. Jealousy kicked hard in Rob's gut.

"I heard someone else say something almost word-for-word identical this morning. Now, who was that?" Sean tapped his chin. "Oh, yeah, here she is now."

When Sean and Reyna turned toward the parking lot, Rob looked to find Mira wearing the same beautiful dress she'd worn in Key West. Her hair was loose. No purse to ruin the lines of the dress, so her phone and her car keys were clenched in one hand. When she saw him, she stopped.

"Rob. What are you doing here?" she asked.

He tried not to think about how this greeting matched the one she'd given him when he'd first shown up on her Concord Court doorstep.

"He's moving into your old place," Reyna said. "I haven't decided… Is that romantic or creepy?"

Sean grinned. "Could be both. We'll have to wait and see."

Then they faded away as he moved closer to Mira. "I was going to call you tomorrow to tell you, but I am moving to Miami. Not because you asked, but because this place, Concord Court, can give me the time to figure out what I want for my life. You were right. Depending on you to make all my decisions for me… That was selfish, unfair, too much pressure on you and on us." She was here. She was safe. She was with him. He could see her and right now he could touch her.

Already he was thrilled with his decision to make the move.

But he would play it cool if he could.

"What about the job and the house?" she asked.

"Well, I went home, to Oklahoma, and I realized that I had already been brave or foolish enough to turn my back on one job that I knew I could do well because it didn't make me happy. The farm is in excellent hands. My sister and brother-in-law have built a happy life there, and if I'd stayed, I could never have done the same." He followed her to a quiet corner. The noise of the movie faded. When she fiddled with her car keys, he held out his hand. Mira stared hard at it for a minute before placing her cell phone and keys in his palm. Rob slipped both in the pocket of his coat and felt a level of satisfaction that made no sense. He was standing in for her purse again, but something about the unspoken routine hit him right in the center of his chest. "Atlanta was the wrong place and the wrong team, that doesn't mean I'm not supposed to be a police officer necessarily. Maybe it's internal affairs, where I help hold the force accountable to the public we serve, or it's training upcoming officers, but I'm going to apply to the Miami Police Department. I'll take the tests and attend the academy and then I'll figure out where I go next."

Rob watched her shiver as a breeze stirred her hair. He slipped out of his jacket and placed it over her shoulders and did his best to ignore the satisfaction he felt as he did it. Caring for Mira was right. That made him happy.

"I'm sorry I can't give that up." Rob meant it but no matter how many times he'd tried to find a new answer to the old question, nothing changed. He'd found the job he was meant to do.

Mira grabbed his hand. "No, I'm glad. You're good at your job. You're the officer I want showing up when my family or friends need help. This city needs good people who will protect everyone, be fair, follow the law and not look out for their own interests. You have always been that guy, the one who will sacrifice for others." She gave a wry grin. "So much so that it gets annoying sometimes."

Rob appreciated everything she said.

"But the nightmares," Rob said slowly. He knew none of their real problems had changed.

"Yeah, we've gotten reacquainted over the past week, but nothing like before," she said and shook her head as he started to apologize, "and I realized something important, thanks to my mother. Whatever you do, do not tell her I said this. She would be insufferable." Mira relaxed into his arms. "A bit of trouble sleeping is nothing compared to loving you in the sunshine. It just isn't. She talked to me about worrying about the people she loved, but how she knew that no matter how long she had with them, they knew they were loved. That is something everyone should be lucky enough to have." She laughed and Rob was sure he heard tears but he didn't want to interrupt what she was saying. "Love is something we never had to worry about. I knew you loved me, Rob. I love you, too. And I'm not going to let anything or anyone keep me from the peace and joy of loving fully."

So then that sounded like…

"Are we not divorced?" he asked.

"Oh, no, I filed the paperwork. I felt awful to do it but it's done." She wiped a finger under her eyes to brush away the tears.

"Good." Rob smiled at her as she frowned.

"This time we're going to do it the right way. No rush. Would you like to watch the last half hour of *Forrest Gump* with me? We'll find a blanket and some shrimp, which I have been told is available in unlimited quantities."

Mira laughed. "And then what?"

Rob pretended to consider it. "As long as we're both eating shrimp, I'm thinking a kiss at midnight."

Her giggle made him feel like a giant.

"And then what?"

"One day at a time. We're in charge now, with no one setting the schedule." Rob stroked her cheek. "All we have to do is enjoy the sunshine together."

"Two divorced people dating." Mira nodded. "We're going to have to get back out there in the dating scene some time. Might as well do it together."

Rob couldn't contain his grin as he filled up a plate with a heaping scoop of shrimp for two and followed Mira and her water bottles to a crowded blanket with Wade and Brisa. He met Brisa's stare when he sat down. Her grin was huge and so satisfied.

"I used to be bad at keeping secrets

but this time, I nailed it." She clapped her hands but immediately quieted when people around her shushed.

"You did," Rob said, "and this was better than I expected. I like shrimp."

Brisa rolled her eyes. "Get ready to be romantic, soldier. It'll be midnight soon and you can celebrate the New Year with a kiss with your wife. Well, technically your ex. But, that's not romantic, so…whatever. As a result of this party, you're going to be thanking me."

Rob stretched his legs and realized he had a whole list of people to thank already. Mira's family and friends had helped her come to terms with her fears, and they'd certainly supported him with his own. He realized he'd never felt like this, like tomorrow was going to be a great day, no matter what it held.

It was sweet.

Mira rested her hand on his leg. She used to do that whenever they had a chance to spend time on the couch in front of the TV. It hadn't happened often, but that gesture was the kind of thing that convinced him they had what it took to get through this together. Whatever life tossed at them, as long as they stayed connected somehow, they could come through it.

When the movie ended, Brisa joined Marcus at the front of the group. "And now it's time for our special midnight countdown. Marcus Bryant is the man you need for all your landscape design and outdoor party decor. He did this for us. I'll let him take over."

"Everybody find someone to ring in the New Year with," Marcus said. "Ten." He hit a switch and one of the glittering palm trees went dark.

"What happened? That's one of your favorite trees," Mira whispered in his ear in a scandalized tone. Rob wrapped his arms tightly around her. He was ready for his kiss.

"Nine," Marcus called out and another palm tree went dark. He continued the countdown until only one tree remained. Rob was certain the rest of the crowd was anticipating that final switch as much as he was. Mira had turned to press her hand to his chest. Her eyes were locked on his.

"One." Marcus hit the last switch. The

palm trees were all dark, but the paper lanterns strung overhead lit in a warm glow that perfectly fit the soft, muffled cheer of the crowd.

Mira pressed her lips to his in a sweet, easy kiss that reminded him of a hundred other times she'd done so out of the blue, just because she could. Sunlight. Warmth. Easy road trips. Breakfast for dinner. They were all in that kiss, but for the first time in a long time, Rob could feel the promise of a future.

When she eased back, Mira said, "My mother told me it was too soon for me to be kissing someone new. I can't wait to tell her she was wrong." Then she laughed. "How do you feel about grapes? We're going to follow all of my parents' instructions for good luck for this New Year."

Rob had no idea what she was talking about, but he didn't really care, either.

"If you have a minute, try writing down some of your family's rules, please." He pulled her closer. "I want to get them all right the next time I ask you to marry me."

EPILOGUE

MIRA STOOD WITH her father behind the curtains that Sean and Marcus had rigged around her parents' back patio and checked for any nervous energy, but the only emotion she could name was happiness. In a few minutes, she'd walk down an aisle, and meet Rob at the end of it. This time, they were doing everything right.

"I suppose we should not count on rain," her mother muttered to herself, fussing with the bouquet of white roses she'd made for Mira to carry. "Although it is June, and afternoon showers are standard here. No, not today, not when it would mean so much to my beloved older daughter's second and final marriage."

"Gina, did Mom say that at your wedding?" Naomi asked. "I distinctly remember her saying it at mine, and so far, so good, you know?"

Her mother snapped, "Marriage is hard. You need all the luck you can get. Ask this one! She already knows."

"Your beloved older daughter has never once fallen out of love with that husband of hers. This second marriage ought to be airtight, Mum," Gina answered.

Mira waited for the irritation to hit, but she couldn't get upset with any of them.

Not today.

"June brides are happy their whole married lives just like they are on their wedding day. This girl has not stopped grinning yet." Kris claimed her bridesmaid bouquet and raised it as if victorious. Her mother had insisted on wrapping the bouquets in new blue satin ribbons with sparkling bells tied on the ends.

The music began. "Everyone starts on their right foot," her father said. "Don't mess this up, girls."

Gina saluted and arranged everyone in line from youngest to oldest.

The first time she and Rob had gotten married, they'd pulled a few friends together and stood in front of the base chaplain a world away from their families. It had felt right then, but nothing like this.

Having the chance to do it over and do it perfectly was amazing.

This event was going to be a family affair in every way. She and Rob had planned every detail.

"Did you and Rob have a good talk last night, Dad?" Mira asked as Naomi stepped through the curtains to lead the way down the aisle.

"We did. He's a good kid." Her father cleared his throat. "Made a nice recovery, that one. Gotta admire a man who gets back up after he's knocked down."

Mira swallowed a smile at either one of them being called kids, but it was a father's prerogative.

"His mother…" Her father tilted his head from side to side. "Well, she's very nice."

Mira was so glad everyone was getting along. "I'm looking forward to a long visit with his sister this summer. Now that school is out, I have some time. After Rob finishes the police academy, he's going out to help 'put up hay.'" When her father raised his eyebrows, she shrugged. "That's all I know about it. I might not even be saying it correctly."

He patted her hand. The bells dangling from her bouquet jingled softly. More luck threaded through the ceremony courtesy of her family.

Kris stepped through the curtains. Before she went, Gina raised a hand and blew Mira a kiss. "Love you." Then she was gone. That left only her parents.

Mira had asked them both to walk with her down the aisle.

"Mom, thank you for all you've done to make this night perfect." Mira pressed a kiss to her mother's cheek. Touching the earrings her mother had loaned her reminded Mira of how much tradition meant to her parents. Gina, Kris and Naomi had all worn these earrings. Her mother had borrowed them from Nan and worn them at her wedding. Mira had missed this tradition with her first wedding. She appreciated having a second chance to complete the circle. "I'm happy we can do this together."

When her mother blinked rapidly, Mira wondered if she'd gone too far.

"No making the mother of the bride cry,"

her mother muttered as she tugged the skirt of the red sundress Mira had chosen to wear for the occasion. Her mother had pushed for the whole nine yards of white lace in a wedding dress, but Mira had wanted casual, and opted for red and gold. Since it was now eighty degrees after sunset, Mira knew she'd made the right decision.

"Or the father," her father said as he tugged them to the opening in the curtains. After a peek, he nodded. "Time for the main event, ladies." Mira felt her parents wrap their hands around her arms and together they stepped out into the grass that sometimes served as a flag football field, sometimes a baseball diamond.

Tonight, rows of chairs held Mira's family, Rob's family and their friends from Concord Court. Marcus had come up with a beautiful temporary pavilion at the end and had covered it in roses. Only a few were from the rosebushes behind her garage, but the connection was nice. She'd grown something and contributed it to this marriage.

Their guests provided the only additional light in the form of candles.

Family. Friends. And Rob. All made for a beautiful scene.

As she stepped up beside him, he bent close to her. "Are you jingling?"

Mira remembered the sweatshirt she'd been wearing when he popped up on her doorstep. "I am jingling. Do you have a problem with that?"

The justice of the peace they'd hired cleared his throat.

Were they interrupting his flow? Mira didn't care.

"Nope. I love it. I don't even have to know why you have bells on." Rob smiled at her. "I've got a lifetime to figure it out."

* * * * *

For more compelling romances in the Veterans' Road miniseries from Cheryl Harper and Harlequin Heartwarming, visit www.Harlequin.com today!

Get 4 FREE REWARDS!

We'll send you 2 FREE Books plus 2 FREE Mystery Gifts.

Love Inspired books feature uplifting stories where faith helps guide you through life's challenges and discover the promise of a new beginning.

FREE Value Over $20

YES! Please send me 2 FREE Love Inspired Romance novels and my 2 FREE mystery gifts (gifts are worth about $10 retail). After receiving them, if I don't wish to receive any more books, I can return the shipping statement marked "cancel." If I don't cancel, I will receive 6 brand-new novels every month and be billed just $5.24 each for the regular-print edition or $5.99 each for the larger-print edition in the U.S., or $5.74 each for the regular-print edition or $6.24 each for the larger-print edition in Canada. That's a savings of at least 13% off the cover price. It's quite a bargain! Shipping and handling is just 50¢ per book in the U.S. and $1.25 per book in Canada.* I understand that accepting the 2 free books and gifts places me under no obligation to buy anything. I can always return a shipment and cancel at any time. The free books and gifts are mine to keep no matter what I decide.

Choose one: ☐ **Love Inspired Romance**
Regular-Print
(105/305 IDN GNWC)

☐ **Love Inspired Romance**
Larger-Print
(122/322 IDN GNWC)

Name (please print)

Address   Apt. #

City   State/Province   Zip/Postal Code

Email: Please check this box ☐ if you would like to receive newsletters and promotional emails from Harlequin Enterprises ULC and its affiliates. You can unsubscribe anytime.

Mail to the **Harlequin Reader Service:**
IN U.S.A.: P.O. Box 1341, Buffalo, NY 14240-8531
IN CANADA: P.O. Box 603, Fort Erie, Ontario L2A 5X3

Want to try 2 free books from another series? Call 1-800-873-8635 or visit www.ReaderService.com.

Get 4 FREE REWARDS!

We'll send you 2 FREE Books plus 2 FREE Mystery Gifts.

Love Inspired Suspense books showcase how courage and optimism unite in stories of faith and love in the face of danger.

FREE Value Over $20

HARLEQUIN SELECTS COLLECTION

19 FREE BOOKS IN ALL!

From Robyn Carr to RaeAnne Thayne to Linda Lael Miller and Sherryl Woods we promise (actually, GUARANTEE!) each author in the Harlequin Selects collection has seen their name on the *New York Times* or *USA TODAY* bestseller lists!

Get 4 FREE REWARDS!

We'll send you 2 FREE Books plus 2 FREE Mystery Gifts.

BRENDA JACKSON — Follow Your Heart

ROBYN CARR — The Country Guesthouse

RICK MOFINA — SEARCH FOR HER

B.J. DANIELS — FROM the SHADOWS

FREE Value Over $20

Both the **Romance** and **Suspense** collections feature compelling novels written by many of today's bestselling authors.

YES! Please send me 2 FREE novels from the Essential Romance or Essential Suspense Collection and my 2 FREE gifts (gifts are worth about $10 retail). After receiving them, if I don't wish to receive any more books, I can return the shipping statement marked "cancel." If I don't cancel, I will receive 4 brand-new novels every month and be billed just $7.24 each in the U.S. or $7.49 each in Canada. That's a savings of up to 28% off the cover price. It's quite a bargain! Shipping and handling is just 50¢ per book in the U.S. and $1.25 per book in Canada.* I understand that accepting the 2 free books and gifts places me under no obligation to buy anything. I can always return a shipment and cancel at any time. The free books and gifts are mine to keep no matter what I decide.

Choose one: ☐ **Essential Romance** (194/394 MDN GQ6M) ☐ **Essential Suspense** (191/391 MDN GQ6M)

Name (please print)

Address   Apt. #

City   State/Province   Zip/Postal Code

Email: Please check this box ☐ if you would like to receive newsletters and promotional emails from Harlequin Enterprises ULC and its affiliates. You can unsubscribe anytime.

Mail to the **Harlequin Reader Service:**
IN U.S.A.: P.O. Box 1341, Buffalo, NY 14240-8531
IN CANADA: P.O. Box 603, Fort Erie, Ontario L2A 5X3

Want to try 2 free books from another series! Call 1-800-873-8635 or visit www.ReaderService.com.

---

*Terms and prices subject to change without notice. Prices do not include sales taxes, which will be charged (if applicable) based on your state or country of residence. Canadian residents will be charged applicable taxes. Offer not valid in Quebec. This offer is limited to one order per household. Books received may not be as shown. Not valid for current subscribers to the Essential Romance or Essential Suspense Collection. All orders subject to approval. Credit or debit balances in a customer's account(s) may be offset by any other outstanding balance owed by or to the customer. Please allow 4 to 6 weeks for delivery. Offer available while quantities last.

Your Privacy—Your information is being collected by Harlequin Enterprises ULC, operating as Harlequin Reader Service. For a complete summary of the information we collect, how we use this information and to whom it is disclosed, please visit our privacy notice located at corporate.harlequin.com/privacy-notice. From time to time we may also exchange your personal information with reputable third parties. If you wish to opt out of this sharing of your personal information, please visit readerservice.com/consumerschoice or call 1-800-873-8635. **Notice to California Residents**—Under California law, you have specific rights to control and access your data. For more information on these rights and how to exercise them, visit corporate.harlequin.com/california-privacy.

STRS21R2

COMING NEXT MONTH FROM

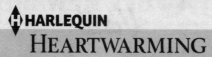

#399 SNOWBOUND WITH HER MOUNTAIN COWBOY

The Second Chance Club • by Patricia Johns

Angelina Cunningham gets the surprise of the season when her ex-husband appears on her doorstep. But Ben has lost his memory—and forgotten how he broke her heart! Can braving a blizzard together give them a second chance?

#400 HIS HOMETOWN YULETIDE VOW

A Pacific Cove Romance • by Carol Ross

Former baseball player Derrick Bright needs a PR expert—too bad the best in the business is his ex Anne. He'll do whatever it takes to get her help...and reclaim her heart by Christmas!

#401 HER CHRISTMASTIME FAMILY

The Golden Matchmakers Club • by Tara Randel

Widowed officer Roan Donovan needs to make merry for his kids in time for Christmas. But he's more grinch than holiday glee. Good thing the girl next door, single mom Faith, has enough Christmas spirit to spare!

#402 A MERRY CHRISTMAS DATE

Matchmaker at Work • by Syndi Powell

Melanie Beach won't spend another holiday alone. But when she confesses her love to longtime friend Jack, he doesn't return her feelings. Can the magic of the season mend broken hearts and point the way to love?

Visit
ReaderService.com
Today!

As a valued member of the Harlequin Reader Service, you'll find these benefits and more at ReaderService.com:

- Try 2 free books from any series
- Access risk-free special offers
- View your account history & manage payments
- Browse the latest Bonus Bucks catalog

Don't miss out!

If you want to stay up-to-date on the latest at the Harlequin Reader Service and enjoy more content, make sure you've signed up for our monthly News & Notes email newsletter. Sign up online at ReaderService.com or by calling Customer Service at 1-800-873-8635.